Hannah might be his ~~later~~ she was carrying his brother's child.

Maybe she'd decided to refuse his proposal. Judd had to be prepared for that.

"Let's walk. When you're ready you can tell me what you've decided."

Judd waited for Hannah to speak. He'd promised he wouldn't rush her, but it wasn't easy to keep still. It was as if she held his life in her hands.

"I don't suppose you've heard from Quint," she said at last.

Judd exhaled slowly. "You know I'd tell you if I had."

She clasped her hands, her fingers flexing and twisting. "There's not much we can do except wait, is there?"

"You and I can wait. It's the baby who can't."

"I know." She turned to face him. The setting sun cast her features in soft rose gold. "That's why I've decided to accept your offer, Judd. Until Quint comes home, I'd be honored and grateful to be your wife."

* * *

The Borrowed Bride
Harlequin® Historical #920—November 2008

ELIZABETH LANE

The
Borrowed
Bride

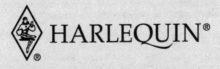

HARLEQUIN®

TORONTO • NEW YORK • LONDON
AMSTERDAM • PARIS • SYDNEY • HAMBURG
STOCKHOLM • ATHENS • TOKYO • MILAN • MADRID
PRAGUE • WARSAW • BUDAPEST • AUCKLAND

ISBN-13: 978-0-373-29520-3
ISBN-10:   0-373-29520-0

THE BORROWED BRIDE

Copyright © 2008 by Elizabeth Lane

This edition published by arrangement with Harlequin Books S.A.

® and TM are trademarks of the publisher. Trademarks indicated with
® are registered in the United States Patent and Trademark Office, the
Canadian Trade Marks Office and in other countries.

www.eHarlequin.com

Printed in U.S.A.

For my mother, and for mothers everywhere

forehead, the tiny bump on the bridge of his nose, the alert brown eyes, fixed now on the distant curve of tracks where the train would appear. A smile tugged at the corner of his mouth.

It wasn't fair, Hannah thought. Quint was happy, and her own heart was on the verge of shattering like a mason jar dropped onto a stone floor.

Hannah had loved Quint Seavers for as long as she could remember. They'd been sweethearts since their school days, and the whole town had expected them to marry. So why couldn't he have just let nature take its course? Why had he gotten this crackbrained urge to run off and seek his fortune in the Klondike goldfields?

At first she'd hoped it was just a whim. But the Klondike was all Quint had talked about for the past year. Only one thing had kept him in Dutchman's Creek. His older brother, Judd, had joined the Theodore Roosevelt's Rough Riders and gone off to the Spanish American War, leaving Quint behind to tend the family ranch and look after their invalid mother. But that was about to change. After four months with the Rough Riders and five months in a Virginia military hospital, Judd was coming home. He'd be arriving on the train that had just appeared around the distant bend—the train that would be taking Quint away.

"Do you think he'll be changed?" Edna Seavers's white hands gripped the woven cane arms of her wheelchair. A cheerless wisp of a woman clad in widow's black, she'd been wheeled around in that chair for as long as Hannah could remember.

"War changes everybody, Mama," Quint said. "Judd's

been through a bad time with his wounds and the malaria. But he'll come around once he's been home awhile. You'll see."

"I wish it was you coming home and Judd leaving." Mrs. Seavers had never hidden the fact that Quint was the favorite of her two children. "Why do you have to go anyway? You're too young to go rushing off on your own."

Quint sighed. "I'm twenty-one, Mama. You promised me that I could go when Judd came home. Well, Judd's coming. And I'm going."

Hannah glanced from Quint to his mother, feeling invisible. She'd been Quint's girl for years, but Edna Seavers barely acknowledged her existence.

The train whistled again, its shrill voice a cry in Hannah's ears. She shifted her weight, conscious of the raw ache between her thighs. Her mother had lectured her about men's appetites and made her swear, with her right hand on the Bible, that she would keep herself from sin. But last night with Quint, in the darkness of the hayloft, her good intentions had unraveled like a torn sweater. She had given herself willingly. But the act had been so awkward and painful that when Quint had moaned and rolled off her, she'd been secretly relieved. Later that night, in the room she shared with her four younger sisters, Hannah had buried her face in her pillow and wept until there were no tears left.

Pistons pumping, the engine glided into the station. Half-glimpsed faces flashed past in the windows of the passenger car. For an instant Hannah held her breath, as if she could will the train to keep moving. Then the mail sack thumped onto the platform. The brakes moaned as the line of cars shuddered to a full stop.

There was a beat of silence, then a stirring inside the passenger car. A door swung open. The lone figure of a tall man in a drooping felt hat emerged onto the step. Veiled by misting rain he moved down onto the platform.

Hannah hadn't known Judd Seavers well. Eight years Quint's senior, he'd been too old to be counted among her playmates. She remembered him as a taciturn young man with somber gray eyes and hands that were always working. In the years Hannah had been coming around the Seavers place, he'd shown no more interest in her than Edna had.

Now he walked toward them, where they waited under the shelter of the eave. He moved slowly, heedless of the rain that beaded his tan coat and trickled off the brim of his hat. A battered canvas field bag, the sort that a soldier would carry, dangled loosely from one hand. He looked old, Hannah thought. Old before his time. Maybe that was what war did to people.

But why was she thinking about Judd? Minutes from now, Quint—*her* Quint, the love of her life—would be gone. Certainly for months. Maybe for years.

Maybe forever.

Judd clenched his teeth against the pain that shot through him with each step. Most of the time it wasn't so bad, but the long, jarring train ride had roused every shard of metal that the doctors had left in his body. He was hurting like blazes, but he wasn't about to show it. Not with his mother and brother looking on.

The nurse had offered him laudanum to ease the trip, but he had turned it down. He'd had enough opiates to know what they could do to a man, and he'd sworn he was finished. Still, sitting up those long nights with the rhythm of iron wheels rattling through his bones, he'd have bargained away his soul for a few hours of relief.

But never mind all that, he was home now, walking down the platform through the soft Colorado rain. Home from the war with two legs, two arms and two eyes. He could only wish to God that some of his friends had fared as well.

At least the malaria had abated—for now. The miserable, recurring chills and fever, along with infections from the wounds, had kept him in the hospital for what seemed like an eternity. By rights, he should be dead. He'd lost track of how many times he'd teetered on the brink and fought his way back. Maybe someday he'd figure out why.

No one rushed out into the rain to meet him—not even Quint. The gangly boy Judd had nurtured from babyhood had grown into a fine-looking man. His pack rested beside him on the platform, ready to be flung onto the train at the first call of "All aboard!" After a year of running the ranch and putting up with their mother's complaints, he was like a young red-tailed hawk, fledged and ready to soar. Judd couldn't begrudge him his chance. Quint had earned it.

His mother looked even grayer and thinner than he remembered. Aside from that, she didn't appear to have changed much. The same black dress, woolen cape and prim bonnet. The same purse-lipped frown. Maybe she was wishing he'd come home in a box. If he had, Quint would never be able to leave.

Then there was the girl. Dressed in a thin shawl and a faded red calico dress, she clung to Quint's hand as if trying to meld their fingers. She'd be one of the Gustavsons—the family that eked out a living on the small dirt farm that bordered the Seavers Ranch. The whole tribe of youngsters had the same round blue eyes and corn silk hair. This one had grown up pretty. What was her name? Hannah, that was it. He'd forgotten about her until now.

Quint worked loose from her and came out toward him. Rain misted on his hair as he held out his hand. "Glad you're home, Judd," he said awkwardly. "I've tried to take care of the place the way you'd have wanted."

"I imagine the place will be fine." Judd clasped the callused fingers. The boy had developed a man's grip. "How's Mother?"

"The same. And Gretel Schmidt is still taking care of her. You won't find much of anything changed."

Except you, Judd thought as he trailed his brother back to where the women waited under the eave. His mother made no effort to smile. Her hands were colder and thinner than he remembered. The girl—Hannah—murmured a shy hello. Her honey-gold hair was plaited like a schoolgirl's, in two thick braids that hung over her shapely little breasts. Judd caught the glimmer of tears before she lowered dark blue eyes.

"Are you quite recovered from your wounds, son?" Judd's mother had grown up in a well-to-do Boston family. She took pride in her formal speech and expected her sons to use it in her presence.

"Quite recovered, Mother. Only a twinge now and then." Judd's body screamed as he lied.

"Your father would have been proud of you."

"I hope so."

"You won't have much time to rest up," Quint said. "We've got a couple hundred cows waiting to drop their calves. But then, I reckon you know what to expect."

"Reckon?" His mother sniffed with disdain. "People will judge you by your speech, Quint. Remember that, if you don't remember anything else I've taught you."

"I'm gonna say 'ain't' every other sentence when I get out of this place," Quint muttered in Judd's ear.

The train whistle gave two short but deafening blasts. "All aboard!" the conductor shouted.

"Well, I guess this is it." Quint cupped Hannah's face between his palms. "I'll write when I can," he promised. "And when I come back rich, you and I will have a wedding like this county's never seen!"

The girl was weeping openly. "I don't care about rich. Just come back to me safe."

He kissed her quick and hard, then caught the pack by one strap and swung it onto his shoulder.

"Mother." He pecked her cheek. Her mouth was pressed thin. She didn't reply.

Last, Quint turned to Judd. "You can send letters care of General Delivery in Skagway," he said. "I'll pick them up when I can, and I'll write back."

Judd shook his proffered hand. "Just take your girl's advice. Come back safe. Come back to us all."

"All aboard!" The engine was building up steam. As it began to move Quint flashed a grin, leaped onto the step and vanished into the jaws of the closing door. Seconds later he reappeared at one of the windows, smiling and waving his hand.

Reaching toward him, the girl raced along the platform. She kept even until the train picked up speed and left her behind.

Laboring for breath, Hannah walked back the way she'd come. A stitch clawed at her side. Wind chilled a patch of skin where she'd ripped the shoulder seam of her outgrown dress. She tugged her shawl over the gap.

Mrs. Seavers and Judd waited for her under the eave of the platform—so proud, so cold, both of them. They were nothing like Quint, who'd loved her and made her laugh and hadn't cared that her family was poor.

What would she do without him?

What if he never came back?

Slowing her step, she tried to imagine what Alaska would be like. She'd heard tales of giant grizzly bears, wolf packs, howling blizzards, avalanches, bottomless lakes and lawless men who'd stop at nothing to get what they wanted. The thought of Quint in such a place sickened her with dread. She wanted to fly after the train, stop it somehow and bring him back to the people who loved him.

Judd had stepped behind his mother's wheelchair and taken the grips. As they moved out into the drizzle, she opened her tiny black umbrella and held it over her head. Rain-soaked and fighting tears, Hannah trailed them to the buggy. They would let her off at her home. After that, she wouldn't likely set foot on the Seavers place until Quint returned. The Seavers were quality folk, with a fine ranch, a big house and money in the bank. Hannah's own parents had emigrated from Norway as newlyweds. They worked hard on their little farm, but it was all they could do to feed the seven robust children they'd produced. As the oldest, Hannah would have plenty to do while Quint was away. But she was already planning the letters she would write him by candlelight at day's end.

The buggy was waiting in a lot behind the depot. Judd guided the wheelchair over the bumpy ground, tilting it backward to keep from spilling his mother into the mud. His big, scarred hands were pale, most likely from long months in the hospital. Hannah's gaze was drawn to those hands. She found herself wondering how badly he'd been hurt. He moved like a strong man, but she noticed the way his jaw clenched as he lifted his eighty-five-pound mother onto the buggy seat. His storm-gray eyes were sunk into shadows. They had a wearied look about them, as if they'd seen too much of the world.

While Judd loaded the wheelchair into the back of the buggy, Hannah climbed onto the single seat beside Edna Seavers. The buggy's oiled leather cover kept off the rain but the wind was chilly. She huddled into her shawl, her teeth chattering. Her eyes gazed straight ahead at the gleaming rumps of the two matched bays.

She thought of the train, carrying Quint to Seattle, where he would board a steamer for Alaska—a mysterious place that was no more than a name in Hannah's mind. Maybe she could ask the schoolteacher to show her a map, so she could see where he'd be going.

Judd came around to the left side of the buggy and climbed onto the seat. Without a word, he flicked the reins onto the backs of the horses. The buggy rolled forward, wheels cutting into the mud.

Hannah shivered beneath her damp shawl as they passed along the main street of the awakening town. By now, the sun had risen above the peaks, but its rain-filtered light was gray and murky. The stillness of her two companions only added to the gloom. Having grown up in a big, noisy family, she was unaccustomed to long silences. Surely Judd or his mother would say something soon.

Crammed against Edna's bony little body, she struggled to keep still. At last, as the buggy crossed the bridge over the swollen creek, Hannah could stand it no longer.

"I'll bet you could tell some good war stories, Judd," she said. "What was it like, galloping up San Juan Hill behind Teddy Roosevelt?"

The impatient sound he made fell somewhere between a growl and a sigh. "It was Kettle Hill, not San Juan Hill. And we weren't galloping. We were on foot and taking a hell of a pounding. The only horse in sight was the one under Roosevelt's fat rear end."

"Oh." Taken aback, Hannah paused, then rallied. "But you were in the Rough Riders. Wasn't that a cavalry unit?"

"Cavalry troops need horses. Ours didn't make it to Florida before we shipped out. The Rough Riders landed in Cuba and fought as infantry. Don't you read the papers?"

Hannah recoiled as if he'd slapped her face. As a matter of fact, her family couldn't afford to buy newspapers. And even if her father had brought one home, she would have been too busy milking, churning, weeding, scrubbing and minding her young brothers and sisters to sit down and read it.

"I'm only going by what I've heard," she said. "But it must have been glorious, charging up the hill, guns blazing at the enemy—"

"Glorious!" Judd snorted contemptuously. "It was a bloodbath! Seventy-six percent casualties, men dropping like mown wheat, all so Teddy Roosevelt could become a damned hero! They could've cut down the Spanish with artillery fire before they sent us up. But no, somebody couldn't wait—"

"Really, Judd!" Edna's spidery fingers clutched her folded umbrella. "All this talk about the war is giving me a headache, and I didn't bring my pills. Can't you just be quiet until we get home?"

Judd sighed and hunched over the reins. Hannah squirmed on the padded leather bench. How could this joyless family have produced her loving, laughing Quint? Maybe he was a changeling. Or maybe he took after his long-dead father. Whatever the explanation, she missed him so much that she wanted to cry her eyes out.

In funereal stillness they drove along the rutted road, through clumps of dripping willow and across the open grassland. To the west, craggy peaks crowned in glittering snow rose above the gray mist. Rain drizzled lightly off the top of the buggy. For Hannah, the silence was becoming unbearable.

"Quint told me that the biggest mountain in North America was in Alaska," she said. "Do you think he'll get a chance to see it?"

Edna Seavers shot Hannah a glare—the first time the woman had actually looked at her all morning. "I asked for quiet," she said. "Please have the courtesy to respect my wishes."

"I'm sorry," Hannah murmured. "I only meant to—"

"That's enough, young lady. And I'll thank you not to mention my son in my hearing. I'm upset enough as it is, and my headache is getting worse."

"Sorry." Hannah glanced at Judd's craggy profile. He was looking straight ahead, his mouth set in a chiseled line. Clearly, he wasn't about to spring to her defense against his own mother.

Stomach churning, she stared down at her clenched hands. This had been the worst morning of her life. And being around these two miserable people wasn't making it any better.

"Stop the buggy," she said. "I want to walk."

Judd turned to look at her, a puzzled frown on his face. "Don't be silly. It's raining," he said.

"I don't care. I'm already wet."

"All right, if that's what you want." He tugged the reins hard enough to halt the plodding team. "Can you make it home from here? It's a couple of miles by the road."

"I know a shortcut. I'll be fine. Thank you for the ride." She clambered out of the wagon, holding her skirts clear of the mud. Tears were welling like a spring flood. She gulped them back, turning away before they could spill over.

Judd watched her leave the road and stride across the open pastureland. Head high, braids flung back, she walked like a queen. The Gustavsons barely had a pot to piss in. But this one had pride.

"We need to get home," his mother said.

"Fine." Judd clucked the team into motion. "You were rude to her, Mother. You should have apologized."

"Why? So she can come over and moon around the house while Quint is gone? I'll miss your brother, but I'm hoping he'll stay away long enough for her to find somebody else. She's a pretty thing, but she's as common as dirt—certainly not of our class."

Judd didn't reply. His mother's views hadn't changed in thirty years. Arguing with her would be a waste of breath.

Looking across the pasture, he could still see the splash of Hannah's red dress against the drab yellow grass. His eyes followed her until she vanished into the trees.

Chapter Two

May 19, 1899
Dear Quint…

Hannah chewed on the stubby pencil to bite away the wood and expose more of the meager lead. If she went for a knife to sharpen it, one of her parents was bound to see her and give her some chore to do. Most days she wouldn't have minded. But this letter couldn't wait. She had to finish it and get it to town before the westbound train picked up the mail.

The shade of new-leafed aspens dappled her skirts as she shifted her knees beneath the notebook. Below the bank, the creek flowed high with mountain snow melt. The rushing water laughed and whispered. A magpie scolded from the crest of a yellow pine.

Steeling her resolve, she pressed the blunted lead against the paper, forced it to form letters, then words.

It's springtime here. Violets are blooming in the pasture. Bessie has a new calf. Papa let me help with the birthing of it…

Hannah paused, chewing her lower lip in frustration. She was wasting precious time and paper. There was no way to soften the blow of what she had to tell Quint. Best to just write it out plain and be done.

But at a time like this, even plain words were as hard to come by as gold coins in a pauper's graveyard.

In the months Quint had been gone, Hannah had yet to receive a single letter from him. But Alaska was far away—so remote that he might as well be on the moon. And Quint had told her that he might be prospecting in remote areas with no postal service. Surely there was no cause to worry. But Hannah did worry. Anxiety had become a constant companion, a parasite that gnawed at her insides day and night.

Especially now.

Only the memory of Edna Seavers's wintry eyes and Judd's indifferent manner kept her from crossing the open pastureland to rap on the door of their big, bleak house. In any case, it would be a wasted trip, Hannah told herself. Since she hadn't heard from Quint, it wasn't likely his mother and brother had heard from him, either.

As for her own letters, the ones she'd written faithfully and carried into town every week, they could be anywhere, lost between here and the frozen North. She could only pray that this one letter would find him and bring him home.

The first month, when her menstrual flow hadn't come, she'd dismissed it from her mind. Her periods had always been irregular. But after the second month the secret dread had sprouted and begun to root. Last week, when she'd started throwing up in the morning, all doubt had vanished. After seeing her mother through six pregnancies, Hannah knew the signs all too well.

So far she'd managed to hide her condition from her family. But her mother had eyes like a hawk. She was bound to notice before long. Another couple of months, and the whole town would know about the secret thing she and Quint had done in that shadowed hayloft.

Ripping the page out of the notebook, Hannah crumpled it in her fist and began again.

Dear Quint,
I have something important to tell you…

The knot in Hannah's stomach tightened. Quint had been so excited about his great adventure. Her news would devastate him. He might even blame her for allowing this to happen. Surely he would consider it his duty to come home and marry her. But he wouldn't be happy about it. Quint had chafed under the burden of caring for the ranch and his ailing mother. Much as he'd professed to love her, Hannah could only imagine how he'd feel about being saddled with a wife and child.

But in the larger scheme of things Quint's feelings, and hers, didn't matter. A baby was coming—an innocent little spirit who deserved a mother and a father and an honorable name. She would do the right thing. So would Quint. It wasn't the best beginning for a marriage, but they'd loved each other for years. God willing, they would be happy.

If only she could get word to him.

Gripping the pencil, she hunched over the notebook.

There's no easy way to say this. We're going to have a child, my dearest. It should be born in December. I know how much you want to find your fortune in Alaska. But we have to think of the baby now. You need to come home so we can get married, the sooner the better.

By the time she finished the letter, Hannah's eyes were blurry with tears. She folded the sheet of cheap, ruled notepaper and tucked it into her apron pocket. Her fingers fumbled for the pennies she'd scrimped to buy an envelope and a postage stamp.

All her hopes and prayers would be riding with this letter. Somehow it had to reach Alaska and find its way to Quint.

It just had to.

June 6, 1899

Judd had been riding fence since dawn, checking for weak spots where a cow could push its way through or tangle its head in a loose strand of barbed wire. Now the midday sun blazed down with the heat of a blacksmith's forge. He was sore and sweaty, and his mouth was as dry as alkali dust. But he had to admit that he relished the work. Anything was better than lying in that god-awful excuse for a hospital, listening to the groans and whimpers of men who would never go home again except in a pine box.

At the watering trough, he dismounted. While the horse drank, he scooped the mossy water in his Stetson and emptied it over his head. The wetness streamed off his hair to soak into his sweat-encrusted shirt. Judd sluiced his arms, savoring the coolness. At rare moments like this he almost felt alive again. But the feeling never lasted. His body might be healing, but the blackness in his soul lurked like a pool of quicksand, waiting to suck him down.

Raking back his damp hair, he gazed out across the open pasture that separated the Seavers ranch from the Gustavson farm. In the distance someone was moving—a dot of blue seen through the shimmering air, coming closer. Judd's throat tightened as he remembered the Gustavson girl—Quint's girl—racing down the platform after the departing train. He could still see her losing ground, faltering, then turning back with stricken corn-flower eyes, as if her whole world had been crushed beneath the iron wheels.

Judd hadn't seen her since that dismal morning. Nor had he heard from Quint. Maybe she'd received some news of him and was coming to share it.

He watched and waited. A bead of water trickled down his cheek to lose itself in the stubble of his unshaven chin. As the figure grew closer, Judd's spirits sank. It wasn't the girl after all. It was a woman, fair-haired and stoutly built. He recognized her as the mother of the Gustavson brood.

She moved wearily, leaning forward as if harnessed to an invisible boulder that she was dragging behind her.

By the time Judd had unsaddled the horse and loosed it in the corral, Mrs. Gustavson had reached the front gate. Remembering his long-forgotten manners, he started down the road to greet her and escort her to the house. Even from a distance he could see that she was distraught. She walked with a dejected slump, dabbing at her eyes and nose with a wadded rag that served as a handkerchief.

At the sight of Judd, she straightened her posture, lifted her chin and jammed the rag into the pocket of her faded chambray dress. In her youth, she might have been as pretty as her daughter. But two decades of poverty, backbreaking labor and constant childbearing had taken their toll. Any beauty she'd possessed had worn away, exposing a core of toughness and raw Norwegian pride. Poor as she was, Mary Gustavson was a woman to be reckoned with.

Partway down the long, straight approach to the house, they met. Judd lifted the damp Stetson he'd replaced on his head. "Good day, Mrs. Gustavson."

"Judd." She nodded curtly. She had the kind of ruddy Nordic skin that stretched tight over the bones of her face. Her tearstained eyes were several shades lighter than her daughter's. "I trust your mother is at home."

"Yes." Judd glanced at the sun, calculating the time. "She usually takes tea in the parlor at this hour. I'll walk you to the door." He offered his arm but she ignored the gesture. Her eyes were fixed on the well-built two-story house with its shuttered windows and gingerbread porch.

Judd's father had built the place fifteen years ago. The summer after his family moved in, Tom Seavers had been trampled to death in a cattle stampede. On hearing the news, his wife had suffered a disabling stroke.

In the intervening years, Edna Seavers had transformed the place into a mausoleum for the living. Judd couldn't blame Quint for wanting to strike out on his own. He might have considered leaving himself. But this was home. He was needed here, especially now. And he had no other refuge when the nightmares came.

"Has your daughter heard anything from Quint?" he asked, making awkward conversation as they mounted the porch steps. Mary Gustavson did not reply. Her posture had gone rigid. Her face had taken on the stoic expression of a soldier marching into battle.

Judd reached out to open the door for her, but she brushed his hand aside, seized the heavy brass knocker and gave three sharp raps as if to announce her presence. The wooden floor on the other side creaked under the weight of heavy footsteps. The door swung inward.

The woman standing in the entry was built like a brick wall, her face so devoid of expression that it might have been cast in concrete. Gretel Schmidt had cared for Edna since the days following her stroke. She had also taken on the cooking, washing and housekeeping duties. What she lacked in beauty she made up in competence. Judd valued her service and paid her enough to keep her from seeking other work.

"Gretel, Mrs. Gustavson has come to see my mother," he said. "I presume she's in the parlor."

"This way." Gretel lumbered back down the paneled

hallway toward the sitting room. Judd turned to go back outside, then hesitated. Mary Gustavson wouldn't have come here on a social call. Something was wrong. If it concerned his family, he'd be well-advised to stay and listen. Tossing his hat onto a rack behind the door, he followed the two women down the hall.

The parlor's tall windows faced east, offering morning sun and a fine view of the mountains. Edna Seavers had covered them with heavy drapes, which she kept drawn against the light. The well-furnished chamber was as gloomy as the inside of a funeral home.

Edna sat in her customary rocking chair, reading the Bible by the light of a small table lamp. Her ebony cane was propped against one arm of the chair. The stroke had weakened her left side. She could hobble around the house with the cane, but for ventures out she preferred the dignity of a wheelchair.

Was she any worse today? Judd studied her now, remembering what he'd learned from her doctor last month. His mother was more fragile than even she realized. But her will seemed as strong as ever.

She glanced up as Gretel entered to announce the visitor. Her bony little fingers laid the black marker ribbon across the page before closing the Bible. "Two cups of hot chamomile tea, Gretel," she said. "Please have a seat, Mrs. Gustavson."

Mary Gustavson lowered her ample frame onto the edge of a needlepoint chair. After her long trek in the sun, she would surely have preferred cold lemonade, or even water, to hot tea. But she sat in awkward silence, blinking as her eyes adjusted to the darkness.

Judd found a seat in a shadowed corner. He had no wish to be part of the drama, only to listen and observe.

"Have you heard from your boy Quint, Mrs. Seavers?" Mary spoke good English but with a thick Norwegian accent.

Judd could almost read the thoughts behind his mother's disapproving frown. The tea had yet to arrive, and this uncouth woman had already brushed aside the social pleasantries and cut to the reason for her visit.

Judd stifled a groan as he realized what that reason must be. Only one thing would have brought Mary Gustavson to this house.

"As a matter of fact, I haven't heard a thing," Edna sniffed. "But why should my son be any concern of yours?"

Mary's reply confirmed Judd's guess. "Our Hannah is with child. I've no doubt that your son is the father."

"How can you be sure?" Edna's voice dripped acid. "For all you know, your daughter could have spread her legs for half the boys in the county. Just because we've got money, and because Quint isn't here to defend himself—"

"Hannah is a good girl!" Mary was on her feet, pale and quivering. "If she lost her virtue, it was because she loved your son, and he took advantage of her."

"My son is a gentleman. He would never take advantage of any girl." Edna took a moment to pour a cup of the tea that Gretel had placed on the table. Her face was a mask of propriety but her hands were shaking. Tea sloshed onto the tabletop, staining the lace doily that covered it. "In any case, you've no proof of your accusation. Until Quint appears to answer for himself, there's nothing I can do."

"Then write him a letter! Tell him he has to come home!"

Edna set the teacup back on its silver tray, its contents untasted. "Nobody wants Quint home more than I do. I've written to him every week, begging him to abandon this silly adventure. But he hasn't replied. I don't know if my letters have even reached him. So you see, Mrs. Gustavson, whether I believe you or not, my hands are tied."

"But this is your grandchild, your own flesh and blood!" Mary's work-roughened hands twisted in anguish. "My Hannah and your Quint, they were sweethearts. There was nobody else for her. You know that. Soon the whole town will see the scandal. Do you want that for Quint's child? To be born without a father? To be called always by that ugly word?"

Edna's hand fluttered to her throat. "Really, Mrs. Gustavson, I don't see—"

"You must get Quint home! My daughter needs a husband! Her baby needs a name!"

Edna had shrunk into her chair like a threatened animal. "But that isn't possible. We don't know how to reach him."

"Then who is going to marry my Hannah?" Mary demanded. "Who is going to be a father to your son's baby?"

"I will."

Judd rose as he spoke the words. Shocked into silence, the two women stared at him.

"You?" Edna choked out the word. "But that's preposterous!"

"Do you have a better idea?" Judd's mind raced, the plan falling into place as he spoke. "The marriage would be in name only, of course. We could have the divorce papers drawn up ahead of time. When Quint gets home, all we'd have to do is sign them. Then he and Hannah would be free to marry."

Mary Gustavson was gazing at him as if he'd just saved her family from a burning house. "Thank you," she murmured.

Judd forced himself to meet her tearful gaze. He'd offered his help out of genuine concern. But what was he getting that poor girl into? Even on a temporary basis, he was no bargain for any woman. And no bride deserved a mother-in-law like Edna Seavers.

"Don't thank me yet," he said. "I'm willing to marry your daughter, Mrs. Gustavson, but Hannah needs to be willing, too. She needs to understand the conditions and agree to them."

"She will. I'll make sure of that."

Judd glanced at his mother. Edna's face was white with suppressed anger. Her lips were pressed into a rigid line. None of this was going to be easy. But he had to do the right thing for his brother's child—and for that child's grandmother. He turned back to Mary.

"If you don't mind I'd like to ask Hannah myself. The least the poor girl deserves is a proper proposal."

Mary looked hesitant. Her mouth tightened.

"I'll come calling tonight, after supper. You can tell her to expect me."

"Should I tell her the rest?"

"How much does she already know?"

"About this? Nothing. I told her I was going to visit a friend across the creek. But she'll find out soon enough."

"Then I'll leave it in your hands. You know Hannah better than I do." Actually he scarcely knew Hannah at all, Judd realized as he spoke. Maybe this wasn't such a good idea.

"I'll be going then." Mary turned back to Edna. "I thank you for your hospitality, Mrs. Seavers."

Edna's only reply was a nod to Gretel, who'd appeared in the doorway to usher the visitor outside.

No sooner had the front door closed than the storm broke inside the parlor. "How dare you, Judd? The idea, marrying that wretched girl! Think of the scandal! What will people say?"

Judd faced his mother calmly. "What will they say if I *don't* marry her? Once she starts to show, the whole town will be counting backward. They'll know it's Quint's baby she's carrying. For us to turn her away when we have the means to help—that would be heartless."

"But why should we have to take her in? Give her some money! Send her away to some home where she can have the brat and place it for adoption!"

Judd willed himself to feel pity instead of outrage. "The brat, as you call it, is your grandchild—maybe the only one you'll ever have. What if something happens to Quint? What if he doesn't come home?"

"Don't say such a terrible thing. Don't even think it." Edna pressed her fingertips to her forehead, then released her hands to flutter like wounded doves to her lap. "In any case, you're here. Surely you'll be wanting a proper marriage, with children of your own."

"Not the way I am now."

"What nonsense! Look at you! You're perfectly fine! You're getting stronger every day!"

Judd sighed. "Mother, sometimes I envy your ability to see only what you want to see. Now if you'll excuse me, I need to get the men started on the new horse paddock."

Without waiting for her response, he strode out of the parlor, down the hall and onto the covered porch that ran the width of the house. On the long train ride home, he'd had plenty of time to sort out the realities of his life. He wouldn't have minded having a family of his own. But his black spells and nightmares were worse than he'd wish on any woman. He wasn't fit to be a real husband—or a real father. But now he had a chance to rescue an awkward situation. What kind of man would he be if he walked away?

He would do his best to stand in for Quint, Judd vowed. He would treat Hannah as a sister, keeping her at a distance, avoiding any physical contact that might be misunderstood. When Quint returned, he would sign the divorce papers and hand her over to the father of her child, untouched.

His behavior would be above reproach.

Hannah washed the supper dishes, rinsing them in fresh water and handing them to her sister Annie to dry. An evening breeze fluttered the flour sack curtains at the window and freshened the torrid air that hung beneath the smoke-blackened rafters. Frogs and crickets chirped in the willow clumps that bordered the creek.

Annie, who was sixteen and pretty, chattered about the dress she was making over and the new boy she'd met in town. Hannah tried to listen, but her thoughts wheeled and scattered like a flock of blackbirds, too agitated to settle in any one place.

Three days ago her mother had broached the subject of her pregnancy. Their confrontation had begun in anger and ended in tears. Hannah knew how badly she'd let her family down. Unless Quint returned to marry her, there would be scandal, expense, and one more Gustavson mouth to feed. Worse, she'd be branded as a fallen woman. Her reputation would cast its shadow on her whole family, especially on her sisters.

Sweet heaven, she'd been so much in love. On that last night, she couldn't have denied Quint anything—not even her willing, young body. But how many lives would be touched by her foolish mistake?

A snore rose from her father's slack mouth, where he lay sprawled in his armchair. Affection tugged at Hannah's heart. Soren Gustavson toiled from dawn to dark, tending the pigs he raised and coaxing potatoes, beets and carrots from the rocky Colorado soil. No doubt he'd been told about his daughter's condition. But pregnancy was women's business, and he was too worn-out to deal with it. He was a small man, his overtaxed body already showing signs of age. Hannah's baby would add one more burden to his sagging shoulders.

Overhead, the floor of the loft where the children slept creaked under her mother's footfalls. Mary Gustavson always made time to tuck her younger children into bed and listen to their prayers. Tonight, however, the calm cadence was missing from her steps. She seemed rushed and uncertain.

Over supper, she'd mentioned something about a visit from Judd Seavers. But a neighborly call was no reason to get her in a tizzy. Judd was probably coming to discuss the strip of grassland that bordered his ranch. The Seavers family had been trying to buy it from Soren for years. Soren had always refused. This time would be no different.

Mary came downstairs smoothing her hair. She'd taken off her rumpled apron and replaced it with a clean one. "Wash your face, Hannah," she fussed. "You've got a smudge on your cheek. Then come here and let me comb out your hair. You're getting too old for those pigtails!"

Annie giggled as Mary dragged Hannah toward the washstand. What was going on? Why should it matter how she looked to Judd? He'd certainly seen her in pigtails before—not that he'd ever given her a second glance.

She squirmed on the wooden stool, her thoughts flying even faster than her mother's hands. How would Mary know Judd was coming unless she'd spoken with him? And what could he want, if his visit wasn't about buying land?

Her heart dropped. What if something had happened to Quint? What if the family had gotten word, and Judd was coming to break the news?

She was working up the courage to ask when three light raps on the door galvanized everyone's attention. The brush stilled in Hannah's hair. Soren started from his nap.

It was Annie who flew across the floor to answer the

knock. She flung the door open. Lamplight spilled onto the porch to reveal Judd standing on the threshold. He was dressed in a clean chambray shirt and a light woolen vest. His face was freshly shaved, his hair still wet from combing.

He had the look and manner of a prisoner facing execution.

"Good evening, Judd." Annie spoke politely but with a hint of flirtation in her voice. "Have you come to see my parents? They're both here, and they're expecting you."

Judd shifted his feet. His riding boots gleamed with fresh polish. "Good evening, Mr. Gustavson, Mrs. Gustavson. Actually it's not you I've come to see. I'd like your permission to speak with Hannah—alone."

Chapter Three

"Go on, Hannah. You and Judd can talk on the porch."
Mary Gustavson prodded her daughter with the end of
the hairbrush. Hannah came forward as if she were being
dragged by invisible chains. Her blue eyes were wide
and frightened. How much had her mother told her?
Judd wondered. Did she know what he'd come for?

Maybe he was making a ghastly mistake.

Judd felt his mouth go dry as he watched her. He'd
always thought of Quint's girl as pretty, in a whole-
some, apple-cheeked sort of way. But he'd never seen
her like this, with lamplight falling on her glorious hair,
framing her face in a halo of gold. Even in her faded
gingham dress, Hannah was beautiful.

Lord, what was he thinking? Even poor and pregnant,
this girl could have suitors fighting to marry her. Why
should she accept a man like him, even to give her child
the Seavers name?

"Good evening, Judd." Her voice barely rose above
a whisper.

Judd swallowed the knot in his throat. "Let's go outside, Hannah," he murmured, offering his arm.

She hesitated, then laid her hand on his sleeve. Her touch was as weightless as dandelion fluff, but he could feel the warmth of her flesh through the thin fabric. The contact sent an unexpected—and unwelcome—jab of heat to his loins. Judd swore silently. This was going to be awkward as hell.

They crossed the moonlit porch. As they reached the steps, she cleared her throat and spoke.

"What is it, Judd? Has something happened to Quint? Is that what you've come to tell me?"

"No." He shook his head, thinking how much his arrival must have worried her. "Nothing's happened. Not that we know of, at least. We haven't heard from Quint since he left."

"Neither have I." She moved down the steps and into the yard. Her mother had suggested they talk on the porch, but Hannah appeared too restless to settle in one spot. Judd was restless, too.

"Do you think he's all right?" she asked.

"We have to hope he is. Alaska's a big, wild place. If Quint's out in the goldfields, there'd be no way for him to mail a letter, or to get one."

"I've written to him every week." Her voice quivered as if she were on the verge of tears.

"So has our mother. And I've written a few times myself. He'll have a heap of letters waiting for him when he gets back to Skagway."

They walked a few steps in silence, wandering out toward the corral where the two poor-looking cows drowsed under the eave of the milk shed. Hannah had taken her hand away from his sleeve. She walked with her arms clasped around her ribs, as if protecting herself.

"You said you wanted to talk to me, Judd."

"Yes." Lord, this would be one of the hardest things he'd ever done. "I want to make you an offer, Hannah. You may not think much of it, but hear me out."

She turned to face him. "I'm listening. Just tell me."

"All right." Judd sucked in his breath, forcing himself to meet her questioning gaze. "Your mother paid us a visit today. She told us about your baby."

Hannah reeled as if she'd been kicked in the stomach. She caught the corral fence with one hand, feeling slightly ill. She'd wanted to keep the baby a secret for as long as possible. But her mother had shared that secret with the last two people she'd have chosen to tell.

"You don't have to convince me the baby's Quint's," Judd said. "Seeing the two of you together for so long, I've no doubt of that. The question is, what do we do now?"

"We?" Hannah gulped. "Since when did this become your problem, Judd?"

"Since I found out you were carrying my brother's child—my own flesh and blood."

Oh, blast, he was going to make her cry. Hannah steeled her emotions. "I've written to Quint about the baby," she said. "I've written again and again. Surely, once he gets word, he'll catch the next boat home."

"But when will he get word? And how soon will he

be able to get back? If he's still in the Klondike when winter comes, he might not make it out till spring."

Hannah's heart sank. "The baby could be born before Quint comes home."

"Without a proper father and without a legal name."

A nighthawk swooped through the darkness, moonlight flashing on its white-barred wings. The horse Judd had tied to the fence shifted in the darkness. Hannah gazed up at Quint's taciturn brother, a man ten years her senior. She'd known him all her life, yet scarcely knew him at all. Surely he hadn't meant what had just popped into her head.

No, of course not.

"I'm offering to marry you, Hannah," Judd was talking fast now, pouring out more words than Hannah had ever heard from him at one time. "It wouldn't be a real marriage, of course. Not in the physical sense. But it would be legal. It would give your child the Seavers name and the right to inherit Quint's share of the estate one day. And it would hush up the gossip that's bound to start before long.

"Not entirely. People can count." Hannah responded from a well of stunned silence.

"They can and they will. But you'd be a Seavers. A married woman. And you'd have me to defend your honor."

A married woman.

Judd's wife.

Hannah's legs had gone rubbery. She gripped the fence rail for support. The last thing she'd expected from tonight's visit was a proposal.

Judd was waiting, studying her face with fathomless eyes. What had prompted him to make such an outlandish offer? Had her mother begged him to rescue her daughter from shame?

Had he really thought this out?

With effort she found her voice. "What about Quint? What's to happen when he comes home?"

"I've thought it all out. Our family lawyer can draw up divorce papers before the wedding. When Quint comes home, we can sign them, and you'll be free to marry the father of your child."

Hannah stared at the ground, where the moonlight had joined their shadows. The next question lay unspoken between them, cold and dark and too dreadful for words. Hannah forced herself to give it voice.

"And if Quint doesn't come back? What then?"

"That would be up to you. Anytime you wanted your freedom, we could sign the papers and be done with it. Your child would still be a Seavers with the right of inheritance." Judd exhaled raggedly. "But there's no need to dwell on that now. Unless we hear differently, we have to assume that Quint's fine, and that he'll be coming home."

"Yes, of course we do." The night was warm, but Hannah felt a shiver pass through her body. She turned away from Judd and fixed her eyes on the North Star. She often looked that way when she wanted to feel close to Quint. Where was he now? she wondered. Was he gazing at the night sky, just as she was—maybe thinking of her while she entertained a marriage proposal from his brother?

Would marrying Judd be an act of betrayal or an act of sacrifice, for the sake of Quint's child?

Was she actually thinking of saying yes?

"I can promise you'd be taken care of the way Quint would want," Judd said. "You'd have your own bedroom and anything you needed in the way of clothes, things for the baby and even gifts for your family. Gretel does the cooking and housework and cares for my mother. That wouldn't change."

Hannah's fingers wadded the fabric of her skirt as his words sank in. The Gustavsons had always been poor, but they'd been happy enough. She'd never minded hard work, nor had she wasted time yearning for finery. The idea of having a servant was as foreign to her as living on the moon. As for the rest…

Something shrank inside Hannah as she imagined passing her days in that silent, gloomy house with the waspish Edna Seavers and her huge, grim mastiff of a housekeeper. She'd assumed that when she and Quint married, they would build a home of their own. But for the sham marriage Judd was proposing, that wouldn't be practical. And she could hardly stay with her own family—not if she wanted her child to be accepted as a Seavers.

Behind her, Judd waited in silence. Maybe he thought she'd jump at the chance to have a comfortable life, to live in an elegant ranch house, wear store-bought clothes and sit down to meals she didn't have to prepare. Well, he was wrong. In that great mausoleum of a home she would feel more like a prisoner than a cherished, useful member of the family.

Exasperated, she swung back to face him. "Who

came up with this crazy idea, Judd? Did my mother talk you into saving my honor?"

He shook his head. "Nobody talked me into anything. And my reason for coming here tonight has little to do with your honor—or with you as a woman."

So much for pretty words. Hannah scuffed at a stone, her silence pressing him to continue.

"If Quint doesn't make it home, that baby you're carrying will be all we have left of him—and most likely the only grandchild my mother will ever have. I'm looking out for the next generation of our family."

"But what about you, Judd? Surely you'll want to find a good woman and start a family of your own before long."

He looked away from her, his eyes fixed on the jagged silhouette of the mountains. A falling star streaked through the darkness and vanished. "I'm not a fit husband for any woman," he said. "Chances are I never will be."

"I don't understand."

"There's no need for you to understand. If you become my wife, we'll keep a proper distance like polite friends. My personal demons will be my concern, not yours."

"I see," Hannah murmured, though she really didn't. She was just beginning to realize how little she knew about Judd Seavers.

He exhaled slowly, like a man who'd just set down a heavy weight. "I'm not expecting your answer tonight," he said. "Take time to think about what I've said. Either way, I don't want to rush you."

"Thank you." Hannah moved away from the fence. Thinking too long about Judd's offer would only make her decision harder. It would be just as well to make up her mind and be done with it. "Come back in the morning," she said. "I'll give you my answer then."

"I'll come tomorrow night." He loosed the reins from around the fence rail and eased onto his tall black gelding. The grimace that flashed across his face told Hannah that the war wounds still pained him. "I want to do right by you and my brother and the child. But I won't push your decision. You need enough time to be sure."

For the space of a heartbeat he gazed down at her upturned face. Then, without giving her a chance to say more, he swung toward the gate and nudged the horse to a canter.

Hannah stood watching the dark forms of horse and rider blend into night. Only then did she allow her legs to betray her. Like a wounded animal, she sank to the ground. Her fingers splayed over her face. Her body quivered with unspent sobs.

This couldn't be happening. She was still coming to terms with having a baby, still clinging to the hope that Quint would come home and marry her. Judd's offer had come from nowhere, slamming her with the force of a lightning bolt and leaving her in a state of shock.

Judd meant well, Hannah reminded herself. His plan was well thought out, covering all possibilities. If Quint came back, she could divorce Judd and marry her true love. If the worst happened, and Quint didn't return, the child conceived in that impulsive moment would never know the stigma of bastardy. He or she would have the Seavers name, access to a good education and a share of the finest ranch in the county.

On one hand, how could she even think of saying no?

On the other hand, how could she find the courage to say yes?

Judd Seavers was like a black pool with unknown pitfalls lurking beneath its quiet surface. He'd mentioned his personal demons. What did he mean? Could he be an alcoholic, or even an opium addict? Was he capable of harming her or her child? Surely not—but how could she be certain?

And the women in that big, silent house! Edna Seavers had never shown her anything but contempt. And Hannah had been terrified of Gretel Schmidt since she was five years old. Unless she wanted to spend her time in hiding, she would have to confront both of them. The very thought of it made her knees go watery.

The front door opened, flooding the yard with lamplight. "Hannah?" Her mother's questioning voice rose above the drone of frogs and crickets. "Are you all right?"

"Yes, Mama, I'm fine." Hannah rose and stepped into the light. "Judd's gone. He left a few minutes ago."

"Well?" Mary Gustavson stood on the porch, one hand holding the lantern, the other fisted on her ample hip. She would know, of course, that Judd had come to propose. The fact that he hadn't come back inside to speak with Soren didn't bode for good news.

"Judd's coming for my answer tomorrow night. I can't believe you told him about the baby, Mama—and told his mother! Mrs. Seavers must hate me!"

"I did what I had to, Hannah. There's been a wrong done. For the sake of your innocent babe, it's got to be put right."

Hannah sagged against the porch rail, feeling like a child called on the carpet. "I've written to Quint," she protested feebly. "Surely, when he gets word, he'll come home."

Mary sighed wearily. "Unless those letters are opened and read, you might as well be dropping them down a well. Face up to it, girl. You haven't received so much as a note from the boy. You can't depend on him to come back and marry you."

"But Judd—I barely know him, Mama. And he's nothing like Quint. I might as well be marrying a stranger."

"He's a Seavers and he's willing. For now that's got to be enough. Count your blessings and say yes before he changes his mind. Otherwise there's no help for you—or for us."

Fighting tears, Hannah brushed past her and entered the house. Soren was awake, sitting up in his chair with a worried frown on his face. Annie hovered behind him, wide-eyed and anxious. Hannah's eyes took in the shabby room, the bare puncheon floor and smoke-blackened rafters, the cracked, mismatched dishes stacked on the rickety counter. She forced herself to see Annie's thread-bare hand-me-down dress and the tired shadows under her father's eyes. She thought of her younger brothers and sisters asleep upstairs, the younger ones laid like firewood in a single bed, the older ones on the floor.

Otherwise there's no help for you—or for us...

Her mother's words echoed in Hannah's mind as she forced herself to face reality. The Gustavsons were dirt-poor. Marriage into the Seavers family would give her the means to better their lot—Judd had implied as much himself. Refusing his offer would be foolish. Worse, it would be selfish.

Hannah had no desire to become Mrs. Judd Seavers. But her own feelings were of no importance. The chance to give her family and her child a better life outweighed all other considerations.

She had no choice except to say yes.

Judd lay awake in the four-poster bed his parents had once shared. The night breeze stirred the gauzy curtains at the tall window. The moon cast a ghostly rectangle of light on the far wall.

Had he done the right thing, asking Hannah to marry him? Lord, she'd looked so forlorn, so frightened, as if he were some kind of monster. What had he been thinking?

Punching the flatness from his pillow, he rolled onto his side and stretched his long legs. Maybe he should ride back to the Gustavson house tomorrow morning and tell her he'd changed his mind. That would take the pressure off the poor girl. She could wait for Quint without the awful prospect of marriage to a physically and mentally scarred man looming over her.

He wouldn't have to abandon her entirely. He could offer money to help with the child, maybe even hire her father and a couple of the older boys to help out on the ranch. The Gustavsons were honest and hardworking. He could do worse.

The sight of Hannah's face, with its deep blue eyes and spun-gold halo of hair, lingered in his memory. How could Quint go gallivanting off to Alaska and leave a girl like that? How could any man be fool enough to leave her?

Muttering under his breath, he twisted onto his belly and willed himself to sleep. Things would be all right either way, he reminded himself. If Hannah refused him, he could go his way, knowing he'd at least tried to do the right thing. If she accepted—a quiver passed through his body at the thought of it—he would treat her with kindness and respect, keeping a proper distance between them at all times.

And he would redouble his efforts to find Quint. After hearing the news about their mother's health, he'd hired a detective agency in Denver to look into Quint's whereabouts. With Hannah's pregnancy, the search had become even more urgent. The young fool needed to come home and face up to his responsibilities as a father.

If he was still alive…

Judd could feel himself sinking into a dark fog. It swirled around him, pulling him down like quicksand. From out of the murk came the sharp report of rifle fire and the deep-throated boom of exploding mortar shells. He was charging up the muddy hill, boots sliding, lungs bursting as men fell around him—the men he'd trained with, learned to respect, even love. Blood, flesh and brains spattered his face as the young lieutenant ahead of him disintegrated in a blast of gunfire. With no time to wipe himself clean, Judd clenched his teeth and kept moving forward. When he could see a target he fired. When he ran out of bullets he hacked a path with his bayonet.

On his right was his boyhood friend, Daniel Sims. They'd signed up together and gone through training side by side. Judd was struggling to stay on his feet when he saw Daniel go down, clutching his body at the waist. Blood poured between his fingers. He was gut shot, a guarantee of a slow and miserable death.

"Kill me, Judd…" Daniel's boyish features twisted in agony. "I'm done for. Get it over with, for the love of God…."

Judd's service revolver was still in its holster. Judd drew the gun.

"Do it, friend." Daniel's face was a mask of agony. Blood trickled from one corner of his mouth. "I'll bless you with my dying breath…."

Judd thumbed back the hammer. His blood-slicked finger tightened on the trigger. He gazed down into his friend's face through a haze of smoke. But now it wasn't Daniel he saw. It was…Quint.

No!

Judd awoke with a scream of anguish. The sheets had tangled around his jerking body. They were drenched in cold sweat.

Hannah spent the morning helping her mother do the family wash. It was hot, steamy work, made worse by her queasy stomach. First the buckets of water had to be carried from the pump to the big copper wash boiler. Then, with a fire blazing beneath the iron stand, whittled curls of homemade lye soap were tossed into the simmering water. Once the soap dissolved, the clothes and dirty bed linens were added. It was Hannah's job to stir them with a broomstick until the water cooled enough to use the washboard.

To ease the strain on their hands and bodies, Hannah and her mother took turns. While one hunched over the board, scrubbing the garments and tossing them into the rinse water, the other twisted each piece, shook it out and hung it on the clothesline. The process took all morning.

Hannah ached with the weariness of a night spent tossing and turning, but she knew better than to complain or to plead her condition. Her mother had done laundry up to the last hours of her pregnancies. The same would be expected of her.

While they scrubbed and rinsed, Annie took charge of the kitchen and the small children. After Hannah married Judd Seavers, Annie would likely be promoted to laundry duty while thirteen-year-old Emma took on the child-minding. The boys would help Soren in the fields until they were old enough to take over the farm or leave to find menial jobs that paid a paltry wage. As things stood, none of them would go to school beyond the eighth grade or do any kind of work that didn't involve their hands and backs. It was a hard lot, but it was theirs and they seemed to accept it.

Somehow, Hannah resolved, she would find a way to make their lives better.

With the laundry finished, there was still plenty to be done. Hannah found a rusty hoe and went out to help eleven-year-old Peter finish weeding the vegetable patch. Today she was grateful for the work and for Peter's childish chatter. It helped to keep her mind off Judd's impending visit.

What if he didn't come?

What if he'd changed his mind?

She wouldn't blame him if he backed out. After all, she hadn't given him any encouragement. Judd knew, of course, that she didn't love him. Truth be told, she wasn't even sure she liked him. But that didn't matter, Hannah reminded herself. This was a legal arrangement, to protect her baby's rights until Quint returned. She and Judd would be living together like two polite strangers in a boardinghouse, with his mother and the formidable Gretel as chaperones.

A nunnery couldn't be safer.

She was yanking the last tangle of wild morning glory from among the string beans when she glanced up to see a tall rider approaching the gate. Even silhouetted as he was, against the blaze of the setting sun, there was no mistaking Judd. Hannah's emotions fluttered between dismay and relief. He'd come early, giving her no time to clean up. Her hair was plastered to her head beneath her mother's ugly sunbonnet. Her face was smudged with dirt, and her gingham dress felt glued to her body. But why should her appearance matter? It wasn't as if they were courting. He'd made her a plainspoken offer last night. Now he'd come for his answer.

She could only hope it was the answer he wanted to hear.

Judd eased out of the saddle, opened the sagging gate and led his horse through. It was early yet, barely sundown. The family would still be at evening chores. He should have waited until after dark. But never mind, he wouldn't be here long. All he needed was a single word from Hannah—yes or no.

Turning, he closed the gate behind the horse. He could

see Hannah now, standing in the family garden, clad in the faded gingham she'd worn to see Quint off on the train. A blue sunbonnet dangled by its strings from her left hand. With her right hand, she was hurriedly finger-combing her hair back from her face. The motion strained the fabric of her bodice against one swollen breast.

Judd tore his eyes away from the sight. Hannah might be his future bride, but she was carrying his brother's child. He'd be well-advised to discipline his gaze.

Hannah had seen him. She hesitated, shading her eyes against the sunset. Then she started down the slope. She was tall like her mother, with a graceful stride that no one else in her family possessed. Just watching her walk toward him was a pleasure.

"Hello," she greeted him as she came within speaking range. Judd could feel the tension in her voice. Maybe she'd decided to refuse his offer. He had to be prepared for that.

"Let's walk," he said, tethering his horse to the pasture fence. "When you're ready you can tell me what you've decided."

With a silent nod she turned onto the footpath that led along the creek. The tall wheatgrass rustled in the wind. From somewhere beyond the willows, a bobwhite quail piped its plaintive *lay-low, lay-low.*

Judd waited for Hannah to speak. He'd promised he wouldn't rush her but it wasn't easy to keep still. It was as if she held his life in her strong, young hands.

"I don't suppose you've heard from Quint," she said at last.

Judd exhaled slowly. "You know I'd tell you right off

if I had. I went into town and checked the mail myself. There was nothing."

"But he's got to be alive, don't you think? Surely, if the worst happened, somebody would notify his family."

"One would hope so. I'm already working with an agency in Denver. They've got a good reputation for finding people. But anything they can do is going to take time."

She clasped her work-reddened hands. Her interlaced fingers flexed and twisted. "Meanwhile, there's not much we can do except wait, is there?"

"You and I can wait. It's the baby who can't."

"I know." She turned to face him. The setting sun cast her features in soft rose-gold, like a Renaissance painting. "That's why I've decided to accept your offer, Judd. Until Quint comes home, I'd be honored and grateful to be your wife."

Chapter Four

Hannah and Judd were married by a Justice of the Peace the following Sunday afternoon. The ceremony took place on the spacious front porch of the Seavers house with Edna Seavers, Gretel Schmidt and the nine Gustavsons attending. Annie, in the pink Sunday dress she'd made over for herself, served as bridesmaid.

Hannah wore the yellowed satin wedding gown that Mary Gustavson had put away and saved for her daughters. In place of a veil, her unbound hair was crowned by a simple garland of wildflowers that Annie had picked and woven half an hour before. She carried the same flowers in a bouquet.

The mood of the little gathering might have been better suited to a funeral than a wedding. Edna sat poker-straight in her wheelchair, looking as grim as Whistler's portrait of his mother. Gretel, in gray, stood like a granite pillar behind her. Mary, in a mismatched skirt and jacket with an out-of-style hat, wept through the entire ceremony. Soren simply looked lost. Only pretty, romantic

Annie seemed to see the wedding as a cause for cele-
bration. But she was too busy shushing the younger
children to pay close attention to the ceremony.

Hannah stood beside her bridegroom, fighting tears.
For as long as she'd been in love with Quint, she'd
dreamed of their wedding. She'd imagined looking up
into his twinkling brown eyes, clasping his hand as she
vowed to love, honor and cherish him for the rest of their
lives. She'd imagined their first kiss as man and wife,
long and tender, filled with sweet anticipation of the
wedding night to come.

Now the wrong man stood at her side, his low voice
speaking vows that were more mockery than truth. "I,
Judd, do take thee, Hannah, to be my lawfully wedded
wife…to love and to cherish…in sickness and in health…
as long as we both shall live…"

Their divorce documents lay locked in Judd's desk,
awaiting only two signatures to dissolve the marriage.
There would be no wedding night, no intimacy of any kind.

*Where are you, Quint? Why can't you come home
and put an end to this travesty?*

"With this ring I thee wed…" Judd was sliding a thin
gold band onto her finger. The metal felt cold and strange.
It was all Hannah could do to keep from tearing herself
away, leaping off the porch and dashing for the gate.

"I now pronounce you husband and wife. You may
kiss the bride." The justice was an elderly man who'd
performed hundreds of weddings. Judd had taken him
aside and asked him to leave out the kiss, but the old
fellow had clearly forgotten.

Hannah had scarcely glanced at Judd during their

vows. Now she looked up into his questioning gray eyes. Theirs might not be a real marriage, but it was a genuine partnership, bound by a spirit of cooperation. To turn away from the kiss would end the ceremony on a sour note. Hannah understood this. So, she sensed, did Judd.

Giving him the barest nod, she tilted her face upward. Her breath stopped as his hand braced the small of her back. She had never kissed any boy except Quint. Maybe if she shut her eyes and pretended…

His lips closed on hers, smooth and cool and gentle. For an instant Hannah froze. Then she found herself stretching on tiptoe, leaning into the kiss, prolonging it by milliseconds. Something fluttered in her chest. Then Judd released her and stepped aside.

She had just kissed her husband. And it hadn't been the least bit like kissing Quint.

Little by little Hannah began to breathe again. Her mother came forward to hug her, swiftly followed by Annie. Soren pumped Judd's hand. It was all for show. Every adult, even Annie, knew what was happening and why.

Edna Seavers did not join in the congratulations. While Gretel hurried off to fetch lemonade and dainty apricot tarts, Edna sat in her wheelchair as if she were carved from granite.

Let her be, Hannah thought. But Judd, it seemed, was determined to have things his way. Seizing her elbow in an iron grip, he steered her toward his mother's chair. "Aren't you going to welcome Hannah into the family, Mother?" he demanded.

Edna's gaze remained fixed on her hands.

"Mother?"

She sighed. "I'm getting one of my headaches, Judd. Please take me to my room."

Judd's eyes flickered toward Hannah. "It's all right," she murmured. "Go on."

She stood watching as he opened the front door and eased the chair over the threshold. This, Hannah sensed, was just a small taste of things to come. How could she face living in this house with a woman who hated her so?

Come back, Quint, she pleaded silently. *Come back and take me away from here.*

Judd wheeled his mother to her room at the rear of the house's main floor. The door opened to whitewashed walls hung with black velvet draperies that blocked the light from the tall windows. After the brightness of afternoon sunlight, Judd could barely see the narrow bed with its black canopy and coverlet and the photograph of his father that sat on the nightstand in a black-edged frame. The room was like a crypt for the living.

It was the gloom of existence in this house, as much as Daniel's urging, that had driven him to enlist in Roosevelt's Rough Riders. He'd returned carrying burdens of his own. Now, after three months, it was as if he belonged here, one more shadow in a house full of shadows.

His mother's bones were weightless, like a bird's. Judd lifted her in his arms and lowered her to the bed. She lay propped on the pillows, waiting for him to cover her legs with the merino shawl she kept folded on a nearby chair.

In her younger days, Edna Seavers had been a beauty,

with chestnut hair and laughing dark eyes. But grief over her husband's death had transformed her into a husk of her former self. Judd couldn't imagine what it must have been like, loving someone that much. Seeing what it had done to his mother had taught Judd an early lesson. Love walked hand in hand with devastating loss.

"You've always prided yourself on your fine manners, Mother," he chided her. "You had no call to be rude to Hannah and her family."

Edna made a little sniffing sound. Her jaw remained stubbornly set.

"Hannah's your daughter-in-law. She's a fine girl from an honest, hardworking family. Since she'll be living under this roof, the sooner you accept her, the easier it'll be for all of us, including you."

Edna glared up at him. "A fine girl, is she? Then why is she strutting around with one man's ring on her finger and another man's child in her belly?"

"Mother, that's enough—"

"I won't abide her, Judd. She took Quint away from me. Now she's taken you, as well!"

"I need to get back to our guests. I'll have Gretel bring you some tea." Judd turned and walked out of the room. He loved his mother and did his best to be a respectful son. But sometimes the only way to deal with her was to leave.

Quint was their father's son—handsome, charming, impulsive and generous. Maybe that was why Edna loved him so much. But Judd had come to realize that it was mostly Edna's nature he'd inherited—brooding, melancholy and as stubborn as tempered steel. When the two of them clashed they could remain at odds for weeks, even months.

Now he'd unleashed the devil, marrying Hannah and bringing her home. But it was done and Judd wasn't backing down. For the sake of Quint's child, this was one battle he was determined to win.

He could only hope Hannah was up to the challenge.

Forcing his face into a cheerful expression, he stepped out onto the porch. The festivities had moved to the grassy lawn, where the younger Gustavsons were enjoying a spirited game of tag. Hannah stood with her parents and the old man who'd performed the ceremony. The ivory satin gown was too large for her, but it draped her slim curves with a softness that Judd found oddly becoming. With her flowing corn silk hair crowned by its wreath of flowers, she looked like a creature from another age, a pagan nymph poised at the edge of a meadow.

"Come and play with us, Hannah!" A little boy tugged at her skirt. "It's more fun with you! You can be 'it.'"

She glanced down at her wedding dress. "I'm sorry, Ben, but I really don't think…"

"Please!" His eyes would have melted granite. "Just for a minute!"

She hesitated, then laughed as she set her glass on the porch step. "Why not? Here I come!"

Kicking off her slippers, she lifted her skirts clear of the ground and charged into the mob of children. They scattered, shrieking and giggling as she darted after them.

Watching the play of sunbeams on her hair, Judd felt an ache rise in his throat. Hannah was so vibrant, so full of life and light. How would she survive in this house?

Watching her with Quint, in her pigtails and faded cottons, he'd wondered idly what his brother saw in the girl. Now he knew. Hannah had a glow about her, a simple, happy warmth that kindled deep inside and emerged on the surface as beauty, like sunlight through a stained-glass window. Judd couldn't get enough of looking at her.

She was his bride, and the mother of Quint's child.

Lord Almighty, what had he done?

Hannah stood under the porch's broad eave, watching the twilight shadows steal across the lawn. The refreshment table had been cleared away. Her mother's wedding gown had been wrapped in an old muslin sheet and boxed away to await the next Gustavson bride. Her family had kissed her and gone home. The ordeal of her wedding day was coming to its blessed end.

She'd taken her time unpacking the meager possessions that her family had brought over from their house. They'd crammed her clothes, her meager toiletries, and a few precious books—everything she owned—into a single gunny sack. It had struck Hannah as ludicrous, putting her pitiful things into the cavernous dresser drawers and huge cedar-lined wardrobe. The scent of the wood, however, had enthralled her. She had thrust her head deep into the wardrobe and inhaled, filling her senses with the spicy cedar fragrance.

Judd had insisted that she take the large upstairs bedroom where his parents had once slept. She would need the space when Quint came home, as well as for the baby.

Giving Hannah no chance to argue, he had moved his things back to his old room next door. Quint's room, farther down the hall, remained much as he'd left it. Edna and Gretel's rooms were directly below, on the first floor.

Closing her eyes, Hannah pushed back her hair and let the breeze cool her sweat-dampened face. Back home, her mother would be putting the little ones to bed. Her father would be dozing in his chair while Annie and Emma cleaned up in the kitchen. Her brother Ephraim, who dreamed of becoming a preacher, would be reading the Bible by the light of a guttering candle.

Hannah's new home seemed as grand as a palace. But she missed the cheery warmth of the little farmhouse. She missed having her family around her.

From the bunkhouse beyond the barn, the breeze carried the twang of a guitar and the faint aroma of tobacco smoke. Four hired hands stayed at the ranch full-time, with extra men hired on for roundup and branding. Hannah had yet to meet any of them. Even if she did, she knew better than to become too friendly. Her mother had warned her about cowboys and the harm they could do to a woman's reputation. Gretel was so aloof that she barely spoke, and as for Judd…

Her hand toyed with the thin gold band he'd placed on her finger that afternoon. A quiver passed through her body at the memory of him standing beside her in his trim black suit, his jaw freshly shaved, his unruly brown hair wet-combed into place. She remembered the questioning look in his gray eyes as he bent to kiss her, the sudden lurch of her heart as his cool, firm lips closed on hers.

Judd was her husband in name only, Hannah reminded herself. He didn't love her—maybe didn't even like her. But his loyalty to Quint was beyond question. He could be counted on to keep his distance, avoiding anything that might be seen as too much familiarity.

Hannah had acquired a new home and a new family today. But no one here was her friend. She had never felt more alone in her life.

The crickets had awakened in the long grass. In the east, the rim of the waning moon gleamed above the wooded hills. For years Hannah had fantasized about her wedding night, lying in Quint's arms, touching and being touched in ways that made her ache to think of them.

But this wouldn't be the wedding night she'd imagined. She would spend it alone in a bed that seemed as wide and cold as the distance that separated her from the man she loved.

"Are you hungry?" Judd's soft-spoken question startled her. He'd come out onto the porch and was standing a few steps behind her. "There's cold chicken and rice pudding in the kitchen. I can ask Gretel to get you a tray."

Hannah shook her head. She'd declined supper an hour earlier, pleading a queasy stomach. In truth, she hadn't been up to sitting down with her new family. "Don't bother her," she said. "Can I fix myself a sandwich later, or will Gretel chase me out of the kitchen with a meat cleaver?"

He moved forward to stand beside her at the porch railing. "You can do anything you want to, Hannah. This is your home now."

"I don't mean to sound ungrateful, but this place doesn't feel much like home. At home I had things to do. I was allowed to be useful. Here—it's like living in a fine hotel."

He sighed. "Does the room suit you well enough?"

"It seems as big as a barn—although I've never seen a barn with a canopied bed in it. Do you realize I've never spent a night alone in my entire life?"

He cast her a sharp glance. "You'll get used to it. And if you need anything, I'll be right next door. All you have to do is call out."

"I see." Her callused hands gripped the railing. Color scalded her cheeks. What if he'd taken her remark as an invitation? It had certainly sounded like one.

She glanced up at him, feeling vulnerable. Judd was her legal husband. If he decided to exercise his marital rights, who would stand in his way?

The rising moon cast his hawkish features into planes of light and shadow. Quint was the handsomer of the two brothers, but Judd possessed an aura of raw power, a quiet authority that, Hannah realized, had always been there. He was wearing the white shirt he'd been married in, but now the sleeves were rolled up, exposing sinewy forearms. His throat, bared by the open collar, was dark bronze against the white linen. The pale, wounded soldier who'd stepped off the train three months ago was gone. The man who stood beside her now was sun-tanned and healthy, with a strength that Hannah found disturbingly sensual.

Hannah studied his big, scarred hands where they rested beside hers on the porch rail. She could feel his eyes on her, sense the unspoken questions they would hold. A freshet of liquid heat trickled downward to form a shimmering pool in her loins.

What would happen if she were to reach out and touch him?

"Are you afraid of me, Hannah?"

His words startled her. Her eyes flashed upward to meet his.

"You've no need to be," he said. "You're my brother's woman. You're carrying his child—my own flesh and blood. I'd give my life to protect you."

"I know," Hannah whispered.

"Then know that you can trust me. When you agreed to this marriage, I promised I wouldn't lay a hand on you. You'll find me a man of my word."

Hannah groped for a fitting reply, but her tongue felt frozen to the roof of her mouth. The only sound that emerged came from the pit of her stomach—a low, rumbling growl.

Judd stifled a chuckle. "I thought you said you weren't hungry."

Hannah flushed in the darkness. "Maybe just a little."

"Tell you what," Judd said. "Gretel makes the best rice pudding in six counties. I've got a hankering for a bowl of it myself. Have a seat on the steps while I go and get us some." When Hannah hesitated, he added, "That's an order, Mrs. Seavers."

Hearing her married name spoken was enough to buckle Hannah's knees. She collapsed on the top step and sat trembling as Judd crossed the porch and went into the house. Heaven save her, she'd really done it!

She was Mrs. Judd Seavers before all creation—and soon the town would be buzzing with the scandal. She could just imagine the whispers. With Quint gone barely three months, that scheming little Hannah Gustavson had up and married his brother!

She couldn't expect to be treated kindly for it, especially once the baby started showing. But she would learn to hold her head high, Hannah vowed. She was a Seavers, legally and lawfully wed. More important, her baby was a Seavers. No one could dispute that now or ever.

What an unholy mess she'd created.

Scarcely five minutes had passed before Judd returned with two heaping bowls of rice pudding. "I hope you like it cold, he said. "Gretel had already put the pan in the springhouse."

"Cold is fine." She accepted one of the bowls. Her fingers brushed his as she took it. She ignored the tingle of awareness as he took a seat beside her, close enough to talk but not close enough to touch her. The pudding smelled of fresh cream and rich spices whose names Hannah could only guess. When she tried a tentative spoonful, her mouth closed on a raisin.

"Do you like it?" Judd asked.

"It's…heavenly. We had rice at home and a little sugar. But spices and raisins were luxuries my parents couldn't afford."

"Luxuries? A handful of raisins and a sprinkle of cinnamon?"

"I can tell you've never been poor." Hannah tasted another spoonful of pudding. It was all she could do to keep from bolting it down. Since Judd had given her the perfect opening, she summoned her courage and brought up the matter that had been pressing her mind since his proposal.

"You said I could have money for gifts. I hope you were serious, because I want to help my family—school clothes for the boys, some pretty dresses for Mama and the girls, maybe some books—Annie loves to read. And my father could use a new plow…" Hannah's voice trailed off. The list of her family's needs, she realized, was endless. She didn't want Judd to think she was greedy.

"I'll arrange for an allowance, whatever seems reasonable. You can use it any way you like. No questions asked."

"Just like that?" She stared at him, amazed that such a thing could be so easy.

"Just like that. Next time we're in town we'll stop by the bank. I'll have Mr. Calhoun set up a fund for you with monthly transfers from the ranch account. You can draw on it anytime. And when your brothers are old enough, they can come talk to me about jobs on the ranch."

Hannah swallowed the tightness in her throat. "I don't know what to say. I never expected that kind of generosity."

"I'm only doing what Quint would want for the mother of his child."

"And what about your mother? Will she approve of what you're doing?"

"It's my decision to make. Mother's washed her hands of the whole ranch business."

"I see." Hannah lowered her gaze and made a show of enjoying the sweet rice pudding. According to the Bible, her mother and the fiery sermons she'd heard in church, she deserved to burn in hell for what she'd let Quint do. Instead, it was if the gates of paradise had opened, spilling out all the fine things she'd never had. Reason told her there would have to be a time of reckoning.

The risen moon hung like a pearl against the velvet sky. From inside the house came the sound of a door closing and Gretel's heavy footsteps fading down the hall. A floorboard creaked. Then there was only the drone of crickets and the rustle of the wind in through long blades of grass.

Judd hadn't spoken. The silence between them was growing awkward. Hannah set her bowl on the step and cleared her throat.

"How's your mother's headache?" she asked, making a try at conversation.

She sensed a slight hesitation. "My mother's headache will be better when she wants it to be. For now, she's asleep. I'm guessing she'll be fine in the morning."

"Until she sets eyes on me, she will." Hannah shook her head. "Why does she hate me so much, Judd?"

"It's change she hates, not you. Give her time. She'll come around."

"She can take all the time she wants. Meanwhile, I plan to stay out of her way. Not that I'm ungrateful, mind you. This is her home, after all, and she has a right to peace and quiet. It's just…" Hannah's voice trailed off. She stared down at her hands.

"Just what?"

"It doesn't really matter how your mother feels about me. But I want her to love the baby. I want my child— Quint's child—to be happy here."

Judd had been gazing across the yard. Now he turned toward her, his face in shadow. "My mother isn't a bad woman, Hannah. She's old and sad and set in her ways. Give her a chance."

"Will she give *me* a chance?"

"Eventually, I hope. But you may need to make the first move."

Hannah felt her heart shrink inside her chest. "I don't know if I'm ready to do that."

"Suit yourself." Judd rose wearily. "It's getting late. I'll be leaving with the men at first light to drive the herd up to summer pasture. You won't be seeing me for the next couple of weeks. But Sam Burton, the assistant foreman will be staying here to keep an eye on things. He'll know where to find me if I'm needed."

Hannah bit back a murmur of dismay. If not quite a friend, Judd was the closest thing she had to an ally. Now he'd be leaving her alone with those two forbidding old women.

"We'll go to the bank when I get back. Meanwhile, I'll get some cash out of the safe and leave it under the blotter on my desk. Take it. Use it for anything you need."

Hannah gulped back a rush of emotion. "I don't know what to say. No one's ever been so generous with me."

"I'm just doing what any brother would do for his sister. I hope you'll look on me that way. As a brother."

He reached down to help her to her feet. His big hand was leathery with calluses, his skin cool against her fingertips. "Thank you," she murmured. "I'll do my best not to disappoint your family."

"Just be happy here. For now, that's enough."

He loomed above her in the darkness, his eyes hooded. Her hand lingered in his like a small animal seeking safety.

Suddenly she realized she was trembling.

Judd released her and stepped back. "You look all in," he said. "It's been a long day for both of us. Come on, I'll walk you to your room."

Hannah preceded him through the open doorway to the front hall. A glowing lantern hung from a hook on the door frame. Taking it in his hand, Judd led the way up the dark stairs to the second floor. The bedroom doors were closed. His was on the left, hers on the right.

"You'll need this." He opened Hannah's door and handed her the lantern. "Remember, if anything frightens you just call out. I'll hear you."

"I'll be fine. Thank you for everything, Judd."

He stood looking down at her, the lamplight flickering on his face. He was her husband. This was their wedding night. Hannah grappled with a sense of unreality. Maybe tomorrow she'd wake up and discover that the whole day had been a strange dream.

Maybe tomorrow a letter from Quint would arrive, and everything would be put right.

"Sleep well, Hannah." He turned away, went into his own room and closed the door. Hannah did the same. Light from the lantern cast distorted shadows on the papered walls. She could hear Judd moving about, walking across the floor, taking off his boots, opening and closing a drawer. He could hear her equally well, Hannah reminded herself as she peeled off her clothes and dropped her flannel nightgown over her head. He might even be able to hear her using her chamber pot. She would need to be mindful of every sound she made.

Snuffing the lantern flame, she crawled under the covers. After so many years of sleeping with her sisters, Hannah felt lost in the vastness of the double bed. She stretched her limbs, touching all four corners at the same time. The sensation of emptiness was frightening.

She was exhausted after the emotional day. Even so, sleep was a long time coming. The bed was too soft, the room too silent. Hannah missed the sound of breathing and the familiar, warm aroma of her slumbering sisters.

Only when she lay straight along the edge of the mattress, taking up the least possible amount of space, did she finally drift off. Her sleep was restless. The darkness behind her closed eyelids swirled with disjointed dreams and images—the train carrying Quint out of her reach; Edna Seavers's head imposed on Gretel's sturdy body; Judd's somber gray eyes and big, scarred hands; winged babies floating over a full moon….

A sound jolted her awake. She sat bolt upright, staring into the darkness as the confusion faded. As she came fully alert she heard it again—a low keening sound, punctuated by gasps and muttered words. "No… oh, God, no…"

"Judd?" Swinging her legs off the bed, Hannah flung herself toward the wall that separated their rooms. Pressing close, she could hear what seemed to be the sound of a thrashing body. The moaning and muffled curses continued.

"Judd?" Hannah rapped lightly on the wall. She'd heard that some men returned from war with terrible nightmares. If that was happening to Judd, it could be dangerous to wake him. At the very least, it would be imprudent to enter his room.

She rapped on the wall again, harder this time, but Judd gave no sign that he'd heard. The night he'd asked her to marry him, he'd said something about his personal demons. Was this what he'd meant?

Not knowing what else to do, Hannah waited by the wall. The night was warm, but she was shivering beneath her thin nightgown. Was he dangerous? Could she do anything to help him? Did she dare?

Something hard—perhaps the nightstand—crashed to the floor. Then, abruptly, there was silence. Gathering her courage she risked a light tap. "Judd, are you all right?"

There was a scraping sound, like a piece of furniture being righted. "I'm fine," Judd growled. "Bad dream, that's all. Should've warned you about them. Go to sleep, Hannah."

"Can I get you anything?"

"No!" His vehemence warned her not to say more. Still shivering, Hannah crossed the floor and crawled between the rumpled sheets. She expected Judd to do the same, but she could tell by the thud of his boots and the clink of his belt buckle that he was getting dressed. Moments later she heard the opening and closing of his door and the creak of his footsteps on the stairs.

Chapter Five

The next morning Hannah was up and dressed at first light. But there was no sign of Judd. His bed was made up, his study cloaked in silence. Only when she saw the corner of a bill showing beneath the blotter on his desk did she remember his promise to leave her some cash. He'd been more than generous, but Hannah couldn't bring herself to take the money. Pushing the bills back out of sight, she closed the door behind her and tiptoed outside.

Crossing the porch, she strode out into the yard. The first thing she noticed was that Judd's black gelding was missing from the corral. The cowhands had finished breakfast and were saddling up. Two men were hitching the mules to the chuck wagon. Hannah thought of asking them what time Judd had left and why he'd ridden off so early. But then she remembered that she was Judd's wife. The hired hands would assume that their boss and his bride had spent the night together. To hint at the truth would only provide fodder for gossip.

The men tipped their hats, greeted her with a deferential "Ma'am" and swung onto their mounts. Retreating to the porch, Hannah watched them ride off toward the outer pasture where the herd had been gathered for the drive to the grassy upland meadows. The distance wasn't far. But she knew from past years that it would take time to spread the cattle out and make sure they were well settled.

From the kitchen came the clattering sound of Gretel shaking the ashes down through the grate of the big black cookstove. That had been Hannah's job in the place she still thought of as home. Strangely, she missed the dusty chore. But something told her Gretel might not take kindly to an offer of help.

Pal, the shaggy border collie mix that Quint had raised from puppyhood, sidled up to the porch. Sinking onto the steps, Hannah circled him with her arms and pressed her face into his thick fur. "You miss him, too, don't you boy?" she whispered.

Pal thumped his tail and slicked her cheek with his sloppy tongue. Hannah sighed. At least she had one friend in this alien place.

Whistling to the dog, she cut across the yard and found the path that wound through the willows to the place where the creek widened to form a marshy pond. Red-winged blackbirds flitted among the cattails. A muskrat trailed a silken wake through the quiet water. Hannah settled her skirts on a fallen tree trunk. With one arm around the dog, she watched the sunrise fade from flame to pale indigo.

She and Quint had come here often during their growing-up years. It was a private place where they could share dreams and secrets. Seated on this very log, they'd explored their first tentative kisses, lips brushing lips, then clinging with the awkwardness of first passion.

A tear welled in Hannah's eye and spilled down her cheek. For years she'd dreamed of becoming Quint's wife. Now it was as if her whole world had turned upside down. She was Mrs. Seavers. But she was married to the wrong brother.

Rising, she walked back along the path to the corral. Most of the horses had gone on the cattle drive, but a few remained, swishing their tails and munching their morning oats. The two huge Belgians that pulled the hay wagon stood next to the fence. Both of them were hungry for attention. She stroked one, then the other as they butted her with their massive heads. She got along fine with the animals on the Seavers ranch, Hannah reflected glumly. It was the people who kept her in a state of anxiety—the very people whose acceptance could determine her baby's future.

The truth struck her like a shotgun blast. She'd been wallowing in self-pity, making excuses for her own unhappiness. But it was time to grow up. She had a child on the way. For the sake of that child, she needed to do the very thing she dreaded most.

Resolute now, she turned back toward the house. Hiding from Edna Seavers would gain her nothing. And Judd was right. She would have to make the first move. The longer she put it off, the more strained their relationship would become.

Pausing by the outside pump, she ran cold spring-water over her hands and splashed it on her face. Her damp fingers smoothed her tangled hair. As a married woman, Hannah knew it was high time she abandoned her girlish pigtails. But she had no pins to fasten her heavy locks into a style a lady might wear. For now she wove the waist-length mass into a single plait down her back and tied it with the piece of yarn she kept in her pocket. Elegant it wasn't. But for an appearance at breakfast, it would have to do.

Judd had mentioned that his mother rose early and usually took breakfast in the dining room. She would likely be there by now. Hannah could only hope the woman was in the mood for company.

She mounted the porch and opened the front door. The greasy aromas of bacon and fried eggs triggered a spasm of nausea. Rushing down the steps again, she doubled over and vomited behind a scraggly, untended rosebush. Even when empty, her stomach continued to heave. How could she face her new mother-in-law over breakfast when the very smell of food made her gag?

But she was making excuses again. Steeling her resolve, Hannah marched back to the pump where she rinsed out her mouth and splashed her face one more time. Putting off the confrontation with Edna Seavers would only make it that much harder to try again.

Lifting her chin she opened the front door and stepped into the house. The dining room lay between the parlor and the kitchen. Her stomach roiled as the breakfast smells seeped into her senses. But at least she had nothing left to throw up.

The dining room was on her left. Hannah forced herself to turn in the doorway. The fleeting hope that Edna wouldn't be there vanished as she saw the sparrowlike figure seated at the head of the table. Not a sparrow, she thought; more like a kestrel—a tiny sparrow hawk with all the instincts of a predator. Her eyes—gray like Judd's—narrowed as Hannah stepped into the room.

"There you are," she said, nodding to indicate an empty chair on her left. "I wasn't sure you'd have the good manners to show up."

Only then did Hannah notice that a place had been set for her—fine gold-edged china on a fresh linen table-cloth, with a folded napkin tucked under the fork.

Hannah took her seat in a high-backed Queen Anne chair. "I apologize for being late," she murmured. "My stomach isn't on its best behavior these days."

"I see." Edna's voice was blade thin. "After this, I hope you'll refrain from discussing bodily functions at the table." She glanced toward the kitchen. "Gretel!"

"Yes, ma'am?" Gretel appeared in the doorway, wearing a charcoal-hued dress with a ruffled white apron and cap. The costume was as ludicrous as a chris-tening gown on a bulldog, Hannah thought, but she knew better than to comment. If Edna Seavers wanted to dress her housekeeper like a fancy parlor maid that was her business.

"Some peppermint tea, if you please, Gretel. A cup for the poor girl, and I'll have one, as well."

"My name is Hannah, Mrs. Seavers."

"Yes, of course." Edna waved her hand dismis-sively. "Have a biscuit. That should settle you until the tea arrives."

"Thank you." Hannah selected a hot biscuit from the

napkin-lined bowl, lifted it to her mouth and took a small bite. It was fresh and flaky. She certainly couldn't fault Gretel's cooking.

"Merciful heaven, do you always eat like that?" Edna was staring at her in horror.

"I'm sorry, I don't know what you mean." Hannah had helped herself only when invited and certainly hadn't stuffed the biscuit into her mouth.

"That! Taking a bite out of the whole biscuit. I won't have such atrocious manners at my table!"

Hannah battled the urge to jump up and leave. Whatever happened, she vowed, she wasn't going to let Edna Seavers unsettle her. "Maybe you could show me the correct way to eat a biscuit, Mrs. Seavers." she said politely.

Edna dabbed at her mouth with a corner of her napkin. "Knowing that family of yours, I'm not surprised that you never learned. I didn't invite you to join our household, but as long as you're here you're going to acquire some decent table manners. Otherwise you can sleep in the barn and eat with the pigs."

Hannah recoiled as if she'd been scalded. True, she'd grown up poor, but no one in her family had ever spoken so unkindly to her. She forced herself to hold her tongue. She was enduring this humiliation for the sake of her child, she reminded herself.

"First the napkin," Edna said. "It goes on your lap, folded in half, like this."

At home, Hannah's father had eaten with a dish towel tucked into the bib of his overalls. Mary and the girls had worn aprons to protect their dresses. The folded napkin appeared so small as to be useless. "What if I spill?" she asked.

"A proper lady doesn't spill," Edna said, frowning. "Now for the biscuit. Watch me and do exactly as I do."

Hannah mirrored the motions of Edna's little squirrel hands, placing the biscuit on a saucer that sat to the right of her plate. Her stomach was getting queasy again. A bite of the biscuit might have eased the nausea, but she knew better than to take so much as a nibble.

"Now, with the butter knife..." Edna demonstrated and Hannah followed, placing a dab of butter on the edge of the saucer. Next Edna showed her how to break a small piece off the biscuit, apply a minuscule amount of butter with her own knife and slip the morsel daintily into her mouth.

The whole process struck Hannah as impractical. People who ate this way clearly had a lot of time.

"Now, you do it with me watching." Edna sat back in her chair and impaled Hannah with her hawkish eyes. Hannah's hands trembled as she buttered the fingertip-sized chunk of biscuit. As she raised it to her lips, it slipped from her fingers and dropped onto the immaculate linen tablecloth.

"Oh—" Hannah snatched up the morsel and put it in her mouth, hoping Edna wouldn't see the ugly grease spot the butter had left behind.

She did see it, of course. One thin eyebrow slithered upward. Fingers drummed ominously on the tabletop. "How such a clumsy dolt could have bewitched any son of mine is beyond my understanding. Now, again, and this time do it right!"

By now Hannah's nerves were so frayed that she could barely hold the knife. It slipped out of her buttery fingers and clattered to the floor. Only the arrival of Gretel with the tea saved her from an all-out tongue-lashing.

Hannah forced herself to sit quietly while Gretel brought her a clean knife. Edna was teaching her how to be accepted as a Seavers. She would grit her teeth, by heaven, and learn all she could.

She studied the way her mother-in-law sipped from the fragile teacup and mirrored her every motion. Little by little, she managed to get through the next few minutes without disgracing herself. Yes, she was learning. And the peppermint tea was actually helping to settle her stomach. She was even able to down a few forkfuls of scrambled eggs.

"I've arranged for a seamstress to come and fit you for some new clothes," Edna said. "Heaven knows, we can't have you walking around in those rags you brought from your home. You look like you've spent the past ten years hitched behind a mule—for all I know you have!"

Despite her resolve, Hannah was rankled. After all, her parents had done their best to keep their family clothed. "Not everyone can afford fine gowns, Mrs. Seavers. Since I don't plan on attending any fancy dress balls, my own clothes will suit me fine."

"Nonsense! People are going to see you! What will they think of me if I let my daughter-in-law dress like a ragamuffin? Priscilla Hastings is the best seamstress in three counties! She's also an excellent hairdresser." Edna frowned at Hannah's hastily done braid. "That head of yours is a disgrace! I've seen horses' tails that were better groomed!"

"You really don't need to—"

"Not another word, young lady." Edna rose shakily and reached for the cane on the back of her chair. "You wanted to be a Seavers, and you've managed to accomplish that. Now, by heaven, you're going to look and act like a Seavers, not the spawn of some ignorant Norwegian dirt farmer!"

Hannah's head went up. Criticizing her clothes and manners was one thing. Disparaging her family was quite another.

"My parents are honest, hardworking people!" she retorted. "I don't care who you think you are, Mrs. Seavers. I won't have you talking about my family like that!"

Edna had reached the doorway to the hall. She turned, one eyebrow tilted disdainfully. "Well, at least you have some spunk in you, girl. There may be hope for you yet. I've some letter writing to do. Priscilla will be here at ten o'clock. Have Gretel fetch me when she arrives."

Edna's cane thumped awkwardly on the hardwood floor as she made her way back to her room. Hannah sat quivering in her chair. She was doing her best to get along with the woman. But it seemed her mother-in-law was out to humiliate her in every possible way.

Blast Judd! How could he have gone off to the mountains, leaving her here to fend for herself against his sniping, miserable mother?

Maybe that was the whole idea. Throw them together and get out of the way until the flying fur settled. If he'd

done it on purpose, there were going to be words when
he got home!

Gretel entered through the swinging double doors that
separated the dining room from the kitchen. Her narrowed
eyes surveyed the table and came to rest on Hannah.

"Are you finished, miss?"

Hannah's napkin dropped to the floor as she stood.
"I'm quite finished, thank you," she said, fighting tears.
"And my name isn't *miss*. It's Hannah. Or if you want
to be formal, it's Mrs. Seavers. Mrs. Judd Seavers."

Leaving her words to hang on the air, she stumbled
out of the dining room and fled toward the front door.

By the time the buggy carrying Mrs. Priscilla Hastings
pulled up to the Seavers house, Hannah had regained her
composure. She had taken another walk with the dog
and returned in time to rinse the tears off her face and
brush the tangles out of her hair. She was braced and
ready for whatever came next, she told herself. But as
she stood at her upstairs window, watching the matronly
seamstress climb down from the buggy seat and hitch
her horse to the iron ring on the post, Hannah felt her
heart begin to sink.

Quint had always claimed he loved her just as she
was. But with every day that passed, she could feel herself changing, becoming older, sadder and wiser. Now
Edna was forcing her to change in other ways.

Who would she be before this day was over?

Who would she be when Quint finally came home?

Knowing she'd be summoned if she didn't appear
on her own, Hannah was waiting in the parlor when

Edna entered with the seamstress. Priscilla Hastings, a widow in her late forties, was plump and bustling, with pink cheeks and smartly coiffed gray hair. Hannah had been prepared to dislike her on principle, but she found herself warming to the woman's friendly manner.

"I do believe I've seen you in town, Hannah—usually on your way to the depot with a letter, as I recall. But never mind that, let's get started."

Plopping onto an ottoman, she opened the large carpetbag she'd brought. Inside were some well-thumbed copies of *Harper's Bazaar,* a quilted case filled with fabric swatches, a measuring tape, scissors, a pad of notepaper and a cushion full of pins.

"You'll need something for going out, of course, and several dresses to wear around the house," she said, flipping through the magazine pages. "I've marked several styles I think might work for you."

Hannah cast a panic-stricken glance at Edna, who'd settled herself in the rocking chair. Surely the woman was aware that in two months time, none of these clothes would fit. Why didn't she say something?

Edna gave a barely perceptible nod, and Priscilla smiled. "I understand you're going to have a little one. I'll make your dresses with double seams that can be let out by snipping a few threads. After the baby, I'll come back and take them in again. And don't you worry about my spreading gossip. How long do you think I'd stay in business if I carried tales from one house to another?" She opened one of the magazines. "Now let's look for some styles that you'll be comfortable wearing."

The next two hours flew past. After choosing the style and fabric for four dresses—two calicos, one demure chambray and a dark blue silk with a white collar—Hannah was carefully measured. Priscilla chatted while she plied the tape and wrote down the numbers.

"This should be enough to get me started on your new wardrobe, dear. You'll need petticoats and under-things, as well as shoes and stockings. Now that I know your size, I can pick some up in town and bring them when I deliver the first dress."

"Thank you so much," Hannah said. "I never thought I'd have such pretty clothes to wear."

"You can thank your mother-in-law," the seamstress said. "She's the one who hired me to come. What do you think, Mrs. Seavers? Will the dresses be all right?"

Edna waved her hand. Her face looked as if she'd just bitten into an unripe quince. "They'll do as fine as any, I suppose. And there's no need to thank me. I can hardly have a member of my household wandering about in rags, can I?" She picked up her needlepoint from a side table. "Now take the girl upstairs to her room and do something about that dreadful hair!"

June 27, 1899
Dear Quint,
If my letters have reached you, then you know about the baby and my wedding to Judd. It's not like we're really man and wife, you understand. We're just waiting for you to come home so we can put things right.

Hannah laid the pen on the blotter. Her lips moved silently as she reread what she'd written on the pretty linen stationery she'd found in the desk. What would Quint think when he learned she'd married Judd? Would he understand the sacrifice his brother had made to give his child a name?

Oh, why did things have to be so complicated? Why couldn't Quint just come home and marry her?

Judd says he wrote you a letter explaining things. He left two weeks ago on the summer trail drive so I haven't seen much of him. But your mother has been generous with me. She brought in a seamstress to make me some new gowns. I'm wearing one of them this morning. The woman also showed me some ways to pin up my hair. She said I had the most beautiful hair she'd ever seen, but I'm sure she was just being kind. I still need a lot of practice on the hairstyles. This morning I tried a coiled braid…

But why was she telling Quint about her hair? Why should a man be interested in such trivialities?

Things are fine here on the ranch. Judd says you did a good job while he was gone. Pal misses you. He has become my best friend. We take walks down to the pond and remember how nice it was having you with us.

My clothes are getting tight around the waist. I haven't felt the baby move yet, but maybe in a few weeks it will happen. How I wish you were here, sharing all this with me. If you read this, please let us know you're all right. I worry. Judd worries. Your mother worries. We all care about you.

Tears misted Hannah's vision. She'd always been emotional. Now it seemed her pregnancy had magnified that trait. Even the thought of Quint, so far away, raised a lump in her throat.

She finished the letter on a cheerful note, sealed it and took it down to the front hall. Since Edna didn't approve of her daughter-in-law wandering into town alone, Hannah had little choice except to send it with Gretel, who took the buggy into Dutchman's Creek every week for supplies.

Hannah would have preferred carrying the letter herself. For one thing, she liked being sure her message was safely in the mail. For another, she missed the pleasant shortcut across the fields, with blackbirds circling overhead and the long grass singing against her skirts. The Seavers home was as sumptuous as a mansion. But since Judd's departure, she'd felt more like a prisoner than a guest, let alone a member of the family. For the first time in her life, Hannah found herself with idle time on her hands, and she hated it. She wanted to be of use. She wanted to be needed and valued.

So far she'd discovered just one project she could work on without getting in the way. Edna's long-neglected roses had been planted below the porch, on either side of the front steps. When Hannah first noticed the six bushes, they'd been scraggly with deadwood and withering from lack of water and fertilizer. Without bothering to ask permission, she'd rummaged for gloves and tools in the shed and enjoyed hours of pruning, digging, carrying water from the trough and raking in manure from the corral. So far, the rosebushes had rewarded her with new leaves and a profusion of tight green buds. If Edna had noticed the change, she'd made no mention of it. But at least she hadn't complained.

As Hannah passed through the front hall, she glimpsed her reflection in the gilt-framed mirror. Last week Priscilla Hastings had delivered three of her dresses. Today Hannah had chosen an airy gingham in soft hues of pink and blue. Now she stopped to stare at the fashionable young woman in the glass, with her hair fluffed and pinned into an upswept pompadour. Who was she? With every passing day, Hannah was becoming less certain.

She hadn't seen her family in nearly a week. Only now, as she pictured each loved face, did she realize how much she'd missed them. She would go today, Hannah resolved. The Gustavson farm wasn't far—thirty minutes, more or less by the footpath she and Quint had worn bare over the years. Edna would probably welcome her absence for a few hours.

Cheered by the prospect of a visit, she hurried back to the kitchen to tell Gretel where she was going. Then with renewed energy she set out across the pastures.

Judd sat on a wooded knoll astride Black Jack, his tall gelding. The sun was warm, the pine-scented air crystal clear. Bees and butterflies, foraging for sweetness, darted among the wildflowers. A pair of mating ravens, their talons clasped in a wild embrace, made dizzying spirals against the sky.

Judd's eyes scanned the horizon of white-capped peaks. Nature had been generous this year. Winter snows had been deep, spring rainfall abundant. There would be plenty of food and water for cows and wildlife alike.

In the grassy meadow below, cattle grazed belly-deep in summer grass. Spring calves, growing fast, chased and frolicked in the sunlight.

Judd shifted in the saddle, resting his hand on the horn. The cattle should be fine here until fall roundup. He had run out of excuses to stay on the mountain. It was time to take the men and go back to the ranch.

He wasn't looking forward to the return. Here under the roofless sky Judd had felt himself healing. The bloody nightmares that plagued him at home had not followed him here. Only the memory of Hannah's angelic face and trusting blue eyes had haunted his dreams. Hannah—the wife he couldn't allow himself to touch.

Here, separated by time and distance, he almost felt safe. But as soon as he saw her, Judd knew that the devil would start whispering in his ear. The urge to reach out, to brush her shoulder or cup the curve of her face in his palm, would be like a cry in him. Beyond those simple gestures lay the hellfires of temptation—lying in his bed at night, hearing her little sleep sounds through the wall, imagining her in his arms.

Hannah didn't love him, Judd reminded himself. She belonged heart, body and soul to Quint. He had promised to return her, untouched, to her rightful husband. Until that day came he was her guardian, the holder of a sacred trust. It was a trust he was determined not to betray.

Nudging the horse to a walk, Judd started down the slope to the meadow. It was time to call in the men, pack up the gear and head out.

He was nearing the meadow when he heard a sound that made his heart sink—the frantic bawling of a calf in trouble. Judd's eyes scanned the grassy flat below. At first he could see nothing amiss. Then he looked toward the meadow's far side, where the land had crumbled away to form a steep precipice. The calf must have stumbled over the edge.

Judd spurred his mount to a gallop and shot across the flat. No one else was close by, so it would be up to him to find the calf. He could only hope he wouldn't end up having to put an injured animal out of its misery.

Reaching the edge of the meadow, he flung himself out of the saddle. From somewhere below the crumbling bank he could hear the calf bawling piteously. Now the mother, missing her young one, had joined in the ruckus. Judd swore as he drew his pistol and fired three shots into the air. The signal would summon his men to help. The four-month-old calf would weigh more than a grown man and it would be crazy with fear. If he had to go down over that edge and haul it to safety, Judd didn't want to be alone.

Dropping flat to distribute his weight, he bellied his way to the crumbling rim. Now he could see the calf. Its body had fallen against the base of a scraggly pine that grew out of the cliff side. Below it was a sheer fifty-foot drop.

Judd's breath expelled in a low whistle. The calf was

thrashing helplessly, bawling and rolling its eyes. At any second it could struggle free, or the tree could pull loose, sending the animal plunging to its death. There was no time to wait for help. He had to get a rope on the calf now.

Moving as fast as he dared, he scrambled back from the cliff, raced for his horse and seized the coiled lariat that hung on his saddle. As his fingers unwound the rope, his eyes cast around for a place to anchor it. Except for a few saplings, the meadow was bare of trees. Only a hefty boulder, left by a winter avalanche, appeared solid enough to hold the calf's weight.

Judd anchored one end of the rope to the boulder with two wraps and a sturdy knot. Then, with the loop in his hand, he eased forward to the cliff's fragile rim.

The calf was still there, bawling in terror. Judd dropped the loop over its head. But he knew that wouldn't be enough. The calf's weight on the single rope would tighten the loop around its neck, causing it to strangle. He would need to get a second rope sling-fashion around its body. That would mean going over the edge himself.

Relief swept over him as he heard a shout and the sound of a galloping horse. It was Al Macklin, the grizzled foreman. A wise and capable man, he didn't need to be told what to do. Edging forward, he tossed Judd a second rope and anchored the other end to his horse's saddle.

Judd tied Al's rope around his waist, leaving plenty of length on the end to secure the calf. "Keep it tight," he told the older man. "When I've got the calf on, I'll give you a holler."

"Be careful."

Judd eased over the crumbling edge. His boots loosened showers of gravel. Pebbles clattered onto the scree at the foot of the cliff. Judd could hear them fall, but he knew better than to look down.

The calf thrashed in terror, tightening the noose around its throat. With no time to lose, Judd put his full weight on the second rope and swung toward the animal's hindquarters. Wild hooves bruised his ribs as he wrapped the rope's free end into a sling and jerked the knot tight.

He could hear voices topside as other men arrived. "Got it!" he shouted. "Pull us up!"

The sling rope jerked tight. Then the earth groaned and the top of the ledge gave way. The calf screamed as dirt and gravel came crashing down. Judd felt the rope almost pulling him in two. Then his mind imploded into blackness.

Chapter Six

Hannah's shoulders drooped as she trudged back across the fields. The late-afternoon sun blazed in a cloudless sky. The motionless air was stifling. Even the insects had fallen silent.

The visit to her family had left her disheartened. The little ones had stared at her fine clothes as if she were a stranger. Her father had mumbled a greeting and wandered off to repair a broken slat on the pigpen. Her mother, busy with the laundry, had refused Hannah's help, declaring, "Heaven's dear, I can't let you spoil your pretty new dress."

The remark had stung. Hannah would have gladly worn one of her old dresses to visit her family, but Edna had consigned her old clothes to Gretel's ragbag. Her new dresses were all she had.

Only Annie had seemed truly glad to see her. While she plied the butter churn on the porch, she'd peppered Hannah with questions about her new life. What was her room like? How was the food? How had she come by that new dress? And finally, what was it like being married to Judd Seavers?

Only the last question had been difficult for Hannah to answer. "He's been out with the herd for the past two weeks. But when he's around, he's more like a brother than a husband." She paused, groping for more accurate words. True to his promise, Judd hadn't laid a husbandly hand on her. But her feelings for him were far from sisterly. The darkness in him frightened and fascinated her. Part of her wanted to fling up protective walls between them. Another, deeper, part of her wanted reach out to the troubled man she'd married.

"It's awkward—as much for Judd as for me, I think. We've both needed time to get used to the situation. Maybe that's why he went off to the mountains."

"Do you miss him?"

Annie's question had startled Hannah. She did miss Judd, even more than she cared to admit. He was the only member of the Seavers household who treated her as if her presence mattered. "It does get lonesome," she'd replied. "But you could come and visit me. You'd be welcome anytime."

"Welcome?" Annie had snorted daintily. "I'd be less surprised if that old harpy Edna Seavers ran me off with a pitchfork!"

"I'm a member of the family, not a prisoner," Hannah said. "I can certainly have visitors if I want to. If Mrs. Seavers makes you nervous, we can talk in my room or go for a walk. But I'd love to have you come for afternoon tea. Gretel makes these lemon tarts that just melt in your mouth!"

A look of horror had flashed across Annie's pretty face. "*Afternoon tea?* Oh, Hannah, I could never be fine enough for that!"

The noon meal had been an equal disaster. Hannah's mother had squeezed in an extra place at the table. But when Hannah took a furtive peek into the cooking pot, she saw that there was barely enough stew to go around. To join her family would be to take precious food from all their mouths.

Pleading her queasy stomach, she had kissed them all and taken her leave. The next time she came, she vowed, she would not come empty-handed. Judd had told her, after all, that she could use her allowance to buy gifts for her family.

But it would take more than a few presents to raise the Gustavsons out of their poverty.

At the barbed wire fence that divided the two properties, Hannah paused to look back at the place she'd called home for nineteen years. The roof was sagging and the rough log walls barely kept out the winter wind. The farm scarcely produced enough to keep the family fed, let alone a surplus to sell for cash in town.

How could she allow her family to live like this while she was surrounded by comfort and plenty? There had to be something she could do. Her parents were too proud to take handouts, but maybe she could find some way to help them do better for themselves, or at least for the children.

If only she dared talk to Judd about the matter. But he'd already been so generous with her. How could she ask him for more help?

There was no gate in the fence. Over the years, she and Quint had grown adept at scrambling between the wires. Avoiding the nasty barbs of the fence, she pushed the lower wire to the ground with her foot and raised the upper one with one hand. The widened space was just big enough for her to duck between. Gathering her skirts, she lowered her head and shoulders and eased into the opening.

She was partway through when the unthinkable happened. A harmless gopher snake, about the length of her arm, emerged from the grass and slithered across her shoe.

Hannah was used to seeing snakes in the pasture, but this one startled her. Instinctively she shrieked and jumped back. Too late she heard the sound of ripping cloth and felt the barbs gouging into her flesh. She was caught fast, and the new dress, paid for with Seavers money, was ruined.

Little by little she worked herself loose from the barbed wire. The wounds on her back weren't deep, but they were oozing blood. Her skirt was torn as well where the bottom wire had sprung up as she jumped away. What a disaster! Edna Seavers would give her the tongue-lashing of her life!

Head down, Hannah trudged along the path. She would wash the dress and mend it as best she could. But it would never look pretty again. Worse than the damage was the thought of how ungrateful she would appear to be. Edna had been generous enough to buy her something nice. And she had gone right out and carelessly ruined it.

The big house loomed in the distance, whitewashed and gleaming like some heavenly gate where she would be compelled to answer for her sins. She would face the punishment she deserved with no evasions. That was the least she could do.

As she neared the house she realized that something had happened. Men and horses were milling around the corral. Now she recognized the chuck wagon that she'd last seen headed for the mountains. Her pulse leaped. The men were back.

Judd was back.

Heedless of her torn dress and bleeding shoulders, Hannah broke into a run.

Only as she reached the back gate and burst into the yard did she notice that the horses were coated with lather and dust. The men were hauling something out of the back of the wagon—a makeshift stretcher fashioned from two straight aspen trunks and a woolen blanket. On the stretcher, half-hidden by its sagging sides, was the rangy figure of a man.

Hannah's gaze darted around the circle of whiskered faces, seeking the one face that wasn't there. Her throat felt as if she were being strangled by invisible hands.

The man on the stretcher moaned.

She forced herself to look at him.

Judd was still dressed in his bloodstained clothes. Every part of him that Hannah could see was a mass of scrapes, cuts and bruises. She swallowed a gasp.

His swollen eyelids opened. His battered lips moved. "Hullo, Hannah…sorry I'm not much to look at…" His eyes closed as he drifted away again.

Hannah fixed her gaze on a wiry young cowboy. "You—get a fresh horse and go for the doctor! Hurry!

The rest of you, let's get him inside. Then one of you can tell me what happened."

Judd's mother had come out onto the porch with her cane. Her face was ashen. She stood ramrod straight, her lips pressed tightly together. Quint had told Hannah how his father had died in a stampede, and how the men had brought his trampled body in off the range to his wife. Now, Hannah thought, the poor woman must be reliving that fifteen-year-old nightmare.

"No, Mrs. Seavers!" Hannah cried, racing toward the porch. "Judd's alive! He's hurt, but he's not going to die! We won't let him die!"

Edna turned her back and hobbled into the house. A moment later, through the open doorway, Hannah heard the firm closing of her bedroom door.

The young cowboy had saddled a spare horse and was already thundering toward the gate. Hannah turned back to the men who carried the stretcher. She wasn't used to being in charge, but somebody needed to make some fast decisions.

"Take him into the dining room and lay the stretcher on the table," she said. "If the doctor needs to work on him that will be the easiest place. We can put him to bed later."

Al Macklin, the foreman, gave Hannah a respectful glance. "Good idea. You heard the lady, boys. Keep him level. The worse you jar him, the worse it'll hurt."

Judd's jaw clenched as the stretcher carriers mounted the porch. He was clearly in pain and trying not to show it. Her hand crept under the sheet and into his palm. His fingers tightened around hers and held on.

"Judging from where he hurts, I'd guess he's got broken ribs and Lord knows what else," Al said in a low voice. "But after what happened, ma'am, your husband's lucky to be alive."

In a few short sentences he told her what had happened. "The calf was banged up and scared, but it should be fine. It was the boss here who took most of the damage when that bank caved in. The trip down the trail in that bumpy wagon had to be hell. But Judd Seavers has been through worse. He's a tough man."

"Yes." Hannah's fingers curled tighter into Judd's big, palm. "Yes, I know."

They reached the dining room and, moving the chairs aside, laid the stretcher on Edna's white linen tablecloth. The rough aspen logs would likely tear the fabric and scratch the polished mahogany surface beneath. But what lay on the stretcher was infinitely more precious. Leaving Judd on the makeshift carrier would make it easier to move his injured body when the time came.

Macklin motioned the men to leave. "We did all we could just getting him here," he said. "I reckon you can tend him till the doctor takes over. Some whiskey might ease his pain. I'll be outside if you need me." He walked back toward the parlor, then paused in the doorway. "Don't think too badly of Edna. She'd help if she was able, but she's not a strong woman."

"Thank you. I'll do my best here." Hannah turned back to Judd. His eyelids were closed, his breathing labored. For all she knew, he could be dying. And she was no doctor. She had no experience with critical injuries.

But she had to do something. If the doctor was busy

with a sick patient or a woman in labor, he could be hours getting here. Find Gretel—that would be the sensible thing to do. She'd taken care of Edna for years. Surely she'd have some nursing experience.

With a last worried glance at Judd, Hannah darted into the kitchen. She was met with gleaming silence. Gretel's apron hung on its customary hook. Her large raffia shopping bag was gone. Only then did Hannah remember that this was Gretel's day to go into town. She had a friend there, another German woman. Quint had mentioned that they often spent the afternoon knitting and playing cards. If Gretel was visiting, she could be gone till suppertime.

Rushing back to Judd, Hannah leaned over him. His face was bruised, his hair matted with blood and dirt. For now, she was all he had. Her help might not be worth much. But at least she could clean him up and try to make him more comfortable until the doctor arrived.

"Judd, can you hear me?" She touched his cheek.

His eyelids twitched and, with effort, opened. "So, am I the main course?" he muttered.

For an instant Hannah thought he must be delirious. Then she realized he was making a feeble joke about being on the table. "I had the men put you here so the doctor could work on you. But until he comes, you're stuck with me. Tell me where you hurt."

He mouthed a curse. "All over. But don't start planning my funeral yet. I'm a long way from making you the prettiest widow in Dutchman's Creek."

Hannah glanced away to hide a flush of color. The Judd she knew would never pay her such a flowery compliment. Clearly he wasn't right in his head.

"Can you move your arms and legs?" she asked.

Judd grimaced with effort. One foot moved, then the other. Knees flexed, then hands and arms before he collapsed with a grunt of pain. "Satisfied?"

"Your foreman thinks you might have broken ribs."

"Could be. Hurts to breathe."

"Then you'd better lie still until the doctor gets here. Meanwhile I'll do my best to get you cleaned up. Where can I find some whiskey?"

"Sideboard. Bottom left," he muttered between clenched teeth. "And I hope to hell you aren't planning to give me a bath in it."

"Be still and rest." Hannah found the whiskey behind a low cabinet door, along with two unopened bottles of wine and a cut glass decanter of what she assumed to be brandy. Her parents hadn't allowed liquor in the house, but once Quint had sneaked a few samples for her to try. As she recalled, she hadn't cared much for the taste.

Twisting the stopper out of the whiskey bottle, she moved to Judd's side. "Will it hurt you if I raise your head?"

His jaw clenched. "Just do it."

Hannah worked her palm under the back of his skull, cradled his head against her waist and gently lifted his head. His hair smelled of earth and blood.

"Careful." She tilted the bottle to his cracked lips. "Not too fast. You don't want to choke."

"You telling an old soldier how to drink, Mrs. Seavers?" His voice rasped like a rusty saw blade. His throat rippled with each swallow. Hannah waited for the whiskey to do its work, dulling his senses, lessening the pain. When his body relaxed against her she eased the bottle away from his mouth. Judging from the lightness of the container, he'd downed most of its contents.

Where to begin? Next she needed to get him clean and determine the extent of his injuries. To do a proper job, Hannah realized, she would have to get him out of his clothes.

"Judd, can you hear me?"

He mouthed something unintelligible.

"I'm going to try and pull your boots off. If something hurts, like a broken bone, stop me."

"Believe me, lady, I will." His speech was slurred. Maybe she'd given him too much whiskey.

"Here goes." She took the toe and heel of his left boot between her hands and began to work it off his foot. Pain flickered across his battered face, but his lips remained pressed in a line. She'd seen that same expression on his mother's face.

Why wasn't Edna here, hovering around the table, tending and soothing her son?

The boot released with a suddenness that sent her stumbling backward. Dirt and pebbles from the collapsed ledge clattered onto the floor. She was better prepared for the other boot and it came off more easily. Beneath the grimy socks his feet were long and pale. The boots had protected them from bruising. If only the rest of Judd had fared as well.

But she was wasting time. Before she could clean his wounds she needed to get his clothes off. The only way to do that without worsening his injuries would be to cut them away from his body.

Edna kept a pair of scissors in her needlepoint kit. Racing into the parlor, Hannah fished them out of the basket. The blades were as sharp as their owner's tongue.

Judd's eyes opened as she bent over him. "What're you doing?"

"Getting you out of this filthy shirt. Hold still. I'll open it up, then I'll need to cut away the sleeves." Her hands shook as she started on the buttons of his brown canvas shirt and the stained underwear beneath. Here and there, dried blood had glued the fabric to his skin. What couldn't be cut away would have to be soaked away, or left in patches to heal.

Unfastening his belt, she pulled the fabric loose from the waistband of his denims. His skin was pale gold, with a dusting of light brown hair. Livid purple bruises mottled his ribs. The rope that had jerked tight around his waist, saving his life, had left a deep red burn.

"I take it I'm not a pretty sight." His eyes were glazed, his mouth slack.

"You're alive. That's all that matters. Hold still." Hannah trimmed around a patch of blood-soaked cloth, fearful of pulling it loose. Her knuckle brushed one taut mauve nipple. The contact triggered a surge of awareness. This man was her husband. The job of nursing him would fall to her. By the time he was well, his body would be as familiar to her as her own.

Plying the scissors, she cut underneath the tattered sleeves, exposing his arms. His flesh was ravaged with scrapes and bruises. Once she got him clean she was going to need salve to disinfect the wounds and stop the bleeding. Oh, where was the blasted doctor? Why didn't he come?

Judd's eyes were closed, but he seemed very much aware of her. "I'm going to get some soap and warm water to wash you," she said. "Does your mother have anything I can put on your wounds?"

He opened his eyes and shifted his weight on the stretcher. Pain triggered a mouthed curse. "Go out and ask Al Macklin for some wire-cut salve. That'll do the job."

"But isn't that for horses and cows?"

"It is. And it's ten times better than that snake oil Gretel keeps in the house. Go on. Al can get you some wrappings, too."

Hannah hurried outside to find the foreman. He was waiting by the corral and quickly got her the things she needed. She suppressed the urge to ask him to come inside and help.

In the kitchen she filled a basin from the kettle on the stove and found some clean rags under the washstand. Judd's head had taken the brunt of the cave-in. He could have head wounds. But she wouldn't know for sure until she got him clean. Taking a sliver of soap and a tin cup to dip water, she returned to the table to start on his hair.

His eyes opened as she leaned over him. He shook his head. "You didn't sign on for this when you married me, Hannah. Leave me be. I'll be fine till the doctor comes."

"I'm not a child. I can do this." Hannah folded a cloth and slipped it under his head. Lathering her hands, she wet his head and gently cleansed his hair.

A moan escaped his lips as the warm rinse water trickled over his scalp. His thick hair had protected him from cuts and scrapes, but not from a swollen lump just below the crown. The foreman had told her that Judd was knocked unconscious by the falling rocks. Along with everything else, he could have a bad concussion.

"Are you an angel or just a saint?" he murmured.

"If I were either one, I wouldn't be in this predicament, would I?" She blotted the water from his hair, laid a dry towel under his head and changed the dirty water in the bowl.

His face was a mess. Judd closed his eyes as she cradled his damp head and sponged the dirt from his cuts and scrapes. The dark, sticky wire-cut salve, which looked like tar and smelled like disinfectant, did a good job of stanching the blood flow. But before long, Judd's face looked as if it had been streaked with black war paint.

Working her way lower, Hannah sponged his throat, shoulders and chest. He watched her in silence, his eyes following every move. Her lips parted as she touched the angry thumb-sized indentation in his side and the puckered pinkish scars that ringed it like a storm circle around the moon. Quint had told her that either the shot or the infection that followed could have killed him. And then there'd been the malaria. Judd Seavers was indeed a tough man.

His bruised ribs were so tender that the slightest pressure made him wince. The ribs needed to be stabilized with wrappings. But Hannah didn't dare try it herself. Any wrong move on her part could puncture a lung or worse. Only a doctor could perform the task safely.

If only he would get here soon.

She lifted his arm slightly. "Don't let me hurt you," she said.

"It's all right. You're doing fine."

"Why isn't your mother here, Judd?" she asked impulsively. "Why did she take one look at you and shut herself in her room? Did the sight of you give her bad memories?"

"More than that, I'm afraid."

His answer left Hannah puzzled. "Quint told me how your father died. It must have been an awful shock for her. But she's your mother! You'd think she'd want to be here with you!"

"Quint didn't tell you the whole story. I'm not sure he even knows it. He was only six at the time." He drew a deep breath, clenching his jaw against the pain. "I was there when my dad was killed. A fourteen-year-old kid without a lick of sense. The cattle stampeded, and I decided to be a hero and head them off. My horse spooked and threw me right in their path."

Hannah forgot to breathe as she waited for what came next.

"Dad came after me. He got me on his horse, and then something went wrong. One minute he was there, and the next he wasn't. I'll never know what happened. Just that when we found him…" His voice broke, then trailed off. "Sorry to get maudlin on you. Must be the whiskey."

"You were only a boy, Judd. You couldn't have known what would happen."

"Dad was my mother's whole life. She doesn't talk about that day, but I know she's never forgiven me. The black clothes, the dark house, the wheelchair—they're all there to remind me of what I did to her."

"But that's monstrous!"

"Is it?" He shuddered as she touched a sensitive spot on the underside of his arm. "At least she's honest about her feelings. Today, when they hauled me out of that wagon, I'd bet good money she took one look and decided I'd finally gotten what I deserved."

Hannah sponged the ugly rope burn that ran along his beltline, skimming his navel. Where human nature was concerned, she was far from wise. But she sensed that Edna wasn't the only one who'd never forgiven Judd for his father's death. Even after fifteen years, Judd hadn't forgiven himself.

He'd revealed more to her in the past twenty minutes than in all the time she'd known him. Maybe the whiskey had loosened his tongue. Maybe when he came fully to himself, Judd would regret being so open with her. But she was part of his family now. If she was to survive the bitterness and tension that hung over the house like a miasma, she needed to understand the people who lived here.

She surveyed his gashed denims. One bad spot on his inner thigh was still bleeding through the fabric. This was no time for modesty. The pant legs, at least, would need to be cut away. Steeling herself, she picked up the scissors and moved to the foot of the table.

"I can't help wondering why you stayed here so long." The blades cut through a thick seam, parting the cloth at the ankle. "You could have left. Better yet, you could have gotten married, built a home and started a family of your own."

"How could I? Somebody had to take my dad's place and run the ranch. Quint was too young, and even with a foreman to boss the work, Mother didn't have the first idea about managing the place. I'd had hopes of going to college, maybe seeing a little of the world…" His breath eased out as the scissors slid upward along the inseam of his trousers.

"So you joined the Rough Riders."

He sighed. "I'd reached the end of my rope. Needed to get away, wanted to do something for my country. And my friend Daniel was wild to go. We signed up together."

"Yes, I know." Hannah remembered Daniel Sims, a cheerful, red-haired young man. His coffin had been shipped home and buried while Judd was still in the hospital.

"Maybe I was looking for redemption—I don't know. Quint was finally old enough to look after things, but he was clamoring to leave, too. I asked him to give me a year. After that, I promised I'd come back and take over."

"And you kept your promise," she said, recalling that Judd's absence had been closer to ten months. Would Quint keep his promise to her? Would he come home, be a husband to her and a father to their child?

"It wasn't a hard promise to keep," Judd said. "Where else would I have—"

The words ended in a growl of pain as the scissors uncovered the crimson patch on his thigh. It appeared he'd been struck by something hard and sharp—a knife-edged rock or a jagged root. It had gouged his flesh all the way up to the groin. The ugly gash was still oozing blood.

His leg would have to be cleaned and wrapped. To get at the entire wound, she would have to trim away the fabric around it, almost to the hip.

So much blood. She could barely find the wound's

ragged edges. Hannah battled light-headedness as she worked the blade of the scissors, exposing more damage. She should have started here. If only she'd realized—

The viselike clamp of fingers around her wrist shattered her train of thought. The sudden awareness of Judd's masculine strength jolted through her body. The scissors clattered to the table.

"You've done enough, Hannah," he growled. "You may be my legal wife but I'm not expecting you to undress me."

His eyes held flecks of granite. In the deepest part of her body, a molten sensation stirred and began a soft throbbing. "Surely you had female nurses in the hospital," she managed to say.

"That was different. Leave me for the doctor. I'll be fine."

She shook her head. "You can't see the wound. It's worse than you think. And the doctor might not get here for hours—long enough for you to bleed to death, or for infection to set in. I need to clean and dress it now."

"One of the men—"

"They turned you over to me. I'm your wife, after all. Now hold still."

With a shaking hand, Hannah picked up the scissors.

Chapter Seven

Judd fixed his eyes on the glass chandelier that hung over the dining room table. Hannah was not innocent, he reminded himself. She'd experienced enough of a man's body to have conceived a child. Still, the thought of subjecting those girlish eyes to the sight of his nakedness was enough to make him blush with shame.

He swore under his breath as the steel blades snipped higher. It was indignity enough, having her see him uncovered. Worse was the fact that, despite his injuries, he'd managed to become aroused. Maybe it was the whiskey—or more likely having a woman's hands touch him so intimately. Whatever the cause, he was as hard as a brick. Only the tight fastenings on his jeans kept him from jutting straight up like a flagpole. The fact that this woman was his legal and lawful wife only made matters worse. He'd entered into this hellish arrangement with the best of intentions. Now, for all her sisterly behavior, Hannah was driving him crazy. She was about to discover just how crazy.

Judd groaned inwardly. He wouldn't blame the poor girl if she lit out for home and never spoke to him again.

Hannah kept her eyes on the vital task at hand—the careful cutting, the gentle cleansing and the smearing of the wire-cut medicine along the edges of Judd's wound. According to the label on the tin, no stitches would be required to close the gash, only tight wrapping. But she wasn't sure whether she should believe it—especially if that belief could cause Judd serious harm. If only the doctor would get here!

The blades snipped higher along Judd's inner thigh, parting the bloodstained denim and the cotton long johns beneath. Only then did Hannah notice the telltale bulge that pulled the fabric as tight as a drumhead against his crotch. Her stomach flip-flopped. The same thing had often happened to Quint when they'd done too much kissing. It was usually a signal for her to pull away. She remembered all too clearly what had happened the night she *hadn't* pulled away.

But this was Judd. And she certainly hadn't been kissing him. As far as she knew, he didn't even like her. Confusion washed over her in a dizzying wave. Heavens to Betsy, how could a woman who'd conceived a baby know so little about men?

"Hannah, are you all right?" Judd's voice cut into her thoughts. She stared down at the soiled tablecloth, her cheeks scalded with crimson. It was all she could do to keep from flinging down the scissors and plunging blindly out of the room.

Judd cleared his throat. "You look ready to drop," he said. "Sit down and rest. You've done enough."

"No—it's all right. I'm nearly finished," she stammered. Maybe if she ignored the obvious, it would go away. To react to what she'd seen would embarrass them both. She squeezed out the rag in the basin and began sponging the blood from Judd's skin. Her knuckle brushed the barely covered ridge. His body jerked.

"Enough!" His voice was a guttural, animal growl. "Stop this and sit down."

"I'm just—"

"Sit down, damn it! That's an order!"

His eyes blazed up at her. She dropped the rag back into the basin. "Fine. Lie here and bleed. See if I—"

The sound of voices outside galvanized them both. Hannah heard the snort of a horse and the tread of heavy footsteps across the porch. Her knees went limp with relief. Dr. Marlin Fitzroy had arrived.

Seconds later he strode into the room, a portly middle-aged man with a bald head and a ginger-colored moustache that covered his upper lip like the whiskers on a walrus. His smallish hands were pink from scrubbing. Their examination of Judd's injuries was swift and sure. A furtive glance assured Hannah that Judd was no longer straining the crotch of his jeans.

"You could've been a nurse, Mrs. Seavers," the doctor said. "This is right fine work you've done. All I'll have to do is stitch up the gash on his leg and bind his ribs. Then we can have the men carry the stretcher up to his bed."

Hannah flushed at the unaccustomed praise. Only now, as she stepped away from the table, did she realize how tired she was. Her legs felt rubbery. The chandelier above her seemed to be wobbling like a loose wagon wheel. The doctor's face dissolved and reappeared before her eyes.

"I can take over now," he said. "You're looking pale. Why don't you go into the parlor and lie down?"

Those were the last words Hannah heard before her legs folded under her and she pitched into blackness.

Hannah opened her eyes. The first thing to meet her gaze was the parlor's tin-paneled ceiling. As she came fully awake, she realized she was lying on the settee with one of Edna's needlepoint pillows supporting her head and a towel under her shoes. For a moment the house seemed eerily quiet. Only as she tried to sit up did she hear the murmur of masculine voices from beyond the closed door to the dining room. She froze.

"Not that it's any of my business, Judd, but your bride appears to be under a strain. Is she all right?" The speaker was Dr. Fitzroy.

"As far as I know, she's—" Judd muttered a mild curse. "Not a word to anyone, hear? You're our doctor, so you need to know. Hannah's expecting a child."

"I see." There was a beat of silence. Hannah closed her eyes and lay still, her pulse racing.

The doctor cleared his throat. "Since you've only been married a couple of weeks, I take it…"

"She's not quite four months along. Draw your own conclusions."

Another silence followed, this one broken by the tearing of the cloth into strips. "You came home in

March, and Quint left the same day. So I take it the father is—"

"The baby's a Seavers, a part of our family. The rest is nobody's else's business."

"So you did the noble thing. Lord, does Quint know?"

"We've written to him at General Delivery in Skagway. But there's been no word from him. No way to know if he's received a single letter—" Judd took a ragged breath "—or if he's even alive."

"So he might not know about your mother, either?"

"If he'd received any news at all, Quint would be on his way home. I think it's the hope of seeing her boy again that keeps her hanging on."

"Then you can only pray he'll get word. I'll look in on Edna before I head back to town."

"She should still be in her room. If she's taken her pain medicine, you may have to wake her."

"Leave that to me." In the silence that followed, Hannah heard the scrape of a chair leg against the floor. She stared up at the pattern on the pressed tin ceiling tiles. Evidently, Edna's condition was more serious than she'd realized. Why hadn't anyone told her?

"I'll just check on your wife," the doctor said. "Then we'll see about getting you upstairs."

Hannah could hear him moving toward the door. She closed her eyes, pretending to be asleep. It wouldn't do to let Judd and the doctor know she'd been eavesdropping.

The thick parlor rug muffled the doctor's footsteps as he entered the room. Hannah lay still, taking deep, even breaths as he walked around the settee and paused in front of her. Then his footsteps retreated toward the front hall. Seconds later she heard him going outside.

Feeling foolish, she lingered on the settee, still feigning sleep. Judd was in the adjoining room. If she got up to leave, he would hear. It was a silly predicament she'd gotten herself into. But the least awkward way out of it would be to stay right here and finish her nap. The cushions were soft, the afternoon drowsily warm. And she seemed to need more rest of late, with the baby draining her strength.

One hand slipped down below her waist to cradle the growing mound. Her baby. Hers and Quint's. She had already come to love the little creature.

Hannah's eyelids had grown deliciously heavy. Her body seemed to be sinking through a wine-dark fog. With a long sigh, she drifted back into sleep.

The chime of the grandfather clock startled her awake. Her body jerked. Her eyes shot open. What time was it? How long had she slept?

Still foggy, she staggered to her feet. A finger of daylight probed a crack between the dark curtains. Judging from its angle, it was late afternoon. She'd been asleep for an hour, perhaps, no longer. But she felt an odd sense of disorientation, like a child coming awake after being carried into a strange house.

She yawned. Her fingers massaged the small of her back, feeling the raw flesh and the ripped fabric where she'd gouged herself on the barbed wire.

Her bodice was stained with dirt and blood. As she fingered the dark red splotches the memory returned—

Judd's injuries, his head cradled beneath her breasts, the unsettling bulge that had strained the buttons on his trousers....

She flung open the door to the dining room. The tabletop was bare. Its oiled surface bore faint marks from the stretcher poles. But Judd was gone.

From the other side of the kitchen door came the clatter of pans and dishes. Gretel must have returned. But when? And what had she found on her arrival?

Hannah was about to go into the kitchen and ask when she heard the creak of a floorboard overhead and the tread of heavy footsteps across the landing. Rushing out into the hall, she saw Dr. Fitzroy coming down the stairs with his medical bag.

"So you're awake." His bespectacled eyes assessed her from head to foot. "You gave us a scare when you fainted. How are you feeling, Mrs. Seavers?"

"All right. I think I was just tired. But now I've had a lovely nap. Where's Judd?"

"I had the men carry him upstairs on the stretcher. He's in bed now, and none too happy about it. I'd have given him a sedative, but with that bump on his head it could be dangerous. You'll need to watch him, make sure he doesn't sleep too much."

"Yes, I've heard that about concussions."

"Keep him in bed for the next couple of days, and quiet for the next week or so. Too much activity, especially riding, could open that nasty wound on his leg." The doctor frowned, his eyebrows meeting above his spectacles. "Come outside onto the porch. We can talk there."

He opened the door, standing aside for her to pass.

Hannah had known Dr. Fitzroy most of her life. Although her family had been too poor to afford his services, he was a familiar figure in the town, known for his discretion. She knew she had little to risk by being forthright with him.

They stood at the porch rail, looking out over the yard. At the hitching rail, a dappled mare dozed between the traces of the doctor's chaise. Someone had brought the animal a pail of water. Hannah was grateful for that.

Gathering her courage, she spoke. "I'm afraid I have a confession to make. While you and Judd were talking, I woke up. I heard him telling you about the baby."

The doctor nodded. "Then you already know you should be examined to make sure everything's all right. We can take care of it the next time I drop by. That'll save you a trip to my office in town."

"Thank you." Hannah could imagine how tongues would wag if she were to pay the doctor a public visit. Sooner or later her secret would be out, but she wasn't ready to expose it yet.

"One more thing," she said. "Forgive my eavesdropping, but you mentioned something about Mrs. Seavers. Is she ill?"

"Judd hasn't told you?"

"Not a thing. Please, I deal with her every day, and it isn't getting any easier. If something's wrong, I need to know."

Hesitating, the doctor took off his spectacles and polished the lenses on his sleeve. "I'd rather Judd be the one to discuss it. But given that he's had a rough day, and that you're family…" He rubbed the bridge of his nose and replaced his glasses.

"Not a word to anyone, all right? Edna doesn't know. Nobody knows except Judd and Gretel—and maybe Quint if he's read his mail."

Hannah's fingers tightened around the porch rail. A horsefly buzzed in the silent heat.

"Edna has a tumor in her brain," the doctor said. "She's dying."

Hannah sucked in her breath as the words penetrated. She'd never felt comfortable around her mother-in-law, let alone liked her. But this was tragic news for the family—and she was part of that family.

"You're sure?"

"As sure as I can be, given what I've got to work with. I've seen the same symptoms before. The headaches. The numbness. The way her pupils react to light. It's subtle, but it's there."

"How long?" Two innocent words, dark with meaning.

"There's no way to be sure. My best guess is six months. But it could be closer to a year. Or it could be tomorrow."

"And you say she doesn't know?"

"I discovered the tumor a few weeks after Quint left. Another doctor I telegrammed confirmed my diagnosis. It was Judd's decision not to tell her. I concurred. With no hope for a cure, why burden the poor woman with more grief?" Dr. Fitzroy glanced down at the slight bulge below Hannah's waistline. "Seeing her grandchild could ease her passing when the time comes. Let's hope for that much, at least."

"Yes, I'll hope with you." Hannah spoke mechanically, still reeling from the news. "And I'll do my best to make things easier for her. Heaven knows, I haven't been a very understanding daughter-in-law."

"I know Edna can be difficult. But she's going to need you in the times ahead. So is Judd. There'll be a lot of responsibility on your shoulders. Will you be all right?"

"I'll have to be, won't I?" She shook the doctor's hand as he prepared to leave. "Thank you for telling me the truth."

"You needed to know. Send for me if anything doesn't look right. I'll check back in the next few days."

From the shade of the porch, Hannah watched the doctor's chaise roll down the long drive and through the gate. A few hours ago her most urgent concern had been a ruined dress. Now she stood like the lone survivor on a battlefield. Quint was lost. Judd was hurt. Edna was dying. Only one member of the Seavers clan remained present, whole and strong—that was Hannah herself. But would her untested strength be enough to get the family through the days ahead?

She pressed the porch rail with her body, shading her eyes against the low sun. The doctor's rig had vanished around the bend. The cowhands were coming in from riding fence. The smell of fresh biscuits and Mexican chili drifted up the slope from the bunkhouse kitchen.

Hannah filled her senses with the comforting aroma. Little by little, she was becoming part of this ranch, and it was becoming part of her. So far, she'd been nothing but a burden. Now it was time to earn her place here as a member of the Seavers family. It was time to pay back what she'd been given. But how could she do it alone?

As if in answer to her unspoken question, Hannah felt a twitch below her navel, like the flutter of a tiny fish. Transfixed, she laid a hand on her belly and held her breath. There it was again—her baby, alive and stirring.

Wonder and gratitude flashed through her with the clarity of sunlight. She wasn't alone after all. Her child would be a link to bind this family through the hard times ahead—a tiny, precious piece of the future.

But hadn't Judd been aware of this all along? Of course he had, Hannah told herself. Why else would he have offered to marry her, a poor farm girl with an eighth grade education and another man's child in her belly?

So why should that bother her? Judd had never professed to care for her. He had made this sacrifice for his family—most likely to atone for his role in his father's death. Maybe he was hoping that, once she held her grandchild in her arms, Edna might finally forgive him.

She had married Judd with her eyes wide-open, Hannah reminded herself. He didn't love her. And she certainly didn't love him. As long as she and her baby were well taken care of, his motives shouldn't concern her.

Should they?

Never mind. It was time she stopped brooding and made herself useful. First she would go up to her room and put on a clean dress. She wanted to look nice for Edna. That was the least she could do.

Once her clothes were changed, she'd take a moment to check on Judd. Hopefully he'd be asleep and she could let him be. But not for long, she reminded herself.

People with head injuries had been known to go to sleep and never wake up.

Hurrying inside, she mounted the stairs to the landing. The door to Judd's room was closed. For a moment Hannah was tempted to open it and go in. But first things first. Changing her dress, splashing her face and smoothing her hair would only take a few minutes. Judd could wait that long.

The door to the master bedroom stood ajar. Hannah entered, closed the door behind her and crossed the floor to the wardrobe. Her sun-dazzled eyes could barely see in the darkened room. The heavy window drapes, which she'd left open, were now closed. Gretel must have come in to put things in order. Hannah made a mental note to speak to her after supper. The woman had enough to do without serving as her personal maid. She would insist on keeping her own room clean, and Judd's, as well. Maybe she could even take over the laundry.

Lost in thought, she fumbled with the buttons at the back of her ruined dress. They were small and miserably awkward to manage. Worse, where the barbed wire had jabbed her back and shoulders, dried blood had stuck the fabric to her skin. As she tugged, one button popped loose, bounced to the floor and rolled under the wardrobe. Hannah muttered a mild oath.

"Do you need any help?"

The deep voice behind her almost stopped her heart. Hannah spun around to see Judd lying in the shadows of the canopied bed. Plump feather pillows supported his bandaged head and shoulders.

Seconds ticked past before she found her tongue. "What are you doing here?" she demanded.

"Trying to behave myself, and you're not helping." Irony laced Judd's voice. "Just in case you're wondering, it wasn't my idea to be here. The men who carried me upstairs assumed this was still my bedroom. Evidently, so did the doctor."

"You didn't tell them?"

"Tell them I'm not sleeping with my bride? That would give them something to talk about, wouldn't it?" He sighed. "Sit down where I can reach you, Hannah, and I'll help you with those buttons. Believe me, you're in no danger whatsoever."

Hannah hesitated, but only for the space of a breath. She needed help, and Judd was right—she was in no danger. Not from him, at least. So why was her heart fluttering like a trapped moth as she moved toward the bed?

Ignoring her racing pulse, she lowered herself to a sitting position, with her back toward him. He shifted behind her, and she felt the brush of his raw fingertips on her skin. She remembered being told how he'd hung on to the rope while the ledge caved around him. "This can't be easy for you, with your sore hands," she said.

"It's fine. Hold still. And I'm not inexperienced with buttons."

The implication of his words brought a rush of color to her face. She knew so little about this man. Did he mean to tell her he knew how to make love to a woman? Her blush deepened.

Hannah's tongue had become a useless lump in her mouth. She struggled to form words, pouncing on a topic she'd meant to bring up for some time. "Speaking of talk, there's something we need to discuss, Judd," she said.

"What's that?" His voice sounded thick and muzzy, most likely the effect of the whiskey she'd poured down him. He had opened her dress down the back to the top of her camisole. Now he was gently working the fabric loose from her skin.

"It's complicated," she said. "I'm concerned about you and me, and what people will be saying about us."

"I'm listening." His finger traced a line between her shoulder blades. Hannah willed herself to ignore the shimmers of liquid heat that trickled downward from the point of contact. The man wasn't in his right mind. He wasn't accountable for his actions. But *she* was.

"Our families know that we're not living as man and wife," she said. "So does Gretel. And I imagine Dr. Fitzroy has figured it out. But what about everyone else—for instance, the men who put you in this bed?"

"What about them?" His hands moved down the row of buttons, approaching the lightly corseted curve of her waist.

"Don't you think we should agree on what to tell them?"

"Why tell them anything? It's none of their business."

"But do we really want them to assume that we're—"

"That we're sleeping in the same bed? Is that what you want them to assume?"

Hannah studied the narrow gold band that circled her finger. "I suppose that would cause the least amount of gossip. We *are* married, after all. But people do talk. I just need to know what you're telling them."

"Not a damn-blasted thing." Judd's hands paused. "What happens, or doesn't happen, in this room is between you and me—and maybe Quint, wherever he is. The less we say to anybody else, the better."

"And when I can't hide the baby anymore? What then?"

"Maybe Quint will be back by that time." His fingers loosened the last two buttons. "Whatever happens, Hannah, people are going to talk. The best we can do is hold our heads high and keep still. Sooner or later the scandal will fade and they'll find something new to gossip about."

"I see." Hannah rose and walked away, conscious that her dress was open down the back. She could feel his eyes on her as she opened the wardrobe. Partially concealed by the open door, she let the ragged remnant slide off her shoulders and fall around her feet. Hastily she chose another dress, a lace-trimmed blue dobby weave that buttoned down the front. Pulling it over her head, she made herself presentable and stepped into sight once more.

Judd was lying back on the pillows. He watched in silence as she splashed and dried her face and smoothed her hair. She was battling a stubborn hairpin when he spoke.

"When you agreed to marry me, Hannah, I promised myself I'd treat you like a sister. Whatever people think or say, that's what I mean to do."

She turned to face him. "That's fine, Judd. But since I'm part of this family, why didn't you tell me about your mother? I had to pry the truth out of Dr. Fitzroy today."

Pain rippled across his beaten face. "I meant to tell

you, Hannah. Certainly you had the right to know. I was just waiting for the right time."

She jabbed the errant pin into her hair. "Is that why you married me—for your mother? To give her a grandchild before she died?" It wasn't what Hannah had meant to say. But thoughts had a way of becoming words.

"Yes, for my mother. And for the baby. And for Quint. Maybe even for you."

"But not for *you!*" The words spilled out before Hannah could stop them. "For you it was a sacrifice—an atonement for what happened to your father! You think you're so noble, Judd Seavers! But what about me? Don't you think I have feelings? Don't you think I have pride?"

"Hannah—" He strained forward on the pillows, then fell back with a grunt of pain.

Unable to face him, she spun away and plunged toward the stairs. The words had come bursting out of her from a place so dark and deep she hadn't even known it was there. What was wrong with her? Judd had given her everything—a home, an honorable name, freedom from the grinding poverty she'd known all her life. What more could she ask of him?

Merciful heaven, did she want him to love her?

Chapter Eight

Judd cursed the stabbing pain that lanced his ribs with every breath. At any other time, he'd have charged after Hannah, grabbed her by the shoulders and done his best to shake some sense into her.

And then what? Would he have caught her in his arms and bruised those soft, ripe strawberry lips with his kisses?

Hurting, he sank back onto the pillows. Lord, what had possessed him to think he could handle this situation. For all his good intentions, he must have been out of his mind! Right now all he wanted in this world was for Quint to come home and take the whole mess off his hands!

He listened to the sound of her light, swift footfalls descending the stairs and crossing the entry. An instant later he heard the opening and closing of the front door. In the silence that followed, her words drifted back to haunt him.

For you it was a sacrifice—an atonement for what

*happened to your father! You think you're so noble,
Judd Seavers! But what about me? Don't you think I
have feelings? Don't you think I have pride?*

She was right, he conceded. He'd married her for all
the reasons she'd flung at him—as if bringing her and
her child into the family could make up for his mother's
loss of a husband and Quint's loss of a father. He'd
done it to ease his mother's passing and to save an innocent babe from the stain of bastardy. He'd done it—
heaven forgive him—to ease his own guilt.

But his damned self-righteous logic hadn't included
the things a woman needed to hear.

He'd made every effort to be generous with Hannah.
But he'd done nothing to make her feel welcome or
wanted. He'd made no effort to help her fit into his
broken family. And now that the damage was done, he
knew of no way to make things right—not without
crossing lines he'd sworn not to cross.

Had she wanted him to court her? To hold her hand
and bring her flowers and tell her how beautiful she
was? Judd would gladly have done it all. But she was
Quint's girl, and she was carrying Quint's child. Their
marriage was a business arrangement, sealed by a mockery of the sacred ceremony her wedding to Quint would
have been.

No wonder Hannah had flayed him with words and
gone storming out of the house. Judd had heard that
pregnant women were easily upset. But in this situation
he could hardly blame her.

He lay back against the pillows, staring up at the
canopy and hurting like hell. He'd be laid up around the

house for the next week, at least. For much of that time, Hannah would likely be his nurse. He would be the soul of patience and gratitude, Judd vowed. And no matter what temptation the devil might dangle in front of him, he would not lay an unbrotherly hand on the woman.

He could only pray that Quint would return before he lost his mind and his immortal soul.

Judd could feel himself beginning to drift. He was sinking into sleep when the sound of footsteps roused him to wakefulness. Was Hannah coming back? His pulse leaped, then slowed again as he recognized the heavy tread on the stairs. A moment later Gretel appeared in the doorway with supper on a tray.

"Chicken and dumplings. Your favorite, *ja?*"

Forcing a smile, he thanked her in his rudimentary German, which always pleased her.

"My favorite, *ja. Danke,* Gretel. If anything can make me well, it'll be your cooking."

Pleasure flickered across Gretel's grim-looking face. "Your pretty wife is in the dining room. Should I send her up to feed you?"

"Leave her be. I can feed myself." He inched upward on the pillows, wincing at the slightest motion. He hadn't eaten since breakfast, but for some reason he didn't have much appetite. Not even for Gretel's savory chicken and dumplings. As for Hannah ladling food into his mouth… No, he wouldn't have minded that. But in her present state, she'd be more likely to shove the spoon down his throat.

"I will be back for the tray when I finish downstairs."

"No need to hurry." Judd took a spoonful of the tasty

stew. He didn't feel hungry but he knew she was watching and would be disappointed if he didn't eat. Behind Gretel's stern facade beat a tender woman's heart. A little appreciation went a long way with her.

Why couldn't he remember to show the same regard for his beautiful wife? Around Hannah, he was like a clenched fist, afraid of reaching out except to strike. Kind words that came easily around others seemed to stick in his throat when he spoke to her.

But he knew the reason why. The plain truth was, he didn't trust himself around Hannah. He didn't trust his mind or his tongue. And he trusted his hands least of all. When she'd sat on the edge of the bed and allowed him to unfasten her torn dress, only his injuries had kept him from seizing her in his arms and doing what he had the legal right—though not the moral right—to do.

Maybe over the next few months, as her body grew heavy with Quint's child, the danger would lessen. But for now, the urge to touch her, to run a caressing finger along the curve of her spine and lose his fingers in the tangle of her glorious hair, to cup one swollen breast in his palm and feel the nipple harden under his thumb stroke... Lord almighty, every thought of her went straight to his loins. He was beginning to understand why those old-time saints flagellated themselves with whips. He'd be tempted to do the same if he thought it would drive out the forbidden images that played through his mind.

Judd forced himself to finish Gretel's chicken and dumplings, then, with effort, moved the tray onto the nightstand. It had been a hellish day, and he was just beginning to realize how weary he was. His eyelids were growing heavy. He could feel himself sliding into a darkness that pulled him down like quicksand. He sank willingly, wanting only to rest and forget.

Hannah was in his arms, as he'd known she would be. They lay on their sides, chest to chest, their bare legs languorously intertwined. The naked little mound of her belly jutted against his erection, driving him to a frenzy of arousal. His hands clasped her ripe buttocks, pulling her tighter to heighten the pleasure. She moaned, parting her thighs and curving her hips inward to stroke against him. He could feel her wetness, feel the crisp nest of curls surrounding moist folds of flesh, softer than rose petals.

He jerked her closer, his body demanding more. She whimpered with need as the tiny pearl-hard nub glided against the surface of his shaft. Her hips butted and bucked. Her fingers clawed his hair, pulling him down to nuzzle her tautly swollen breasts. His mouth found her nipple. It was as warm and sweet as a summer raspberry. He sucked and laved and nipped, drinking in the smell of her, the taste and feel of her, the sheer intoxication of her womanly curves molding to his.

The unbound glory of her hair surrounded him like a tangled net. Where her honey nest quivered against him, he could feel the slickness spilling out of her, lubricating him for the thrust they both craved so desperately.

Turning onto her back and pulling him with her, she raised her knees. "Please," she whispered, opening herself to him. "Please, Judd…I'll die if you don't make love to me."

Even if she'd said no, Judd would have been beyond

stopping. Wild with long-denied hunger, he pushed between the satin-slick folds and entered her in one long stroke. He heard her gasp. Then her legs wrapped his hips, pulling him deeper into her warm darkness.

She was wet and tight, fitting the length of him like a silken glove. He thrust, pulled back and thrust again, deeper and harder as her flesh closed around him in an intimate embrace. She met his every stroke with her own, drawing him closer, higher. Then he was lost in her, spiraling out of control, until he burst, filling her with the hot, thick jet of his seed....

He heard the heavy pounding of a fist on wood and the voice—a voice he would know anywhere.

"Judd! What the devil's going on in there?"

The door crashed open. Silhouetted by lamplight, Quint stepped across the threshold and strode into the room....

"Judd! Wake up!"

He felt a hand shaking his shoulder. Her voice. Her fragrance. Dazed, he opened his eyes.

"Wake up. You were dreaming." She was leaning over him, her face lit by the candle she'd set on the nightstand. Her wheaten curls tumbled loose over her shoulders, one fairy lock brushing his face.

Judd blinked himself awake. Dreaming—for a moment it was all he could do to believe it. Loving Hannah had felt absolutely real—a sticky dampness beneath the sheet told Judd just how real it had been for him.

And the guilt when Quint had walked into the room. That had been real, too. Lord, he never wanted to feel guilt like that in his life.

"What time is it?" he muttered.

"Almost ten. You were asleep when I came in to get your supper tray for Gretel. I was tempted to let you sleep all night, but the doctor told me it might be dangerous."

"I hadn't thought of that. Thanks for waking me." He noticed then that she was clad in her nightgown and flannel robe. "Were you already in bed?"

She settled in the rocker, wrapping the folds of the robe over her knees. "I was going to sleep in your room, next door. But I was afraid I might not be able to hear you. For tonight, I can sleep right here, in this chair."

Judd eased himself up against the pillows. Spending the night with Hannah in the same room was the last thing he needed. Tomorrow morning, he swore silently, he would get out of this bed if it killed him. He would get dressed, go outside and try to do some useful work. Tomorrow night he would move back into the smaller bedroom. This big, soft bed, with Hannah just within reach, was a dangerous place.

"I'll be fine," he said. "Go on back to bed."

"You have a bad concussion. Somebody needs to be here with you." She sank deeper into the chair, signaling her intent to stay. "Besides, I wanted to apologize. I behaved like an emotional fool tonight. The things I said to you were unkind and unfair."

He sighed. "We'd both had a long, hard day of it, Hannah. And much as the truth hurts, you were right. I should've known I couldn't fix the past by marrying you."

"You've been very generous with me. I can't fault you for that."

"Generosity can't bring Quint home. And it can't

bring peace to my mother. The divorce papers are locked in my desk. Say the word. I'll sign them and see that you and the baby are provided for."

She hesitated long enough to stop Judd's heart. Then she shook her head. "No, it hasn't come to that. Not yet."

His pulse resumed its normal beat. "Thank you for that," he said. "For all my bungling ways, I want you to know that you're needed here."

It had been the right thing to say. He saw that in the softening of her expression. And it had been a true thing. His mother would need Hannah in the days ahead. And he needed her now—more than he dared admit, even to himself.

But he was treading on forbidden ground. Hannah was his brother's woman. He had no right to the thoughts that kept invading his mind. It was time to put an end to them, once and for all.

Only one thing could resolve this mess. For the sake of everyone concerned, he had to make it happen.

The candle had long since guttered out. Hannah sat huddled in the rocking chair, watching Judd sleep. She had kept him awake as long as she could, talking about her parents, their Norwegian roots and their constant struggle to feed and clothe seven children. She'd hoped he might come up with some way to help her family, but as time crawled past he'd grown less attentive and finally dropped off to sleep.

Hannah had opened the heavy curtains and raised the window sash, flooding the room with moonlight and fresh air. She could see Judd clearly where he lay against the pillows, his head sagging wearily to one side. His eyes were closed, his battered face was streaked with the tarry wire-cut ointment. She ached with an unaccustomed yearning to cradle his head in her arms, smooth back his straight brown hair and kiss the bruises that marred his golden skin. He had come close to dying today—and all for the sake of a stranded calf.

She shifted in the chair, tucking her knees against her chest in an effort to get more comfortable. Drowsiness had tempted her to go into the next room and lie down. But she knew she'd never forgive herself if Judd needed her in the night and she was sleeping too soundly to hear him.

The clock in the downstairs hallway struck the hour— one o'clock. From somewhere outside, Hannah heard the haunting screech of a barn owl. Judd's eyes remained closed, but the cadence of his breathing had become jerky. His legs had begun to twitch beneath the coverlet.

Now she could hear him muttering under his breath— words she could barely make out. "No…don't make me do it. Lord, I can't…. We'll get down, get you to a medic…just don't…" The rest was muffled by racking sobs.

"No…" He was becoming more agitated, his movements so violent that Hannah feared he would worsen his injuries. Desperate to quiet him, she stretched out on top of the coverlet alongside his jerking body and gathered him in her arms.

"Hush, it's all right…." She nested his head against the hollow of her throat. Where her palms touched him through the sheet, his body dripped with cold sweat.

"You're dreaming, Judd," she murmured, stroking his hair below the damp bandage. "It's all right. I'm here."

Little by little the shaking subsided. The labored breathing eased. Judd slept in her arms like a tired child.

Hannah brushed a kiss along his hairline. Judd Seavers was a good man, a kind and gentle man. But a vision of hell lived in his mind—a hell he could only have experienced firsthand.

Was there any way to ease the nightmares? Talking about what had happened might be the first step. But Judd was a private man. Without the whiskey, he would never have told her about his father's death and his mother's unforgiving heart. It would take more than whiskey, Hannah sensed, to purge the blackness that fed those hellish dreams. And she was no doctor. She knew even less about the human mind than she did about the human heart.

But she was Judd's wife. If she didn't help him, who would?

He was breathing deeply once more, his body warm and damp in the circle of her arms. The scent of him— a blend of masculine sweat and fresh earth, tinged with the residue of whiskey and the sharp smell of carbolic swam in her head. With the covers between them, Hannah nestled against his warmth, feeling oddly safe and comforted. She was so very tired….

Sleep overtook her at last.

She awakened to the morning sunlight pouring through the open window. The side of the bed where Judd had lain was empty, the sheets cool and dry.

Alarmed, Hannah sat up and bounded out of bed. Judd was nowhere to be seen. The only sign he'd even been here was a bandage that had come loose and fallen to the rug.

Still in her robe, she hurried next door to his bedroom. The bed was empty, the wardrobe open. Judd's boots, which she'd cleaned and put away last night, were gone.

Blast the man, where was he? He belonged in bed!

Without bothering to dress, she flew downstairs and out onto the porch. Her anxious eyes scanned the yard. Seconds crawled past before she spotted him. He was outside the barn, where one of the cowhands was helping him hitch the team of bays to the buggy.

"Good morning, sleepyhead!" he called in a cheerful manner that didn't fool Hannah for an instant. He came toward her, moving like an arthritic seventy-year-old, wincing with every step.

"Get your clothes on and grab some breakfast. We're going into town."

She glared down at him from the porch. "Are you out of your mind, Judd Seavers? You look like a man who just fought his way out of a coffin. You shouldn't be out of bed, let alone driving a buggy."

"Do you want to come, or don't you?"

"Somebody has to look after you! Give me fifteen minutes!"

She raced back into the house and flew up the stairs. For all her worry, she was cheered by the promise of an outing. In the weeks since the wedding she'd scarcely left the ranch except to visit her family. A trip to town would do wonders for her spirits.

Dressing hastily, she washed her face, brushed her teeth and took extra pains with her hair. Edna frowned her disapproval when Hannah flitted past the breakfast table to greet her and snatch up two biscuits. But Hannah was gone before her mother-in-law could launch into another diatribe about her manners.

Her straw hat hung on the rack in the front hall. Catching the ties in her fingers, she dashed out onto the porch. Judd was waiting next to the buggy. He grinned at her breathless state.

"I wouldn't have left you behind. You know that, don't you?"

"Yes, I know." She averted her face to hide the rush of color to her cheeks. Did he remember that she'd held him in her arms much of the night? Or had she been dreaming, too?

He came around the buggy and offered his arm to help her climb up. "I should be the one helping you," she said. "And that bumpy road is going to be murder on your ribs."

"We'll take it slow. I'll be fine." He limped around to the driver's side of the buggy. Pain flashed across his battered face as he hoisted himself onto the seat. His jaw muscles tightened as the wheels jerked into motion. This trip was no lark, Hannah realized. Judd had an urgent reason for going into town this morning. And somehow, she was part of it.

She was burning for answers. But prying, Hannah knew, would get her nowhere. Judd would tell her in his own good time.

He kept his silence as they rolled down the long,

straight drive, through the open gate and onto the rutted road. Judd held the horses to a walk that eased the buggy over the worst of the bumps. Still, now and again, a wheel would strike wrong, and the sudden jolt would stab his ribs with an agony that made his skin whiten around the thin line of his lips.

The morning was sunlit, the air fresh and clear. Meadowlarks caroled from the fence posts that traced the boundaries of pastureland. Bees foraged in patches of deep pink clover and yellow mustard weed. Hannah held her tongue, soaking in the brightness of the day while Judd tended to the driving.

Only when the three-mile ride was nearly over and the town was in sight did he clear his throat and speak. "We'll be going to the bank," he said. "I want to set up your account. For that they'll need your signature. I'll also have you added to our account at the mercantile. Anything you charge there will be billed to the ranch."

"That's very generous," she said. "But do you really want to trust me with so much spending power? For all you know, I could shop your family into the poorhouse."

His gray eyes flickered toward her. "I trust you, Hannah. You're part of our family, and I want to make sure you and the baby have everything you need."

"But I truly don't mind asking you—"

Something in his expression stopped her words. She lowered her gaze to her hands.

By now they were coming into the outskirts of town. Businesses were opening their doors. The boardwalks were crowded with people out to finish their errands before the day warmed. This would be

Hannah's first public appearance as Mrs. Judd Seavers. She sensed curious eyes following the buggy as they rode down the street toward the railroad station. She could imagine what folks were thinking. She'd been Quint's girl for years. Now here she was married to Judd.

Did they view her as a scheming opportunist, one who'd seized her chance to capture the head of the Seavers family instead of the younger brother? Or had some of them guessed the truth?

She glanced down at slight bulge that rose beneath her skirt. She wasn't really showing yet, just looking as if she'd gained some weight around the middle. But people had sharp eyes. They could count—and they would.

Hannah willed herself not to slide down in the buggy seat and hide. She was married to one of the most respected men in the county. And Judd was right. Their private lives were nobody's business. Whatever people were saying about her, she would hold her head proudly.

Judd was drawing stares, as well. He looked a fright, with all those bruises and bandages. But word of his accident would have spread by now. Folks were likely amazed that he was strong enough to drive to town.

At the station, Judd halted the buggy. Climbing down from the seat, he helped his wife to the ground. It was a given that they would pick up the mail and stop by the telegraph office before attending to other business. No member of the Seavers household went into town without checking for word of Quint.

Today, as usual, there was nothing. But Judd surprised Hannah by writing out another message for the operator to send. She shot him a questioning look as he paid for the service.

"That wire went to the agency I hired to look for Quint," he explained as they walked away from the window.

"So what did you tell them?"

"I told them their services were no longer required."

Hannah stared at him, dumbfounded.

"Let's go," he said, taking her arm. "I'll explain on the way home. Then you'll understand what we're doing here today."

They drove back to the main part of town and parked the buggy in front of the bank. Judd helped her to the boardwalk and escorted her into the bank, his manner so gallant that she might have been a princess.

Bypassing the clerks, they went straight into the office of the bank president, Mr. Brandon Calhoun. Hannah had never spoken to Mr. Calhoun, but she knew him. Everyone did. Silver-haired and handsome, he was the wealthiest man in the county, with a beautiful wife and a tall brick house that was even grander than the Seavers home.

Rising from his immense leather chair, he shook hands with Hannah, then with Judd. "How can I help you, Mr. and Mrs. Seavers?" he asked with a smile.

Hannah was dazzled.

Fifteen minutes later she had her own bank account, with a balance so generous that it made her head swim. Judd signed an authorization for monthly funds to be transferred from the ranch account, so she would always have enough for her needs.

"I don't know what to say," she whispered as they left

the bank. "I've never had money, Judd. When I lived at home I had to trade eggs for paper and stamps to send my letters to Quint. I've done nothing to earn this, let alone deserve it."

He glanced down at her, a strange sadness glinting in his eyes. "The money's not for anything you've done, Hannah. It's for times ahead, when you'll likely earn every cent of it."

With that he walked her down the street to Smith's Feed and Mercantile. The elderly clerk behind the counter treated Hannah with the same deference she'd experienced at the bank. In the not-so-distant past, she'd brought her family's butter and eggs to trade for the precious supplies her family needed. Today she was Mrs. Judd Seavers, and she could buy anything she wanted.

Judd had brought along a shopping list from Gretel. After they'd filled a basket with her items, Judd insisted that Hannah pick something out for herself. She chose three bolts of good quality gingham, along with thread, pins, needles and buttons that Annie could use to make dresses for Mama and the girls. The clerk rang up their purchases, and Hannah signed for them—a show, she realized. Most everything that Judd had done this morning had been for show, to demonstrate how she, as his wife, should expect to be treated. But why? And why today, when he belonged in bed?

She remembered the wire he'd sent to the detective agency, terminating their contract, and the way he'd put her off when she'd wondered about it. Judd knew something—something he was preparing her to hear.

The thought of what it might be chilled her to the bone.

Chapter Nine

They walked back toward the buggy carrying their purchases. Judd's limp had eased as the stiffness worked out, but Hannah could see that the pain in his ribs was getting worse. He winced with every step.

What was he keeping from her? Had he received some news, perhaps this morning, while she was still asleep? Was that why she'd awakened to find him hitching the team?

Was he preparing to tell her that Quint was dead?

"It's early yet," he was saying. "But if you'd like to get some lunch at the hotel—"

Hannah shook her head. She'd never eaten at the hotel in her life. On any other day it would have been a treat. But now, with dread clawing at her throat, she knew she wouldn't be able to choke down a bite.

"Please, let's just go home," she said.

He helped her into the buggy, mounted the seat and nudged the horses to an easy walk. Dutchman's Creek wasn't a large town. Before long they'd left the bustling street and curious gazes behind them and were driving through open pastureland once more. Heat waves shimmered across fields of deep green alfalfa. In the distance, the snowcapped Rocky Mountains rose cold and blue against the clouds. Hannah waited, her fingers twisting the fabric of her skirt.

When she could stand it no longer, she forced herself to speak. "Get it over with, Judd. Whatever you're holding back, I need to know. Is it Quint? Is he dead?"

Judd halted the buggy. When he turned toward her, she saw the stark dismay in his eyes. "Lord, Hannah, is that what you've been thinking? If I knew Quint was dead, would I go all this time without telling you?"

The breath went out of her. She sagged on the buggy seat, limp with relief. "So you really haven't heard."

"Not a word. If I had, you'd have known right away."

"But that wire to the detective agency—"

"They've done nothing but send me their blasted bills and tell me they're checking leads. I've lost patience with them. Somebody needs to go after Quint and bring him home." He gazed at the horizon. His hands toyed with the leathers. "I got thinking about it this morning. The shape I'm in, I can't be much help on the ranch. As long as I have to rest, I might as well do it on the train, or on board a ship."

"Judd—"

"No, hear me out. I'm leaving for Alaska in the next few days. I'll follow the routes Quint might have taken and bring a photograph to show people along the way. With luck, I'll discover where he's gone."

"And if you don't?" Hannah whispered the question.

"If I haven't found him by the time the leaves start to turn, I'll come home. With winter setting in, it won't be much use looking."

She reached for his big, scarred hand and squeezed it. "Thank you," she said.

"Don't thank me yet." He flicked the reins, nudging the horses into motion. "You'll have a lot of responsibility while I'm gone. Al Macklin can handle the stock and manage the hired help. But running the household and keeping the accounts will have to be your job. Will you be all right with that?"

Hannah nodded, trying not to feel overwhelmed. She had to do her part. Judd was counting on her. "You'll need to show me some things. Arithmetic was my best subject in school, but bookkeeping will be a challenge."

"My mother may be an even bigger challenge."

"Yes, I can just imagine…" She paused, struck by a new concern. "Judd, what if she—"

"What if she dies?" Judd's breath hissed out in a long exhalation. "Believe me, I've thought about that. So far she's been holding her own. But that could change. If the worst happens, send to town for the undertaker. He'll know what to do about the funeral. Then get word to me, any way you can." He glanced toward her. "You can do this, Hannah. If I didn't believe that, I wouldn't be going."

"Thank you for your confidence." Her laugh was on the raw edge of tears. "I hope you don't come home to find everything in ruin."

"If I can bring Quint back to you, it will have been worth it."

He had turned away from her and was watching the road. She studied his craggy profile, the weathered creases at the corner of his eye, the fine tracery of silver threads at his temple. Judd was a man who shouldered the weight of everything in his world—his father's loss, his mother's bitterness, the ranch, the pregnant girl who should have been Quint's responsibility. And now this. She should have guessed that he'd go after Quint. How could he do anything else?

Her hand reached out to brush his shoulder. "You come back, too, hear?" she said. "Whatever happens, Judd, you come back."

August 22, 1899
Dear Quint,
We've received two short notes from Judd so far, but still nothing from you. He says that when he checked for mail in Skagway, he found all the letters we'd written to you, unopened and tied in a bundle, waiting to be picked up. Since you haven't read them, you don't likely know about anything that's happened here.

You don't know that the doctor says your mother is dying, or that I'm going to have our baby in a few months. You don't know that Judd has married me to give the baby a name, or that he's in Alaska, looking for you. He left here on the 28th of July, took the train to Seattle, boarded a boat and disembarked at Skagway. From there he planned to cross Chilkoot Pass into the Klondike and ask about you in Whitehorse and Dawson. The last time he wrote, he'd found no trace of you. No one recognized your picture, and your name wasn't on any registry. Where are you, Quint? Why haven't you contacted us?

Hannah paused to stand up and stretch her cramped muscles. The baby was growing fast. She already felt huge. How would she look and feel by the time she was ready to give birth?

Massaging the small of her back, she walked to the study's bay window, which looked out on the paddock. Mares cropped the late-summer grass while their foals chased and frolicked like rambunctious children. Beyond the paddock, the outer pastures swept like pale green carpet to the boundaries of the ranch. She imagined her child growing up here, racing through the long grass, fishing for trout in the creek, learning to ride a pony. She pictured a family around the dinner table, talking and laughing, picnics in the hills, trips to town with all of them in the wagon. This ranch could be such a happy place—and would be, she vowed. In the months and years ahead, she would do all she could to make a real home here. If only…

But it was a waste of time to ponder the future when there was so much to be done in the present. So far, with the help of Al Macklin, she'd managed all right. The stock appeared healthy, the fences and outbuildings were in good repair, and the accounts were balanced and up-to-date. Hannah hoped Judd would be pleased. He'd placed a fearful responsibility on her shoulders. She'd done her best to be a good steward, but there was always the fear of the unexpected. She prayed nightly that Judd and Quint would be safe, that Edna's health would remain stable, and that no unforeseen disaster would drop out of nowhere to break all their hearts.

With a sigh she returned to the desk, picked up the pen and dipped it into the inkwell. By now, it seemed, she'd written the same letter to Quint dozens of times. Would he ever read the words she'd penned with so much devotion—or was he already lost to her?

Last night I dreamed you'd died. But I know that can't be true. If you were gone from this earth, my heart would feel it. You're alive, my dearest, and you're out there somewhere. I send my prayers and hopes that we'll hear from you, and that soon you'll come home to us.

She signed the letter, blotted the page and printed the familiar Skagway address on the envelope. Hannah had little doubt that it would join the rest of the unopened mail in the Skagway post office, bundled and waiting to be claimed. But she had promised to write to Quint every week. It was a promise she'd kept faithfully.

Now, if only Quint would keep his.

She glanced at the clock on the mantel of the red brick fireplace. Half an hour remained before Gretel's customary nine o'clock trip to town. There was time to write one more letter.

Opening the drawer she reached for another sheet of

monogrammed linen stationery and dipped the pen nib into the ink. This time the words flowed fast and freely.

Dear Judd,
With luck, you'll find this letter waiting when you get back to Skagway. All is as well as can be expected here. Your mother is about the same as when you left. The headaches plague her, but no more than usual. She's still none too warm toward me, but I'm getting used to her manner. We may never become friends, but at least we're learning to tolerate one another.

You might be surprised when you see me. I've become as round as an October pumpkin. The baby kicks hard enough to keep me awake at night. Priscilla Hastings came last week and let my seams out to their limits. When she complained of having more work than she could do alone, I suggested she hire my sister Annie to help her. Annie is thrilled with her new position. I'm hoping it will provide her with a good livelihood in years to come.

The repairs on the barn roof are finished. I took the liberty of suggesting to Al Macklin that he hire my brother Ephraim to help. Ephraim's only fifteen but he's strong for his age and used to hard work. Al has him building a new weaselproof chicken coop on the far side of the barn. Gretel's taken a shine to him, as well. He's gaining weight from the treats she bakes for him. She's a very kind woman— more shy than grim, when you get to know her. You can't imagine how she used to terrify me.

Hannah paused to turn the paper over and lay it on the blotter. She'd covered the entire page and still had so many things to tell Judd. Jabbing the pen into the inkwell, she continued writing on the back.

The new Hereford calves you ordered for breeding stock came in by rail a few days ago. Al had plowed up the west pasture for a late crop of hay, so I arranged with my father to lease the land that runs along the property line—the one he's always refused to sell you. The calves are there now, and I'm paying my little brothers a bit of pocket change to keep an eye on them.

   I hope you won't mind my making these decisions. I'm trying to do my best by everyone, including you. Every night I pray that you'll find Quint before long, and that the two of you will come home safe and well. I'll be waiting for you both.

Hannah's lips parted as she reread the last sentence. Was that really what she'd meant to say—that she was waiting for two men? That she cared for both of them?

She picked up the pen she'd propped in the inkwell. It might be wise to scribble out the sentence, or better yet, to rewrite the letter. But that would be silly. Of course she cared about Judd—in a brotherly way. There was nothing else to be read into her words.

Was there?

Hastily now, she signed and blotted the letter, folded, sealed and addressed it. Then she hurried into the front hall to hand Gretel both her letters as she bustled out the door to the waiting buggy.

The busy day was just beginning. There were bills to pay and supplies to order. Her father was down with gout, and Edna was running low on her headache medicine. One of the mules had thrown a shoe, and gophers were decimating Gretel's precious vegetable patch. Singly, any of these small crises would have been easy to manage. But their combined weight bore down on her like a load of paving stones. With the baby draining so much of her energy, each day seemed harder to face than the day before.

She'd told Judd a white lie about her relationship with his mother. Dealing with Edna was becoming more difficult every day. Either the tumor was getting worse or she was mourning the absence of her sons. Whatever the reason, nothing Hannah did seemed to please her mother-in-law. But Hannah kept trying. Awareness of Edna's condition gave her an extra measure of patience. Even so, the strain was beginning to tell on her.

"Hannah!" Edna's voice quivered down the hallway from the direction of the dining room. "Where are you, girl?"

"Right here." Hannah popped into sight through the open doorway.

Edna was at the table sipping tea and nibbling on a biscuit. "Why is there no one around when I need something?" she complained. "My tea's gotten cold. And I have a letter for Quint that needs to go out in today's mail. I need you to find Gretel and give it to her."

Hannah sighed. "I can get you more tea. But Gretel's already left for town. Your letter will have to wait until the next time someone goes."

Edna's breath made a little sucking sound. "But I always have a letter for Gretel to take! Why would she leave without it? I declare, the woman is getting more careless every day!"

"No, it wasn't her fault," Hannah said, remembering. "I gave Gretel two letters. She probably thought one of them was yours."

"Two letters?" Edna's eyebrows slithered upward.

"Yes. One for Quint and one for Judd."

"And what business do you have writing to Quint? Judd's your husband. I was there when you married him, you little fortune-hunting chit. Isn't one man enough for you?"

"I'll get you some hot tea." Hannah pushed her way through the swinging doors to the kitchen. It wasn't Edna's fault, she reminded herself as she measured the tea leaves and poured hot water from the kettle on the stove. The woman was ill, and the illness was affecting her mind.

But why did she have to be so mean-spirited? Why couldn't she appreciate the kindness of people around her, like Al Macklin who looked in on her daily? Why couldn't she take some joy in the coming arrival of her grandchild? Even with Hannah's belly jutting out for all to see, Edna ignored the reality of the baby. And this wasn't the first time she'd complained about Hannah's letters to Quint. It was as if she couldn't stand the thought of another woman sharing her beloved son.

Edna wrote faithfully to Quint. But she hadn't penned so much as a line to Judd since his departure. If she were to forgive him, maybe Judd could start forgiving himself. But Hannah was losing hope that it would ever happen. Edna would take her bitterness to her grave.

Hannah strained the brewed tea, added a splash of cream and sweetened it with honey, the way she knew Edna liked it. She was reaching for a saucer when she heard the crash of a chair against the dining room table and the muffled thud of a slight body falling to the floor.

September 25, 1899

Judd rode south, out of Dawson, on a gray Sunday morning. It was only late September, but the air was cold enough to cloud his breath. Half-frozen mud crumbled under the hooves of his horse and pack mule. Smoke hung in dirty clouds above the ramshackle saloons and miners' huts.

Along the creek, where abandoned sluice boxes littered the bank, willows hung their crimson leaves over the water. Judd rubbed at the dark stubble that covered his jaw. He'd promised Hannah that when the leaves changed he would turn for home. It would be wise to keep that promise before a winter blizzard blew in from the North and trapped him here. He wouldn't be sorry to leave this godforsaken country—except that he would be leaving without Quint.

For weeks he'd combed the mining camps and ridden the backcountry, searching for his brother. He'd shown Quint's picture in assay offices, in hotels, in stores, saloons and whorehouses. No one remembered the handsome young man with the open, friendly manner. In his desperation, Judd had checked graveyards, funeral parlors and police reports. He'd checked, as far as he was able, the passenger list of every ship to have docked at Skagway in six months and the registry of men who'd lined up to climb the dangerous trail over Chilkoot Pass.

Quint had vanished as if he'd never existed.

Sick with frustration, Judd turned his back to the wind and headed south through the endless forests of scrubby pine. The long journey home would take him by horse over White Pass and down to Skagway, by steamer to Seattle and by rail back to Dutchman's Creek—and to Hannah.

Missing her was like a blade twisting in his gut.

His days had been filled with searching for Quint. But his nights had been filled with Hannah—her shadowed eyes gazing down at him in the lamplight, her corn silk hair skimming his cheek. Sometimes, in the lonely darkness, he'd felt her arms around him, felt her woman's body spooned against his beneath the blankets, listened to the sweet cadence of her breathing. Once or twice she'd stayed the night, only vanishing when he opened his eyes to dawn. But mostly her presence was a fleeting thing. It faded at the first distraction, leaving him prey to the nightmares that trailed him like hungry wolves.

Judd had left on this quest, in part, to save himself from the hell of wanting her. If he could bring Quint home and see the two of them safely married, he would find the will to walk away. But now he'd be returning alone. The burning would start again as soon as he saw her.

He'd written to her twice along the way. But he hadn't been in any one place long enough to get mail. For all he knew, Quint might have returned. He and

Hannah might be waiting for him to come home and sign the divorce papers so they could wed.

Judd cursed himself for the oversight. He should have signed the papers before leaving. That way, Hannah could have her freedom whenever she wanted it. But it couldn't be helped now. Not unless he died and left her a widow.

He rode south, following the well-worn trail through a land as bleak and vast as an ocean. Now and again he passed other travelers, weary-looking men anxious to escape the Klondike before winter set in. Judd always took pains to show them Quint's picture. But by now he knew what to expect. Not one had seen his brother or heard his name.

He ate sparingly from the supplies in his pack and the fish and berries he gleaned off the land. Once a cow moose and her calf bolted across the trail in front of him. Another time he surprised a grizzly bear on a kill and made a hasty detour to safety.

Often he saw wolves, flashing through the pines on a course that paralleled his own. If they came too close, a gunshot above their heads was usually enough to frighten them off. Judd had no wish to kill them. This was their home, and he'd seen enough death in the war to last him for the rest of his days.

At night he piled his campfire high with wood and slept lightly, with the horse and mule close by. Sometimes the wolf calls kept him awake until dawn. He grew accustomed to the melancholy howls—grew, almost, to enjoy them. It was as if they spoke to something wild and savage in his own soul.

Life on the trail had done wonders for Judd's health.

His injuries had healed, and the pallor from the hospital stay was long gone. The malaria that plagued him for months hadn't returned. He was sun-bronzed and fit, and he'd never felt stronger in his life. Only the nightmares remained—shattering memories of the war that jolted through his system and left him in a cold sweat.

Snow was falling as he crossed the mountains at White Pass. In Skagway he sold his animals and gear for a steamer ticket back to Seattle. Judd would have welcomed the thought of going home. But how was he going to face his mother? How was he going to face Hannah?

How could he tell them he'd failed?

At the post office, the unclaimed bundle of mail for Quint had grown. There were also three letters for Judd, all of them from Hannah. A glance at the postmarks told him they'd been mailed several weeks ago. The news they contained wouldn't be fresh, but Judd was hungry for any word from home, especially if his wife's hand had penned it.

Hannah wasn't really his wife, Judd reminded himself as he searched for a quiet place to read. Not in any of the ways that counted. They had an arrangement, that was all. To want more would be worse than disloyal. It would be treacherous.

He found a sheltered spot in the lee of a warehouse, quiet and out of the wind. Seating himself on a barrel, he selected the most recent of Hannah's letters. He could read the others on the steamer.

Judd's fingers shook slightly as he tore open the envelope. A letter from home was an uncertain thing. The news it carried could be welcome or it could be heart-breaking.

This time it was neither. Hannah's message was warm and chatty, awakening Judd's memories of home, and of her. There'd been no word of Quint, but at least his mother seemed no worse and things were going smoothly on the ranch. Before long he'd be back to take over—but without his brother.

He would take some time to check in Seattle before boarding the train home, Judd resolved. Quint had bought a railway ticket that far, planning to catch a steamer for Skagway. Since there'd been no sign of him in the gold-fields, it was possible that he'd never made it onto the boat.

Judd's blood ran cold at the thought of what might have happened to his brother. The docks of Seattle were teeming with shysters, thieves and cutthroats. Quint was physically strong. But he'd never been away from home before. He was young, naive and far too trusting. Led by curiosity, he would have been easy prey for the vermin that lurked in the shadows, waiting for a mark.

He would start with the police, Judd decided. If that proved fruitless, he would try hospitals, jails, gambling dens, anyplace a young man might have run into bad luck. Money was a great loosener of tongues. If Quint had been there, surely somebody would have remembered him.

The process could take weeks, he realized. And the odds were high that his search would come to no good end. If Quint had made it to Seattle and failed to leave or to write home… Judd blotted the thought from his mind.

He was not ready to face the reality that his brother, in all likelihood, was dead.

Chapter Ten

Seattle, Washington, October 11
My dearest Hannah,

Judd stared down at what he'd written. Good Lord, what was he thinking? It had been a long, tiring day. Maybe he was even more exhausted than he'd realized. Crumpling the sheet of hotel stationery, he picked up the fountain pen and started again on a fresh sheet of paper.

Dear Hannah,
Unless you get a wire to the contrary, know that I'm here in Seattle, still looking for Quint. I spent the day checking the police stations and hospitals. So far I've found no sign that he was even here. Tomorrow I plan to dig deeper. If I hear any news at all, even if it's bad, I promise I'll let you know at once. You may need to prepare yourself for the worst.

Your three letters were waiting for me in Skagway. Thank you for keeping me abreast of things on the ranch. You're doing a fine job, as I knew you would. Your letters for Quint remain at the post office. It may be that he'll come by for them. But after weeks of searching, I've come to doubt that he was ever in Alaska.

I'll leave it to your discretion how much of this news to share with Mother. She's fragile, and she sets great store by Quint. More worry could have a bad effect on her health. But tell her if you think she needs to know.

Now that I'm here, it will be easier to keep in touch. If you have anything urgent to report, you can send a telegram to me at the hotel address shown on this letterhead.

Yours in hope,
Judd

Hannah read Judd's letter sitting on the porch with Quint's dog sprawled against her leg. It was the late afternoon of an Indian summer day. Splotches of red oak and bright gold aspen painted the mountain slopes. Above the tree line, the peaks glittered with the first dusting of snow.

In the fields the men were cutting the tall alfalfa with the haymow and raking it into rows. The fresh, sweet aroma of new-mown hay drifted on the air. Overhead, a trailing V of mallard ducks winged south against the azure sky.

Hannah reread the letter, her eyes tracing each curve of Judd's masterful script. Knowing the truth was a fearful burden, she thought. The awful press of its weight was almost physical.

Inside the house, Edna lay partially paralyzed from the stroke she'd suffered last month. Dr. Fitzroy had estimated her remaining time in days; then, as she rallied and clung to life, in weeks. So far she'd defied the odds. But it was clear that only the hope of seeing Quint again kept her alive.

How could Hannah tell the poor woman that her beloved younger son had vanished without a trace, and that Judd despaired of finding him alive?

And how could she tell Judd about his mother? Knowing Judd, he'd be torn between coming home and continuing the desperate search. It would be an agonizing choice.

Quint's dog thrust its damp nose beneath her hand, begging to be petted. Hannah scratched the scruffy ears. She could feel her baby shifting and kicking, bracing its little feet and pushing off against her bones—Quint's child, maybe all she would ever have of him.

The autumn sun was warm on her skin. Such a beautiful day. Why did there have to be so much sadness in it?

She would not trouble Edna about Quint, Hannah decided. But she had no right to withhold the truth from Judd. She'd written to him, in fact, right after his mother's stroke. But he would have left Alaska by the time her letter arrived at the Skagway post office. According to the last word he'd received, Edna was fine.

Judd had asked her to wire him with urgent news. Edna's condition certainly qualified as urgent. There was only one thing to be done.

Calling for the buggy to be hitched, she hurried inside to tell Gretel she was going to town.

* * *

Rejecting the noisy elevator, Judd toiled up three flights of stairs to his hotel room. It was after midnight. Most of the guests would be sleeping. He would spare them the sound of clunking, squealing gears that had awakened him more times than he cared to remember.

He needed to be in bed himself. After a day of combing Seattle's waterfront, he was dirty, red-eyed and exhausted. He had walked every street, spoken with dockhands, bartenders, gamblers, drunks, pimps and whores. He had long since lost count of the drinks he'd bought and the money he'd spent on information that led nowhere. If Quint had been here at all, nobody remembered him.

Quint was his only brother, his mother's beloved son and the father of Hannah's child. Giving him up for lost was out of the question. But for now, at least, the trail had gone cold.

Maybe he was searching in the wrong place, Judd berated himself. It might be wise to back off and take a fresh look. Something was missing from the puzzle. Until he discovered what it was, he could be wasting precious time.

Weary beyond words, he shuffled down the dim corridor toward his room. Only as he was turning the key in the lock did he notice the yellow Western Union envelope stuffed under the door.

Suddenly he was wide-awake. Switching on the electric lamp, he closed the door behind him, ripped open the envelope and read the telegram inside.

Judd sank onto the bed as his knees gave way beneath him. Emotions churning, he reread the telegram Hannah had sent. His mother was bedridden, her life hanging by a thread. Her single expressed wish was to see Quint again before she died.

Now what? Judd's hands twisted the telegram in frustration. He'd done all he could. Nothing but a miracle could satisfy Edna's last wish. And right now he was fresh out of miracles. He didn't know whether to weep or curse.

Would his mother blame him if he came home without Quint? Would Hannah?

From the clamor in Judd's mind, the voice of one argument rose above the others. His mother needed him. Hannah needed him. The ranch needed him. The one thing worse than coming home without Quint would be not coming home at all.

With a sigh he rose and began packing for the early-morning train. Alive or dead, Quint had to be out there somewhere. But finding him would have to wait.

It was Al Macklin who met Judd's train in Dutchman's Creek. The foreman was waiting in the buggy when Judd stepped onto the platform. His greeting was a simple nod.

Judd tossed his pack onto the rear seat and vaulted up beside him. He'd been hoping Hannah might be here to welcome him. Her absence didn't bode well for things at home. Judd braced himself for bad news.

"How's Mother?" he asked.

"Alive. She sleeps mostly." Macklin's throat rippled. He pressed his lips into a thin line. Although the taciturn old cowboy had never spoken about it, Judd was aware that he'd loved Edna for years. More was the pity that he'd kept his silence. Judd and Quint would have welcomed him as a stepfather.

"And Hannah?"

"Big as a heifer. She's done a right fine job of running things, but with Edna down, she's got more than she can handle, even with Gretel helping."

Judd exhaled slowly, feeling the weariness in every part of his body. "And nobody's heard from Quint?"

"Not a word."

Judd shook his head. "I couldn't find any trace of him, Al. And I don't know where else to look."

"He's a boy. Boys do crazy things. Give him some time, he'll come home."

"I can only pray you're right." Judd settled back in the seat, filling his eyes with the autumn fields, the golden trees and distant mountains. It was good to be home. Given the choice he would never leave again.

He pictured Hannah standing on the porch, her belly round and plump beneath her skirt, her wheaten hair framing her face in windblown tendrils. Was she watching the road, waiting for him? Would he be able to keep himself from bounding up the steps and gathering her into his arms?

A brotherly hug wouldn't be unseemly after his long absence. But Judd knew better than to push the limits. He didn't trust his hands. He didn't trust his lips. He didn't trust his heart.

To keep his mind off Hannah, he made conversation about the business of the ranch—the profits and losses, the storage of winter hay, the health of the new Hereford calves, the pastureland Hannah had leased from her father. The diversion lasted until the buggy rounded the last bend and he saw the house with its long, straight road leading up from the gate. He fixed his attention on the barn with its freshly patched roof and on the sturdy new chicken coop Hannah's younger brother had built. Everything looked fine, as Judd had known it would. But the prospect of what lay inside that gloomy house had weighed on him every mile of the trip home. So many regrets. So many wrongs he couldn't put right.

Hannah was not waiting on the porch. Only the dog came down the steps to greet him, wagging its tail as he climbed down from the buggy and hoisted his pack. The house seemed ominously quiet, the front door closed, the drapes drawn.

Judd's throat tightened as he mounted the steps and opened the front door. "Hello?" he called softly. "Anybody here?"

He saw her then, standing at the far end of the hallway with an empty tin tray in her hands. Her swollen belly rose beneath the white apron she wore over her dress. Her hair was hastily pinned, with one lock falling loose over her ear. Shadows of weariness pooled beneath her eyes. To Judd, she'd never looked more beautiful, not even on their wedding day.

The tray clattered to the floor as their gazes met. Her parted lips shaped his name. Then, as if it were the most natural thing in the world, she sprinted down the corridor and flung herself into his arms.

Judd hadn't meant to hold her, but how could he help himself? As they came together he caught her behind the waist and clasped her close. Her body was sweet and solid, with the bulk of Quint's child pressing between them. Her hair smelled of fresh meadow hay. Her tears wet the stubble on his cheek.

"I'm sorry, Hannah," he murmured against her hair. "I'm so sorry I couldn't bring him home."

"You did everything you could," she whispered. "And we mustn't give up hope. Quint's out there somewhere. Surely, one of these days, he'll come home to us."

Judd had expected her to pull away but she clung to him, her body trembling, her fingertips digging into his shoulders. He held her, letting her womanly warmth flow through every part of him, feeling as if, for the first time in his life, he'd truly come home.

Only when he realized he was becoming aroused did he ease her away, bracing her at arm's length. "You'd better take me to Mother," he said.

"Yes…of course." Hannah blinked as if she were awakening from a dream. "Your mother was dozing a few minutes ago when I checked on her. Maybe knowing you're back will lift her spirits."

Judd followed her down the hall toward the closed door of Edna's bedroom. He knew better than to expect that his mother would be glad to see him. It was Quint, and only Quint, her heart craved. She would never forgive her firstborn son for coming home without him.

Hannah opened the door softly and stepped aside so Judd could enter the room. His mother lay on her back, her head elevated by pillows. Beneath the satin coverlet, her chest rose and fell with the shallow rhythm of her breathing.

Judd walked to the bedside and stood looking

down at her. Clad in a pink flannel nightgown embroidered with roses, Edna looked as fragile as the cast-off skin of a spider. The flesh had shrunk around her bones so that she was little more than a living skeleton.

Hannah had moved to the other side of the bed. Her blue eyes brimmed with tears.

"Can she talk?" he asked in a whisper.

Hannah nodded. "Yes. And she can move a little on her right side. But her mind… You'll see."

Edna made a small moaning sound. Her eyelids fluttered, but didn't open. Judd reached down and lifted her right hand. In the curl of his big palm, her fingers felt no larger than a child's.

"I'm here, Mother," he said softly. "I've come home."

Her eyes opened. A rapturous expression stole over her face. "Quint! Oh, Quint, it's really you!"

Watching Judd, Hannah felt her heart contract. Anguish flashed across his face. "Yes, it's me," he murmured. "I'm here. I won't leave you again."

He lifted his mother's hand and brushed it with his lips. Hannah swallowed the ache in her throat. She remembered how she'd felt in his arms, so safe and protected. Now his tenderness moved her to the brink of tears.

This strong, gentle man was her husband in a make-believe marriage that they couldn't allow to be real.

What a terrible time to discover that she loved him.

Gretel chose that moment to appear in the open doorway with a basin, a towel and a stack of clean sheets and nightgowns. Her eyes lit as she caught sight of Judd; but before she could speak, Hannah rushed to her side with a few whispered words of explanation. Understanding, Gretel backed into the hall and waited.

"Did you find gold in Alaska, Quint?" Edna gazed up at her son with adoring eyes.

"Not much. But it was an adventure." Judd was still holding his mother's hand. "I'll tell you more about it after Gretel's finished with your bath and you've had a chance to rest."

"Don't leave me, Quint!" She clung to his hand with surprising strength.

He made no attempt to loosen her fingers. "I just got here from the train, Mother. I need to clean up and get a bite to eat. But I'll be back soon."

"You promise?"

"I promise. Now be a good girl and let Gretel take care of you. I'll come back later and keep you company."

Little by little her grip relaxed. Judd slipped his hand free and moved back, giving Gretel room to approach the bed. Edna's gaze followed him as he walked out the door and into the hall with Hannah behind him.

As the door closed he sagged against the wall. His face looked as if he'd just walked across a battlefield littered with dead. "Lord, Hannah, I don't know if I can do this," he muttered.

"Would you rather tell her the truth?" Hannah ached for him, but she knew Judd wouldn't want her pity.

He sighed wearily. "What've you got in the kitchen? Except for coffee, I haven't eaten all day."

"Just bread and soup. And I'm afraid you'll have to settle for my cooking. I've taken over the kitchen duties to give Gretel more time for your mother."

"Bread and soup will be fine." He followed her into the kitchen and sank onto a wooden chair next to the well-scrubbed worktable. How tired he looked, and yet how handsome, she thought. The weeks in Alaska had filled out his lanky frame and bronzed his skin to a rich golden tan. His hair curled in thick waves above his collar, and his chin was shadowed with dark brown stubble. Hannah imagined walking over to his chair and cradling his head in her hands. She imagined how his rough whiskers would feel on her skin as she pressed his face into the hollow between her swollen breasts.

But that was a wicked thought. If she were to do such a brazen thing, Judd would push her away in horror.

"How have you been, Hannah?" he asked her.

"Well enough." She moved the soup kettle over the hot front burner of the stove, stirring the rich ham-and-barley soup with a long-handled spoon. "Dr. Fitzroy says everything looks fine with the baby. But of course I don't have the energy I used to."

"How much longer?"

"Six weeks or so. Maybe less. The doctor thinks it might come early." Hannah cut and buttered two thick slices of bread and put them on a blue china plate. Then she dished up the soup, which had just begun to bubble, and added a spoon to the bowl. She had long since given up hope that Quint would be there to see his child born. Worse, she was losing hope that he would ever come back at all.

"Your mother must be excited," Judd said, making conversation. "This will be her first grandchild, won't it?"

"Yes. But she's been busy taking care of my father.

He's been down sick for a couple of weeks, and the whole family is worried. I sent Dr. Fitzroy by to see him. He thinks it's a kidney ailment." Hannah darted out the back door to fetch the cold milk from the springhouse. Bustling back inside, she poured Judd a foaming mugful. "I'll wager you haven't had milk this good since you left home," she said.

"Sit down, Hannah." Judd's fingers closed around her wrist as she set the mug on the table. "You've been flitting around like a hummingbird since I got here. You're going to wear yourself out. Get something to eat and keep me company."

Hannah sank into the chair on the opposite side of the table. Picking up a slice of bread she took a few tentative nibbles. She was too tired and too emotional to be hungry. "So what do you think has become of Quint?" she asked. "Do you believe he's still alive?"

Judd broke off a hunk of bread and dipped it into the soup. His eyes closed as he savored the taste. He seemed so tired and so glad to be home. Maybe she should have waited to bring up the subject of Quint.

He sipped the cold milk, taking his time. "We can't give up hope yet," he said at last. "If Quint had made it to the Klondike, or even as far as Seattle, he would have left some evidence that he was there—a hotel registry, a steamer ticket, people who remembered his face— *something*. But I didn't find a trace of him. Not so much as a hair."

"You're saying Quint might have gone somewhere else?"

Judd set the mug on the table with a click. "Quint is

twenty-one years old, with no more common sense than a blasted—" He broke off, shaking his head. "I'm sorry. I know you love him. But he's never been off on his own before. The young fool could be anywhere. I should never have agreed to let him go."

Hannah's hand crept across the table to rest on his sleeve. "Don't blame yourself, Judd. You couldn't have stopped him. *I* couldn't have stopped him. I know because I tried. I begged him not to go. I even—"

Hannah bit off the rest of the sentence. Heat rose in her face. Her gaze flickered downward to her swollen belly.

"You could have stopped *me,* Hannah."

She looked up to find him watching her, his bloodshot gray eyes brimming with weariness—and raw honesty.

Her lips parted, but her mouth refused to form words.

"If I'd been in Quint's place, and you'd been mine, nothing could have torn me away from here."

Hannah stared down at the table, her cheeks blazing.

"We can't change the past," Judd said. "For now, all we can do is take things one day at a time. Quint could walk through that front door tomorrow. We have to go on believing that."

"Yes, of course we do." Hannah's fingers crumbled a corner of the bread on the table. Judd's unspoken words hung in the air between them. While hope remained that Quint was alive, they owed him their loyalty. Whatever their feelings for one another, to act on them would only bring guilt and shame.

"So, why don't you catch me up on things here while I finish eating?" He changed the subject, closing the perilous door he'd opened between them. "According to

Al Macklin, you've been running yourself ragged. There's no need for that. If Gretel's busy with Mother, why don't you hire some extra help in the house?"

Hannah sighed. "I've thought about it. But the idea of some woman from town carrying tales back and forth about your mother, about me... I couldn't stand that."

"Your family then?"

"Annie has a job she loves. She's bringing home good money. And Emma's only fourteen. Mama needs her help, especially now." Hannah shook her head. "Even if there was someone available, how could I ask a member of my family to work for me as a servant?"

"I hadn't thought of that, but I suppose you're right." He sopped up the last of the soup with the last of the bread, waving away Hannah's offer of more.

"I really don't mind the work," Hannah said. "I've been helping Mama cook and clean all my life, and I enjoy being busy. Now that you're here to take over the business of the ranch, I should be fine."

"Have you forgotten you'll be having a child in a few weeks?"

"How could I?" Hannah glanced down at her belly where the baby was thumping like a young jackrabbit. "My mother managed fine without extra help. So will I."

Judd scowled. "We'll see when the time comes, all right?"

"Fine. There's apple pie. Would you like some?"

He hesitated, then rose from his chair. "Later, maybe. Right now I should take my pack upstairs, clean up a bit and spend some more time with Mother if she's awake."

Hannah rose as well and began clearing away the dishes. She kept her eyes lowered, fearful that meeting his gaze would reveal too much. They'd assumed a formal, awkward manner, but their earlier exchange had left her churning inside. "Let me know when you'd like to see the books," she said.

"Tomorrow will be fine. Right now I'm too tired to make any sense of the numbers."

They came around the table at the same time and collided at the corner. The solid impact of their bodies sent the dishes in Hannah's hands clattering to the hardwood floor. A saucer struck the table leg and shattered into pieces.

"Oh!" Hannah sank to her knees. "I'm sorry, I'll get—"

The words dissolved in her mouth as powerful hands gripped her shoulders and pulled her to a standing position. Judd's eyes blazed into hers.

"Leave it."

She stared at him in confusion. "But I just—"

"Leave it, Hannah. I won't stand for my wife groveling on the floor at my feet. I'll get a broom and clean up the mess myself."

His face was barely a hand breadth from her own. His chapped lips parted slightly as if he were preparing to kiss her. She wanted him to kiss her, Hannah realized. She wanted to feel his arms around her, feel the rough heat of his mouth crushing hers, and more, so much more.

She wanted to be his wife in every sense of the word.

Heart drumming, she strained upward. At the same

instant, Quint's baby moved inside her. She froze as the red tide of shame washed over her. What was she thinking? As the mother of Quint's child, didn't she owe him her loyalty?

Her lips parted as he bent toward her. "Don't," she whispered.

He released her at once and took a step backward. His expression had gone rigid. She sensed that he was about to apologize.

An apology was the last thing she wanted to hear.

Wheeling away from him, Hannah plunged through the swinging doors into the dining room. From there she stumbled into the front hall. At the door, she took a few seconds to compose herself. Lifting her chin, she walked out onto the front porch.

Judd, she knew, would be too proud to follow her. She stood alone in the shadow of the broad eave gazing toward the distant gate. The sun hung low in the autumn sky, brushing clouds with the first rays of twilight color. In the distance, she could see the loaded hay wagon lumbering toward the barn. The big draft horses strained against their collars, turning the wooden wheels over the rutted ground. The smell of fried liver and onions drifted from the bunkhouse.

Hannah gripped the porch rail. Her fingernails dug into the painted wood as she struggled with her emotions.

Quint was her childhood playmate, her first love and the father of her unborn baby.

Judd was her rescuer, her protector, her lawful husband who awakened sweet, secret hungers every time she looked at him.

Two different men, each of them hers in a different way. Heaven help her, was it possible to love them both?

Judd cursed himself as he swept up the broken china and dumped the shards into the trash bin. He'd taken things too far with Hannah. He wouldn't have blamed her if she'd slapped his face before she bolted out of the kitchen.

At least she'd stopped him before he made a complete fool of himself. Kissing her would have been like leaping off a precipice—a long fall with a shattering end. The fragile trust between them would have been broken forever.

Had he been in full possession of his senses, the impulse never would have struck him. But he'd been so weary after long months of searching, so hungry for a taste of warmth and sweetness. And she'd looked so beautiful, with her full lips open and waiting. Temptation had swept over him with the force of an avalanche.

One thing was certain. He could not allow it to happen again. Between his mother's care, the running of the ranch and the need to put up appearances, there was no way he could avoid being with Hannah. But he could train himself to be aware of the danger signals. When either of them was tired or upset, when his mind began to wander forbidden paths, when his body stirred in response to her nearness, he would know it was time to back off—and he would.

Keeping his hands off her would require the discipline of a saint. But Judd had made a promise—to Hannah, to Quint and to himself. He would keep that promise.

Chapter Eleven

November 14, 1899

Dearest Quint,

What little is left of my common sense tells me I should stop writing these letters. I know where they go, and I expect you won't be there to read them. But there's this little bird called Hope, and it's still singing in my heart. If I stop writing to you, I fear that it might fly away.

Judd has been home for nearly a month now. His return has taken a burden off my shoulders, and in good time. With the baby's birth so close, I seem to need more rest than ever. The doctor says it shouldn't be long now—a week or two. I still pray that you will return in time to hold your newborn son in your arms—and it will be a son, I'm certain. No little girl could be so strong. I plan to name him after you and my father: Quinton Soren Seavers. Judd agrees that's it's a fine name. I hope you will like it, and that he will, too.

Seated at the small secretary in her bedroom, Hannah paused to read what she'd just written. She'd mentioned Judd twice in two paragraphs, she realized. Would that give Quint the wrong idea? Laying down the pen she hesitated, her hand poised to crumple the page and start over. Then she shrugged. What were the chances that Quint would ever read this letter?

And what would it matter if he did read it? There was nothing improper in her relationship with Judd. Judd had made sure of that. He avoided being alone with her and spoke to her as if she were a polite visitor. When he helped her into the buggy, his touch was so light that she scarcely felt the pressure of his hands. If she touched him, he froze or drew away.

Picking up the pen again, she continued her letter.

Your mother is no better and seems no worse. She clings to life in the hope of seeing you again.

Once more, she paused. Edna still believed that Judd was Quint. But that could change tomorrow. So far, Hannah had avoided telling Quint about his mother's mental condition. And since he wouldn't likely read this letter, there was no use troubling with it now.

Just come home, Quint, please, wherever you are. Your mother needs you. Your son needs you. I need you most of all.

She signed the letter, folded it and stuffed it into the envelope she'd already addressed. How long would it go on, this waiting, not knowing whether Quint was dead or alive? A word would be enough, a single note, a telegram. All she needed was something to feed her faith that he'd return. Otherwise…

Leaving the thought unfinished, she rose and crossed the room to the bed where, earlier, she'd laid out all the things for the baby. Since Judd's return, she'd spent all her spare time sewing. She'd made nearly a score of little nightgowns and shirts out of clean new flannel. Annie had contributed an exquisitely stitched christening gown and a stack of hemmed muslin diapers. Gretel and her friend had knit sweaters, caps blankets and booties out of soft lambs' wool. There were bibs, belly bands, washcloths and towels. And there was fresh padding for the cradle Judd had brought out of storage and given a coat of fresh white paint. It had been his own cradle, as well as Quint's, he'd told Hannah.

The cradle stood at the foot of the bed now, ready for the next young Seavers. Hannah rocked it lightly with her foot as she tried to imagine what that child would be like. Surely he'd be bright and charming like his father, with Quint's twinkling brown eyes and dimpled smile. She wouldn't mind if he had the wheaten hair that dominated her side of the family. But aside from that she wanted Quint's son to be a miniature of his father—unmistakably his.

Everyone would know, of course. But Judd had been right about one thing—she was respectably married to a Seavers. If the townspeople said anything, it wouldn't be to her face.

Only now, as her time approached, did she fully appreciate what Judd had done for her. She imagined herself pregnant and single with no means of support, a scandal in the town and a burden on her family, with Quint far away and unaware. How would she have managed if Judd hadn't offered to marry her? What kind of future would her child be facing, as little more than another Gustavson mouth to feed?

She owed Judd Seavers more than she could ever hope to repay.

Restless, she walked to the window. By now the leaves had dropped from the trees, leaving the mountainsides bare and brown. Clouds spilled over the western peaks, heralding an early storm. After lunch, when she'd gone outside to bring in the laundry, Hannah had smelled snow in the air. By tomorrow morning the valleys would be dusted with white.

Three days ago Judd had left with the men to round up the cattle and bring them down off the mountain. Worry gnawed at her as she realized they could be caught in a blizzard. The storms that swept over the Rockies could be killers, blinding men and animals with snow and freezing them where they huddled in the open. The day the men had ridden out had been warm and sunny. Had they thought to carry blankets, gloves and warm coats?

As she gazed down the long drive toward the gate, Hannah murmured a prayer for their safety. Almost as if in answer, she saw the thin dark line spilling over the horizon. She watched it spread to become a flood of cattle, men and horses. Soon she could make out the chuck wagon and distinguish individual riders. Straining against the glass, she searched for the sight of Judd on his tall black gelding. Where was he? Dread congealed in the pit of her stomach.

As the cattle poured into the pasture, she saw Judd bringing up the rear. Hannah's spirits leaped as she recognized his buckskin jacket, his dark Stetson and his erect posture in the saddle. But he was riding one of the spare mounts, a sturdy piebald. There was no sign of Black Jack, the splendid horse that was among his most prized possessions.

Quint's dog had bounded off the porch to meet the riders. It ran barking among them, dodging hooves with a skill born of long practice and hard lessons. Finding Judd at last, it danced on its hind legs, scratching at his boot with its paws. Controlling the skittish horse with one hand, Judd leaned down and dragged the scruffy animal onto his lap. The dog wagged and licked, then settled across Judd's knees for the ride to the house.

Taking care on the stairs, Hannah rushed down to the entry and out onto the front porch. Judd waved as he saw her. Leaving his men to take care of the stock, he spurred the piebald and rode up the drive at a canter.

Short of the porch, he reined up and eased the dog to the ground. Only as he lifted his Stetson to wipe the trail dust from his face did Hannah see the haunted look in his bloodshot gray eyes.

"What is it?" she asked softly. "What happened to Black Jack?"

He cleared his throat. "Fool horse broke his leg in a badger hole. Had to shoot him and leave him for the crows. Bad luck happens on the range. How's Mother?"

"The same. She was asleep when I last checked." Judd's gruff dismissal of the horse's death hadn't fooled Hannah. It was plain to see that he was devastated. "You must be starved," she said. "I've got chicken soup hot on the stove."

"Later. When the work's done." He swung the pie-bald back toward the corral, where the men were unloading the horses and the wagon. Hannah watched him go, his head stubbornly high, his back ramrod straight. Her husband was a troubled man—and that trouble went far deeper than the loss of a treasured horse.

Judd had known all day that the nightmares would come. But even though he tried, he knew he couldn't stay awake forever. It was still early when he closed the book of short stories he'd been reading, snuffed out the lamp and stumbled upstairs.

The house was silent except for the sharp keen of wind beneath the eaves. The first storm of the season was blowing in. By morning the ground would be covered with snow.

Hannah had gone to bed soon after supper, exhausted by the weight of her precious burden. Her door stood slightly ajar—a subtle gesture of trust. If she'd known how deeply he hungered to be in her bed, that door would likely be bolted and braced with a heavy piece of furniture.

Succumbing to temptation, he stepped into her room and walked softly to the foot of the bed. She lay on her side, sleeping like an angel with her moonlit hair spread on the pillow and her arms cradling her unborn child. Lord, what he wouldn't give just to slip in behind her and pull her close, smelling the sweetness of her skin and feeling her warm round rump against his belly. She was in no condition for anything more—that much Judd knew and respected. But her nearness might be enough to drive away the roar of exploding shells, the whine of ricocheting lead, the stench of blown bodies and the awful groans of men who couldn't die fast enough.

Putting Black Jack down this morning had damn near killed him. Al had offered to do the job in his place. But the loyal animal deserved a merciful death at the hand of its master. Judd had looked into the horse's trusting eyes and pulled the trigger himself.

Why couldn't he have done the same for his best friend?

Hannah stirred in her sleep, shifting and stretching beneath the satin quilt. Knowing he'd already stayed too long, Judd backed quietly out of the room and left the door as he'd found it.

His own solitary bed was waiting. Stripping down to his long johns, Judd lifted the covers and rolled beneath them. He was drunk with exhaustion. Maybe if he slept deeply enough the nightmares would stay away. But that was wishful thinking. The act of killing his precious horse had triggered memories he'd been struggling for months to bury. Now they were waiting, coiled like venomous snakes in the recesses of his brain just waiting for him to sleep.

Outside, the moan of the wind had risen to a howl. Too weary to resist, Judd turned onto his side, closed his eyes and surrendered to the torment.

Something had awakened Hannah. She sat up in bed, staring into the darkness. Windblown snow peppered the windows, piling whiteness against the night-black panes. A bare elm branch clawed at the side of the house.

Roused by her motion, the baby stirred. A tiny fist landed a solid punch against Hannah's sensitive bladder. With a little mutter, she swung her feet to the floor, dropped to a crouch and fumbled for the chamber pot beneath the bed.

She had finished and was washing her hands when she realized what had awakened her. Over the past months Hannah had become accustomed to Judd's occasional nightmares. She'd come to understand that the last thing he wanted was her interference. But what she was hearing now disturbed her, even terrified her. Judd's breath came in wrenching sobs. He moaned and cried out, uttering muffled curses as his jerking body shook the bed.

He sounded as if he were in terrible pain.

"Judd?" She pressed close against the wall that separated his bedroom from hers. "Judd, are you all right?"

There was no answer but the nightmare continued, growing more vocal and more violent by the second. Judd would want her to leave him alone and let the horror pass. But how could she, when his life might be in danger?

"Judd?" Her bare feet pattered down the hallway. His door was open. From the darkness beyond came the sounds of a soul in torment.

Judd was thrashing in a tangle of covers, his eyes closed, his face beaded with sweat. Hannah found his shoulder and shook it gently. "Wake up, Judd! You're dreaming!"

His arm flailed outward. A fist grazed her head. She shook him harder, her fingers digging into his shoulder. "Wake up!"

He moaned and thrashed, muttering curses that would have horrified her if he'd been awake. She considered striking him or dousing him with water from the washstand. But Judd was a powerful man. In his present condition, that kind of violence could make him even more dangerous.

"No…" His body jerked as if he were being tortured. "No…can't do it…won't. Get a medic over here! A medic, for the love of God…"

He fell to cursing again. Driven by desperation, Hannah did the only thing she could think of.

She lay down beside him on the narrow bed and wrapped him in her arms.

He fought her like a wild animal, struggling and cursing. Hannah clung to his back, her arms clasped around his chest. "There…" she murmured, kissing wherever her mouth could reach, his neck, his shoulder, his sweat dampened hair. "It's all right, my dearest. You're dreaming…"

Little by little she felt his resistance stop. His clenched muscles relaxed. His jerky breathing deepened, became more regular. But the dry, wrenching sobs continued for what seemed like a very long time. At last Judd seemed to rouse himself. Rolling over, he gathered her into his arms and held her against his chest. His body was drenched in perspiration.

"I'm sorry, Hannah." The words were little more than a growl. "You don't deserve to deal with this, with me…."

"Hush." Her lips brushed his stubbled jaw. "It was only a dream. You're all right now."

"For the present." He drew her closer, pressing her swollen belly into the curve of his body. "You shouldn't have come near me. What if I'd hurt you, or even hurt the baby?"

"You wouldn't have hurt me, not even in your sleep. I know you, Judd. You're the very soul of kindness."

She felt the slight shake of his head. "All you know of me is what I let you see, Hannah."

"Then show me the rest!" She pushed away from him, far enough to look into the hooded depths of his eyes. Outside, the wind tore at the house. Snow battered the windows. "Tell me what's in those nightmares, Judd," she said. "I have the right to know. I'm your wife."

His only answer was a long, ragged exhalation. His arms tightened around her. His lips traced a path along her hairline. She sensed that he was struggling with words that wouldn't come.

"The war," Hannah said, trying to help him. "It must have been horrible."

He shook his head. "It was a hundred times worse than you can imagine. I'd give anything I own to blot those memories out of my mind—and my dreams."

Hannah waited, her head resting in the hollow of his throat. He smelled of sweat and wood smoke, his body all muscle and sinew against her softness. If he chose to speak, she would listen. If not, just holding him in the stillness would be enough. Either way, nothing would part her from him tonight.

He drew a deep breath. "Daniel Sims and I signed up together, you'll likely remember. We'd been friends all our lives, and we pretty much talked each other into it. We were going to have ourselves an adventure, serve our country and come home covered with glory. Only it wasn't like that."

Hannah felt the tension building in his body. She nestled closer, easing one leg between his knees so that they lay tangled, warm and intimate through their nightclothes. The contact seemed to relax Judd.

"The Spanish were dug in atop San Juan Hill with their artillery. Kettle Hill lay between. We were massed at the bottom, waiting for the signal that the heavy guns had been knocked out so we could move up the slope. Cuba in July was hotter than bloody hell. A bunch of us were already sick with fever, but that didn't excuse us from being there. The longer we waited the hotter it got, and the sicker we felt. Some of the men could barely walk.

"We were still hearing the artillery fire when Roosevelt got hold of that damn fool horse. He screamed at us, waved his saber and charged up the hill with the ground exploding around him. It was follow him or face a court martial. We ran, in that awful heat with our rifles blazing and artillery blasting the hell out of us."

A shudder passed through Judd's body. "It was a bloodbath. Bullets flying, shells exploding, men dropping everywhere. We were nearly on top when I saw Daniel go down. He'd been gut shot. Bad."

"Oh, Judd…" Hannah's arms tightened around her husband, but he seemed lost now, in the memory of that day. Hannah could feel the quickening of his pulse. His voice had become a grating whisper.

"Daniel was in awful condition, and I knew he didn't have a prayer of getting off that hill alive. But I couldn't just leave him there. I crouched down next to him, tried to give him some water. He was in so much pain. He…" Judd's voice rasped with anguish. "He begged me to take my pistol and shoot him in the head, like I'd do for an animal. He pleaded with me...."

"What happened?" Hannah whispered.

He choked on the words. "I couldn't do it. Lord help me, I knew it would be a mercy, but I couldn't pull that trigger. I was shouting for a medic when the bullet hit me in the side. Couldn't get to the pistol after that. I lay there next to my best friend and watched him die in agony. With his last breath, he cursed me, called me a yellow bastard...."

Judd was shaking. Hannah felt the wetness on her own cheeks as she cradled him in her arms. There was nothing to be said, nothing that would ease Judd's pain. She could only hold him close. She could only love him.

"Rest," she whispered. "I'm here, Judd. I won't go away."

She curled against his chest, kissing the crisp mat of hair where the top of his long johns parted. He clasped her fiercely, hungrily. His lips grazed her hair, her forehead, her closed, wet eyelids. If she were to raise her face, Hannah knew that he would kiss her mouth, as well. But that would open a new door between them—a door that, for everyone's sake, had to remain closed and locked. She was giving him comfort. That was all.

Nothing Judd had ever known was as sweet as the peace of Hannah's arms. Only the fear that she might leave him for her own bed kept him resisting sleep. He lay beside her in the darkness, his senses swimming in the softness of her hair and the womanly aroma of her skin. His body was responding to her—there wasn't much he could do about that. But he needed her in other ways, as well. He needed her tenderness, her beauty, her compassion. He needed the simple joy of having her close to him.

How was he going to stand it when the time came to let her go?

Only when he felt her body relax and heard the little butterfly snore that punctuated each breath did Judd stop fighting sleep. The warm fog surrounded him like a blanket, pulling him into slumber. Hannah's breast lay cradled in the hollow of his arm. Her legs twined with his, one knee resting lightly against his groin. Heaven, he thought as he sank into the bliss of it. A brief and bittersweet taste of a heaven that couldn't be his.

Outside in the darkness, the wind had stilled. But the snow continued to fall, soft and thick and light, like the calm of dreamless sleep.

The frantic clatter of the front door knocker jolted Judd awake. He sat bolt upright. The room was still pitch-black.

Hannah stirred beside him. "What…is it?" she mumbled, rousing herself.

"I don't know, but it sounds like trouble." He swung out of bed and strode toward the landing. "Stay here. I'll take care of it."

He hurried down the stairs, hoping the noise wouldn't wake Gretel or his mother. Glancing back he saw Hannah on the landing, her white nightgown ghostly in the darkness.

The knocking stopped as Judd turned the lock. Cracking open the door, he saw Hannah's fifteen-year-old brother, Ephraim, on the porch. His ragged wool coat and felt hat were blanketed with snow.

Judd drew him inside and closed the door. Ephraim's teeth were chattering with cold. Seconds passed before he could speak. By then Hannah had rushed downstairs and seized her brother by the shoulders.

"What is it?" she demanded.

"It's Pa. He's bad. Ma doesn't think he'll last till morning. If you want to see him—" The boyish voice choked on the words.

Hannah swung toward Judd. "Please, I have to go."

Judd nodded, knowing he'd be with her no matter what the circumstances. "How did you get here?" he asked the boy.

"Rode Pa's plow horse across the fields. The snow's fierce out there."

Judd glanced at Hannah, then back at her brother. "Your sister can't ride safely. We'll take the buggy back to your place. Put your horse in the barn while we get dressed."

Gretel emerged from the kitchen in her blue flannel wrapper, with her hair in braids. The lantern she carried cast flaring shadows on the wall. "I just put coffee on," she said. "It will be hot by the time you're ready to go."

Judd gave her a grateful nod. Hannah had already headed upstairs to put on warm clothes. He followed her as the boy went out to stable his horse. The ride to the Gustavson farm would be miserable in this weather. The distance across the fields was only about two miles. By road it was more than twice as far, but there was no question of going any other way. The buggy couldn't stand up to the rough open land, especially with snowdrifts hiding furrows, ditches and varmint holes that could catch a wheel or worse, cripple a horse.

Judd was pulling on his boots when he remembered a heavy sheepskin coat both he and Quint had worn as teenagers. If he could find it in Quint's room, the coat would have a new owner. Ephraim needed something warmer than the ragged garment he was wearing tonight.

By the time Judd had finished dressing and found the coat, Hannah was dressed and waiting downstairs. Her face was pale, her eyes large and frightened.

"Are you all right?" he asked her.

She shook her head. "I'm just thinking about Mama and the little ones. What will they do if Papa dies, Judd? Who'll take care of them? Who's going to run the farm?"

For the space of a breath he pulled her against him, remembering how sweet she'd felt in his bed. "I'm here, Hannah," he murmured. "I'll be here for you and yours. Now go get some of Gretel's coffee, and maybe some pie, while I hitch up the buggy."

The two broke apart as Ephraim opened the front door and came inside. He was shivering beneath the ragged coat. Judd held out the warm, dry sheepskin. The boy accepted it gratefully. It fit perfectly on his lanky young frame.

Leaving Hannah and her brother with Gretel, Judd went out to the barn. The snow was as high as his boot tops, and the white flakes were still falling. For a moment he eyed the flat-bottomed sledge that stood on end against the wall. It would be easier for the horses to pull over deep snow. But it was used mostly for hauling logs and offered no shelter from the storm. For Hannah's comfort, they would have to take the buggy.

Judd raised the buggy top and loaded the seats with every spare blanket he could find, including an old buffalo robe. Instead of the trim bays, he hitched up the powerful Belgians that were used for heavy work. Their massive bodies would be more resistant to chilling, and they were strong enough to pull the buggy through the deepest snow. He could only hope the light-wheeled vehicle would be a match for their strength.

When he was finished he drove the buggy up to the house and went inside. Hannah was waiting for him, wrapped in a thick woolen cloak that Gretel had lent her. Her face appeared small and pale in the dark recesses of the hood. She looked as if she'd been weeping. When Judd asked her if she was ready to go, she simply nodded.

Ephraim came out of the kitchen wiping his mouth. Judd gulped down the mug of hot coffee Gretel brought him, thanked her, and ushered his charges out to the buggy. An odd foreboding stole over him as he helped Hannah onto the sheltered rear seat and wrapped her in blankets against the cold. Only the foolhardy would be out on a night like this. But Hannah, he knew, would not be dissuaded from going to her father's deathbed. If he stopped her, she would not forgive him in this life.

Ephraim clambered onto the front seat. Judd urged the Belgians forward. Their breath from their huge, warm nostrils raised clouds of white vapor in the darkness. The thin buggy wheels sliced through the snow as they moved down the drive toward the gate.

Snowflakes swirled around the buggy, peppering faces and building white ridges on eyebrows and eyelashes. The horses moved with lowered heads, plowing through drifts that, in places, were almost as high as their bellies. Fence posts, marking the boundaries of pastureland, poked above the snow. Only by driving between them could Judd keep to the road.

Beside him, Ephraim made a little sniffling sound. Judd didn't have to look to know that the boy was weeping. Ephraim wasn't much older than Judd had been when his own father died. Now, years too soon, he would have to become the man of the family. Ephraim was a promising lad. But any dreams he'd had of the future—education, travel, the freedom of being on his own—would have to be put aside for the sake of his family. Judd knew that obligation all too well.

Behind him, Hannah huddled in silence. She'd never talked much about her father. But then, what was there to say about Soren Gustavson? He was a small, quiet man—a good man who'd cared for his family and worked beyond the limits of his strength to provide for them. In all likelihood, he had simply worn himself out. He would leave the world a legacy of robust, handsome children who'd been raised to do right. It was more than could be said for most men at the end of their lives.

In the distance, a light flickered out of the darkness. "There." Ephraim pointed eagerly. "Ma said she'd hang a lantern on the porch for us."

Judd urged the horses toward the light. The niggling worry that had troubled him earlier was still there. He resolved to ignore it. Minutes from now they'd be arriving at the Gustavson farm. His concern would be focused on Hannah and her family. There'd be no time for silly premonitions.

The buggy lurched over a hard bump beneath the

Chapter Twelve

No one was outside to greet them, but lights flickered inside the house. Smoke curled from the chimney, ghostly gray through the falling snow. Hannah felt her stomach clench as the buggy pulled up to the porch. She prayed for the strength to face whatever awaited her inside.

"Help your sister into the house, Ephraim," Judd said. "Don't let her slip in the snow. I'll get the horses under shelter."

Hannah took Ephraim's thin, cold hand and let him assist her out of the buggy. She needed help, since she couldn't see her feet for her burgeoning belly. The snow was almost as high as the porch. She waited while Ephraim kicked the steps clear, giving her thin boots a safer purchase. Under the eave, they stomped the snow off their feet and opened the front door.

It was Annie who met them. Her eyes were red. Her pretty face was blotched with tears. She flung her arms around Hannah's neck. "He's gone," she whispered. "Papa's gone."

Hannah felt something shatter inside her. Too shocked, yet, for the tears that would come later, she let Annie lead her into her parents' bedroom. In the lamplit shadows, she saw her mother slumped in the homemade rocking chair where she'd nursed seven babies. Hannah went to her and put her arms around her shoulders. Her bones were sharp and hard beneath a worn cotton dress that was too thin for winter cold.

She raised her head. Her graying blond hair clung to her scalp. Her face looked old and tired. One chapped hand patted Hannah's belly. "An old soul going and a new soul coming. That's the good Lord's way, I suppose."

Hannah held her, murmuring empty words of comfort. What would the poor woman do now, with no husband and a family to raise? Beneath her grief, Mary Gustavson had to be frantic with worry.

I'll be here for you and yours. Judd's words echoed in her memory. She could only hope he meant what he'd said.

Steeling herself, Hannah turned toward the bed. Her father lay as still as marble, his eyes closed, his mouth slightly open. He looked much the way he used to when he fell asleep in his chair after supper.

Hannah bent and kissed his cold forehead. As tears welled in her eyes, a shadow fell across the bed. She glanced up to see Judd standing in the doorway of the bedroom. He had taken off his coat and stomped off the worst of the snow, but his trouser legs and boots were soaking wet. His skin was ruddy with cold.

"My condolences, Mrs. Gustavson." He crossed the room to Hannah's mother and took her hand. "I'm here to help. If you'll have someone get me a basin and washcloth, and some clean clothes, I'll lay him out for you."

Hannah stared at him in surprise. The laying out of a body for burial was a distressful job, to say the least. In the absence of an undertaker, it was usually done by compassionate female friends and neighbors. It involved washing the corpse, cleaning away the foul wastes and dressing the deceased in proper clothes. With the blizzard cutting off all help, it would be up to Soren's wife and daughters to perform the heartbreaking task. Judd had just offered to spare them the ordeal.

"You'd do that for us?" Mary's eyes glimmered with tears.

Instead of answering, Judd set the work in motion. "Hannah, take your mother into the kitchen and get her something hot. Tell Ephraim I'll need his help. Do you have any planks and nails?"

"Pa's coffin's already made. He had me do it last week." Ephraim had stepped into the room. His efforts to be a man almost broke Hannah's heart. She would have bought her father the finest coffin in Dutchman's Creek. But Soren would be laid to rest in a rough wooden box made by the hands of his eldest son. Somehow that seemed more fitting.

Hooking an arm around her mother's waist, Hannah helped her to the kitchen. The younger children were asleep upstairs with Emma keeping an eye on them. Only Hannah, Annie and their mother were there to sit at the table and sip the fresh barley coffee Annie had brewed. While Judd and Ephraim performed the ablutions behind the bedroom door, the three women talked, wept and did their best to support each other.

Mary looked like a drained husk, her eyes red, her face haggard above the rim of her coffee mug. "You married a good man, Hannah," she said. "I had my doubts when the two of you wed, but he's done well by you."

"He'll do well by you and the little ones, too, Mama," Hannah said quietly. "Judd told me he'd look after our family. He's a man of his word, in every way. Believe me, I know."

"But what about Quint?" Annie interjected. "Surely you haven't given him up for lost."

Hannah shook her head. "I write to Quint every week. It's become like putting notes in bottles and tossing them into the sea, but I still do it. I can't give up hope."

"And you haven't heard from Quint at all?"

"Not a word—and I told you that Judd couldn't find any trace of him in Alaska."

"I pray for Quint every night." Annie's young voice held a surprising note of passion. "I won't stop praying until we find out what happened to him."

"But you haven't torn up those divorce papers yet?" Mary asked.

"There's no chance of that. Not as long as Quint could be alive somewhere. And just in case you're wondering, Judd hasn't laid an unbrotherly hand on me." Hannah stared into her coffee mug, the heat rising in her face. It wasn't a lie. But they'd skirted the edge of truth earlier that night.

"Who'd like more coffee? I made a big pot." Annie rose from her chair and flitted over to the stove. Her spritely little sister was growing up, Hannah reflected. Soon she'd be a lovely young woman with suitors beating a path to her door.

"Save the rest for Judd and Ephraim," Mary said. "They'll be needing it."

Almost as if summoned, Judd opened the bedroom door. He was drying his hands on a towel. Ephraim stood behind him, pale and raw-eyed. "We're going to get the coffin," Judd said. "We'll carry him out to the barn in it. The cold will keep him for as long as we need. As soon as the storm passes I'll get a wagon and take him into town for burial—unless you'd rather bury him here on the farm." He gave Mary a questioning glance.

"Soren never wanted to be anyplace except on his own land," she said.

"Fine, then. When the snow stops I'll send a couple of men over to dig the grave. The ground isn't frozen yet. It shouldn't take long."

"Thank you." Mary stood. "I want some time to say goodbye before you put him in that box. Annie, see if Emma wants to come downstairs. She's old enough to see him if she chooses."

Judd stepped aside so the family could gather in the bedroom. Soren had been washed, shaved, combed and dressed in a clean white shirt and his shabby old suit. Hannah stole a glance at Judd, her heart swelling with gratitude. Her mother was right about him. She'd married a fine man, an exceptional man. In this time of sorrow and uncertainty, Judd was a rock.

By the time the coffin was closed and resting on sawhorses in a safe, dry corner of the barn, everyone was spent. They sat around the kitchen table sipping the last of the barley coffee, and drooping with exhaustion. Mary glanced at Hannah, her eyes narrowing.

"It's time you took my girl home, Judd. She's worn-out and needs to be put to bed."

"I'll be glad to stay if you need me, Mama," Hannah argued, but Mary shook her head.

"You need your rest, and so do I. I'm going to sleep till chore time. You can come back when we put your papa in the ground, if you're feeling up to it."

And that was the way of things, Hannah thought. Even in the face of tragedy there were chores to be done, cows to milk, eggs to gather, clothes to wash, children to feed and dress. Life would go on, but without her father's quiet presence it would never be the same. "I'll send some food over with the men," she said.

"That would be helpful, dear. Now get your cloak on and go home to your own bed."

While Judd fetched the buggy from the barn, Hannah hugged her family, wrapped herself in Gretel's warm cloak, and went out to meet him on the porch. She was exhausted. Her legs ached, her back ached and her swollen belly felt as heavy as a cow's. In the morning she would take stock of what she could do to help her mother. Right now, all she wanted was to lie down and sleep.

The worst of the storm had blown past. Tiny dry flakes, like diamond dust, floated down from an ink-black sky. Here and there, the clouds parted to reveal pin-points of starlight and the thin curve of the waning moon.

Judd helped her off the porch and onto the front seat,

then climbed up beside her. Light from the windows etched deep shadows under his eyes. It had been a long night for both of them.

He turned the buggy toward the gate, following the faint tracks they'd made coming up to the house. Hannah moved closer to him, sagging against his shoulder. "Thank you, Judd," she murmured. "Thank you for helping my family."

"They're good people, and they're my family, too. When your mother's ready, I want to talk to her about leasing the farm for pasture and hay. It would give her enough money to live on and still keep the land in her name. And there's a lot could be done to fix up the house—new windows, plastering on those log walls, cupboards in the kitchen…"

As his voice droned on, Hannah's eyelids grew heavier. Her head sank onto his shoulder, bobbing a little with the motion of the buggy. Lulled by the rhythmic jingle of harness brass, she drifted, dreaming of Judd's arms in the warmth of the bed. This time they were both naked. Her belly was flat and slim, his length huge between her thighs. Her blood blazed hot as she rocked against the swollen shaft, pressing its hardness into her wet, pulsing cleft. The shudders that ripped through her body were so overpowering that she wanted to yowl.

His hands cradled her breasts, cupping them, molding them to his big, calloused palms. His thumbs teased the nipples to aching lumps. The sensation was exquisite, but it wasn't enough. The sweet throbbing between her legs demanded the ultimate satisfaction. He belonged inside her, thrusting deep and hard, filling her, carrying her where she'd yearned to go and had never really been.

"Take me, Judd," she gasped. "Now…please…"

He shifted above her, parting her eager legs. She closed her eyes, waiting for the thrust that would take him into the need-slicked core of her.

It came with a sudden jab, so sharp and painful that she cried out. Her eyes flew open. The handsome face smiling down at her was…Quint's.

Hannah woke with a violent jerk. She was still seated next to Judd. The buggy was still moving along the road, the sturdy Belgians plodding through drifts of glittering snow. She couldn't have been asleep for more than a few minutes. But something, she realized, was happening to her body. Something that frightened her.

"Are you all right?" Judd cast her a worried look.

"I'm…not sure." Hannah had been feeling small contractions for a couple of weeks. The doctor had assured her they were normal. But the cramping she felt now, low in her body, was different, like the clenching of a powerful fist. A warm wetness gushed between her legs, turning icy as it soaked through her petticoat.

Growing up in a big farm family, she'd learned a few things about giving birth. But her mother had been modest and secretive about the process, even with her own daughters. Hannah's memories of childbirth consisted of minding the younger children and listening to the sounds that came from behind the closed bedroom door. She remembered the midwife bustling in and out and, at last, the miracle of that first gasping cry.

Only once had the cry failed to come.

The next pain hit Hannah with the force of a locomotive. She doubled over, clutching her belly in agony. Whatever was happening to her, it was happening fast.

Judd wasted no time with useless questions. "We've got to get you home," he said.

"Yes, hurry," Hannah whispered between clenched teeth.

"Hang on!" He brought the reins down on the Belgians' broad haunches. The snow was deep but lightly packed, offering little resistance to horses and wheels. The buggy jolted ahead, lurching over the rutted road.

"How close to home are we?" She clutched Judd's arm, her eyes scanning a landscape made alien by dark and snow.

"I'd say a little over halfway. Too far to go back to your mother's."

"Hurry!" Hannah felt another contraction building like a giant sea wave. What was wrong? The doctor had told her the baby wasn't due for another week or two. He'd also said that first babies tended to be slow in coming, so there'd be plenty of time to send for him when her pains started. Surely he knew what he was talking about.

But this time he'd been wrong. The pain that ripped through Hannah's body, kneading and twisting her like a lump of bread dough, told her that young Quinton Soren Seavers would be coming soon. Very soon.

Her fingers dug into Judd's coat sleeve, squeezing so hard that he winced. "Bad?" he asked.

"Bad." Hannah forced the words out between her teeth. "I don't know how much longer I can—oh!"

She felt the stretching of flesh and bone and the compulsion to bear down. Summoning all her strength of will, she resisted the urge. Sweat beaded her face and body, soaking into her clothes.

What if something went wrong? What if her baby came into the world white and silent, like the stillborn child that Soren had wrapped in a blanket and buried in the apple orchard? The doctor had said she was strong and healthy and shouldn't worry. But doctors could be wrong, and she was more than worried now. Heaven save her, she was terrified.

Judd was lashing the horses with the reins. The big Belgians plunged through the fallen snow dragging the buggy through drifts as high as the wheel tops. Hannah leaned forward and clutched the dash. Her fingernails dug into the leather as the next pain crested. Flying snow spattered her face. "Hurry…" she breathed. "I don't know if I can—"

Her words ended in a gasp as the buggy's right front wheel shattered.

The horses whinnied, thrashing wildly as the buggy lurched sideways. Judd's arm caught Hannah just in time to keep her from being thrown out into the snow. For the space of a breath they slid across the slick leather seat. Then he managed to brace himself and pull her back to a secure position. They clung together, breathing hard.

He cursed under his breath. "Blast it, I felt something strike that wheel coming the other way. Didn't give it a second thought. If I'd checked it—"

"Hush, you couldn't have known this would happen. But what do we do now?"

He exhaled raggedly. "First we get you comfortable in the backseat. Then I'll get out and have a look at things." His eyes met hers in the darkness. "You and your baby will be all right, I promise you, Hannah."

She nodded, knowing she had to believe him. Her life and the life of her baby were in Judd's capable hands. If need be, she knew he would give his life to save them. But even Judd couldn't perform miracles. Hannah was as frightened as she'd ever been in her life.

The wind had sprung up again, colder than ever. Blowing snow blasted her skin with fine ice crystals, as sharp as sand. She willed herself to hold back the next pain but she was powerless to stop it. It seized her like a set of giant claws, squeezing relentlessly downward.

She was going to have the baby right here, in a broken-down buggy, in the grip of a November blizzard.

Judd folded the blankets to make a bed for Hannah on the floor between the front and back seats of the buggy. It was the most sheltered spot, and probably the most stable, although everything tilted downward toward the broken right wheel. Lord, how could he have allowed this to happen?

Hannah was resting between contractions. He helped her onto the blankets and covered her with the buffalo robe to shield her from the weather. "I'm going to look at the damage," he told her. "Call if you need me. I won't be far."

She clasped his arm in response. Her time, he sensed, was perilously close. Hannah was a healthy young woman whose mother had borne an impressive brood of children. Still, anything could go wrong out here in the freezing darkness. Judd had delivered calves and foals on the ranch. A human birth couldn't be all that different. But he was no doctor, and the stakes were heartbreakingly high.

What if he lost her, or lost the baby? Lord, how could he live with that?

Leaving her, he climbed out of the buggy. Snow had drifted across the road. It whipped around his thighs as he strode forward to check the horses. The Belgians were spooked, but otherwise unharmed. He soothed them, patting their massive necks and brushing the snow off their white-blazed faces. Only when he felt confident they wouldn't bolt did he turn his attention to the broken wheel.

By the time he'd cleared the snow away Judd's hands were numb beneath his leather gloves. His heart sank as he examined the broken spokes and crushed rim. He kept a box of tools under the buggy seat, but the wheel was broken beyond repair. Worse, the front axle had splintered. Even if the wheel could be fixed or replaced, the axle would never hold it.

Hannah was moving in the buggy, pushing against the side with her feet. He could hear her gasps of pain as the contraction surged and crested, but she didn't cry out. She was a tough woman, his Hannah.

But they were in one hell of a fix. They were more than two miles from home. The wheel and axle were beyond mending, and dragging the buggy on its front corner would likely break it to pieces. Hannah was in no condition to ride, or even walk, and he didn't dare leave her alone to go for help.

Judd lifted his gaze to where the Milky Way formed a glittering trail across the sky. It wasn't really a prayer. But he knew he would have to reach beyond his own limits to save this precious woman and her baby. He was going to need help.

Bending, he tested the weight of the sagging corner. If he could brace it somehow, or even walk alongside and carry it—but he could already tell that wasn't going to work. He could lift the side of the buggy but it was too heavy to hold for more than a few seconds. There had to be a better way. All he had to do was find it.

"Judd!" Hannah's cry broke into his thoughts. "The baby—hurry!"

Forgetting everything else, he clambered back into the buggy. Hannah was writhing beneath the buffalo robe. When he reached down to her, she seized his hand, clawing at his knuckles.

"Is it coming now?" Judd's pulse was hammering like a steam piston. He mouthed a wordless prayer. This, he sensed, would be nothing like delivering a foal.

"I…can't tell. It feels like—oh!" She gasped like a drowning swimmer. "How could it hurt this much and not be coming?"

"I'll have to check." Maneuvering around her in the tilted buggy, he found her damp skirts beneath the buffalo robe. The snow lent some reflected light, but not enough. He would have to feel for the baby.

He lifted her skirt. "I'm sorry—" he began by way of apology.

"Just do it!" she hissed through clenched teeth. Her hands clutched his shoulders, as he separated the wet folds of her petticoat, found the opening in her drawers and groped between her moisture-slicked thighs. What he found was unmistakable—between the folds of her straining flesh, the crown of a tiny head.

"It's coming!" he gasped. "Push!"

But she was already pushing for all she was worth. There was a scream of effort, a gush of wetness. Then Hannah's child slid into the world, kicking and squalling like a little wildcat.

Judd felt something soften inside him as he cradled the squirming baby in his hands—so small and wet and feisty. A small miracle had just entered the world.

Even in the shelter of the buggy, the wind was fierce. Get something around the baby. That would be the first thing to do. Seizing a cotton blanket from under the buffalo robe, he swathed the little creature in its folds. The baby continued to shriek.

"Is he all right?" Hannah asked anxiously.

"Listen to those lungs. What do you think?"

"Give him to me," she said. "I want to see my son."

Judd lifted the wriggling bundle toward her, then hesitated. In his hurry to get the baby wrapped, there was one thing he hadn't checked. Lifting a corner of the blanket, he took a quick look. Something was definitely missing. Judd felt a chuckle rise in his throat. Life was full of surprises, some of them wonderful.

Hannah was holding out her arms. "I want my boy! Give him to me!"

"I'm afraid I can't do that," Judd said.

Fear and outrage flashed across her face. "Why not? He's all right, isn't he?"

"Yes, but…" Judd smiled as he placed the baby into her eager hands. "You don't have a son, Hannah. You have a daughter. A beautiful little girl."

"Oh!" Hannah's cry blended surprise and wonder. "Oh, my goodness!" She cradled the baby close. "Just look at her!"

"Are you disappointed?"

Tears glimmered on Hannah's cheeks. "How could I be disappointed? She's beautiful! She has Quint's hair and eyebrows—and look, she even has his dimples!"

The euphoria that had lifted Judd's spirit vanished like the taste of a snowflake. In the excitement, he'd almost forgotten that Hannah was his brother's woman, and her baby was his brother's child. He was only their caregiver, doing his duty until Quint came home to claim them both. He must never let himself forget that.

Finding a string from the blanket, he tied off the umbilical cord and cut it with his pocketknife. The afterbirth could be dealt with when it came. Right now he had even more urgent things to worry about.

"We need to get you home," he said. "Stay covered. Keep the baby close to your skin. I'll think of something."

He climbed out of the buggy again and pondered the broken wheel. He would have to think of something fast. Hannah and the baby were lying on wet, soiled blankets. They would freeze or get sick if they remained here.

"Judd, listen to me!" The urgency in Hannah's voice cut through the blankets. "Take one of the horses and get the baby to the house. You can keep her warm under your coat. Once she's with Gretel, you can come back for me."

Judd took a few seconds to weigh her words. It was

vital that they get the baby to safety. But if anything delayed him in getting back, Hannah could die from the cold. Worse, wild animals roamed the flatland on winter nights. Wolves were rare these days but there were coyotes and packs of half-feral dogs that preyed on sheep and newborn calves. If their noses picked up the scent of blood, she could be in awful danger.

He could take her on the horse, but the sitting and the motion could start her bleeding. Women died that way.

"Judd, did you hear me?"

"I can't leave you here," he said. "It's too dangerous."

"I'll manage. Just take her and go!"

"Not yet." Judd's hand clenched into a fist. Damn it, why had he taken this chance with the buggy in this deep snow? He'd wanted Hannah to be comfortable. But they'd have been safer with the horses dragging the open sledge over the drifts.

The image of the flat-bottomed sledge flashed through Judd's mind. Suddenly he had an idea. Rummaging under the seat, he found the toolbox. He couldn't replace the broken wheel. But he could remove the other wheels, leaving the chassis sitting flat on the snow. The springs and axles underneath would slow it down. But with care, maybe the buggy could be dragged over the snow like a sledge.

Praying his idea would work, he started on the left front wheel. "Brace yourself, it's going to tip," he told Hannah.

She understood at once what he was doing. "Just hurry," was all she said.

Judd labored with half-frozen hands to loosen the wheels and lift each one off its axle. Hannah bore it all patiently, but he knew that she and the baby must be getting cold.

With the wheels gone and the buggy level on the snow, Judd eased the horses to a walk. As the buggy began to move, he twitched the reins on their broad backs, taking them as fast as he dared. Too much speed could break the buggy into pieces.

Time crawled as they moved along the road. After what seemed like an eternity, he caught sight of the high ranch gate and the distant lamp that Gretel had hung on the porch. Beneath the buffalo robe, he could hear Hannah singing and talking to her baby.

By the time they reached the house the sky was fading above the eastern hills. Judd breathed a prayer of thanks. Soon the sun would rise on a new day—and a new life.

Chapter Thirteen

December 12, 1899

Dear Quint,

If only you were here to see your daughter! Clara would melt your heart. She is like you in so many ways.

For all her rough entry into this world, she's thriving. She is healthy, active and already showing a strong will. No wonder I thought she was going to be a boy.

I'm recovering nicely, as well. Annie came last week to take in my dresses. I never thought I'd be happy to get back into a corset, but it's lovely having a waist again.

Your mother still clings to life. The headaches trouble her more than ever, but she's alert enough to enjoy the baby. She even smiles when Gretel lays Clara in her arms. I don't believe I've ever seen your mother smile before. Wherever you are, know that one thing you did made her happy in her last days—you gave her a grandchild.

Hannah frowned as she reread the last sentence. She hadn't meant to imply that Quint had never made his mother happy. After her adored husband, he'd been the joy of her life. As for giving her a grandchild, Quint had accomplished his part in a few furtive seconds. Judd was more of a father to Clara than Quint had ever been. To begin with, he'd given her his name, making her a part of the family. He'd also saved her life on that snowy night, helping her into the world and getting her safely home. Thanks to Judd, Clara would grow up with every advantage—security, social respectability, a fine education and someday, heaven willing, a good marriage. Nothing would be out of her reach.

Still, Hannah mused, what she'd said to Quint in that last sentence was neither kind nor fair.

Impatient with herself, she crumpled the letter and tossed it into the wastebasket. She would try again later, she promised herself. But with a new baby to care for, finding the time wouldn't be easy.

A rap on the door diverted her attention. Gretel stepped into the study, a smile on her face and a squalling bundle in her arms. "The little princess is awake. I changed her diaper upstairs, but I think she wants her *mutti.*"

"She's probably hungry." Hannah reached out and took her squirming baby. "And you don't need to change her, Gretel. Heaven knows you've got enough to do with taking care of Mrs. Seavers."

"Nein." Gretel shook her head. "It's no trouble. I love little babies."

"And what's that heavenly smell coming from the kitchen?" Hannah settled herself in Judd's leather armchair and began unbuttoning the bodice of her dress. Milk from her swollen breasts was already seeping through the fabric.

"Tea cakes. For when your mother comes to visit later. I made them with dried currants, the way she likes them."

"Gretel, you'll wear yourself out! We can't have two women down sick!" Hannah's scolding was gentle. Gretel needed diversions from the dreary job of caring for Edna, even if it meant extra work.

"I better go see they don't burn!" Gretel bustled out of the study. Hannah sank into the soft recess of the chair and lifted the fussing baby to her breast. The hungry little mouth latched on and began to suck. Hannah basked in the warmth of the glowing fireplace. She loved nursing her daughter, gazing down into the tiny face that was so much like Quint's baby picture. Little Clara had her father's thick curls and dark, long-lashed eyes. Her dimples were identical to the ones that deepened in Quint's checks when he smiled. At four weeks, she was already showing signs of her father's alert, restless disposition. Like him, she seemed destined to break hearts.

Hannah felt an unexpected surge of annoyance. Why wasn't Quint here to see his beautiful child? How could he have gone off on that harebrained adventure without a thought for anyone but himself?

What would she say to him if he were to walk through the door this very minute?

Clara finished nursing and dropped off to sleep.

Hannah laid her gently in the basket that served as her downstairs cradle. Buttoning her dress, she rose and stretched. One hand massaged the back of her narrow waist. How lucky she was that the birth had been so easy. By now she was almost fully recovered. Her body was firm and slender, the deep soreness no more than an occasional twinge. But caring for a new baby drained her time and energy. She'd only written to Quint once since the baby's arrival. If she didn't finish a letter now, she might not get around to it for days.

Seating herself at the desk once more, she took a fresh sheet of paper out of the drawer, sighed and picked up the pen.

Dear Quint,
If you read my last letter, you already know that you have a daughter, a beautiful baby girl, born on November 14…

Hannah glanced up. From the porch she heard the stomp of heavy boots, followed by the opening and closing of the front door. The familiar tread of Judd's footsteps creaked along the hallway to pause at the entrance to the study. He'd taken the buckboard to town that afternoon to pick up a shipment of parts for the wrecked buggy. Since he'd planned other errands, as well, it was surprising that he'd returned so soon.

"Hannah?" The strain in his voice told her something was wrong.

"I'm right here." She swiveled the high-backed chair toward him. Judd was still wearing his sheepskin coat.

His face was ruddy with cold. The haunted look in his eyes chilled Hannah like a blast of winter wind.

"What is it?" she whispered as he closed the door behind him.

"This was waiting for me at the depot." He held up a bulky object for her to see. The pen Hannah was holding dropped unnoticed to the floor.

It was Quint's canvas pack, the one he'd carried onto the train the day he'd left Dutchman's Creek.

Hannah's hand crept out to touch it. Aside from some dust, the pack appeared to be full and in good condition. In fact, it looked much as it had the day Quint had slung it onto the train.

"There was a letter attached," Judd said. "Stay where you are. I'll read it to you." Lowering the pack, he worked a crumpled envelope out of his pocket and unfolded a sheet of hotel stationery.

"To Whom It May Concern: My name is Silas Appleton, newly appointed manager of the Bay-side Hotel in San Francisco. This pack was found in a carriage shed where my predecessor had stored some abandoned baggage. Evidently it was left in one of the hotel rooms some months ago and never reclaimed. Being a Christian man, I am shipping it to the address on the tag, in the hope that it will reach its rightful owner. Yours truly…"

His voice trailed off. Hannah's mouth had gone dry. She felt vaguely sick.

"I looked inside," Judd said. "The clothes were definitely Quint's. They were clean and folded, the way Gretel's always folded our laundry. It didn't look as if they'd been worn, or even unpacked."

"Somebody could have stolen the pack, maybe on the train." Hannah made a feeble attempt to deny her fears. There had to be some explanation for this.

"A thief would have rummaged through everything and taken what he could use. He wouldn't have left the pack in this condition, especially not in a hotel room." Judd paused to clear his throat. "Before I left the station, I sent a wire to the Bayside Hotel, asking them to check the registry. But even if they find Quint's name, that will only confirm what I already suspect."

"And what's that?" Hannah whispered. "What are you saying?"

Judd stuffed the letter back into the envelope. "I thought about this all the way home. A young man on his own for the first time, looking for adventure—it would've been like Quint to change his ticket and take a side trip to San Francisco. I'm guessing he arrived, checked into the hotel, left his pack in the room and went out to see the town."

"And…?" She rose shakily from the chair.

"He never made it back to the hotel."

Hannah had understood where this conversation was going. She'd done her best to avoid the truth, but hearing it plain from Judd's lips staggered her like a blow from a sledgehammer. She took a step toward him, but her legs refused to support her. She stumbled.

He caught her in his arms. The room seemed to sway as she sagged against the roughness of his coat. "I'm sorry," she murmured. "Oh, Judd, I'm sorry—for you, for your mother, for Clara. For all of us."

The breath went out of him. He clasped her tight. "All this time, and you kept writing those letters. You never gave up hope. I envied your faith, Hannah, and your constancy. But I've suspected something like this for a long time. San Francisco's a rough place for a young man with more trust than common sense. The fact that we haven't heard—"

"Don't say it!" She drew back and looked up into his stricken face. "I know I have to accept the truth. Heaven knows, we both do, Judd. But don't say it. Not yet."

He was suffering as much as she was, if not more. She could see it in his eyes, hear it in his rapid, shallow breathing. "I'd get on the train and go to San Francisco tomorrow," he said. "But…"

"I know. Your mother needs you." *I need you,* she thought. "We don't have to tell her, do we?"

He shook his head. "In her condition, it would only confuse her."

"And Gretel?"

"Let's wait awhile. Maybe till after Mother's gone. She'll be upset, and it might show. I'll put the pack where she won't see it."

"You could have kept this from me, too," Hannah said. "You could have just let me go on believing."

He shook his head. "How could I? Looking into those hopeful eyes, watching you write those letters… Lord, girl, I could never lie to you."

Hannah lifted her hand and laid it along the side of his face. His stubble-roughened cheek was cold and surprisingly damp. His free hand captured hers and pressed it to his lips. She could sense the emotions that coursed through him—much the same as the ones she was feeling. Shock, grief, uncertainty—and guilt for the bond that had grown between them in Quint's absence. How would they keep that guilt from tearing them apart?

Aching, she leaned against him. Her fingers separated the toggle fasteners on his sheepskin coat. "Hold me, Judd," she whispered. "Just hold me."

He opened the front of the coat and gathered her inside. His warm, solid body surrounded her with its strength. Her arms crept around him, binding him close. She could feel his heart pounding against her cheek and hear the jerky rasp of his breathing. For a long time they simply held each other. A dry sob rose in Hannah's throat, then another and another. Finally the tears came, soaking into Judd's woolen shirt. She wept for Quint's youth and brightness and beauty. She wept for the mother who'd spoiled him, the brother who'd looked after him, and the little girl who would never know her father. She wept herself dry while he held her in his strong arms.

Spent at last, she drew back and lifted her tear-blotched face. "How can we just give up?" she asked. "After all, we don't really know what happened. Quint could be anywhere, still alive and still trying to get home to us. He could come walking through that front door any minute. We can't abandon him, Judd. We have to go on believing!"

Judd released her. His eyes had gone leaden. "We

may never know what happened. But if you choose to keep faith, I won't try to dissuade you, Hannah. That's your decision."

He picked up the pack and stuffed it under his coat. "I'll be in the shed, working on the buggy if anybody needs me."

Hannah listened to Judd's fading footsteps as he walked down the hall. She heard the front door open and close and the sound of his boots as he strode across the porch.

Dry mouthed and trembling, she sank onto the edge of the chair. Her heart was pounding. Her skin felt clammy. What she'd just said was nothing but denial. It was time to face the truth. Quint was gone. He wouldn't be coming home—ever.

Judd was wiser than she was. When he'd failed to find Quint, he'd suspected the worst. He'd spared her his fears, giving her time to reach her own conclusion. But she'd refused to even consider the idea of Quint's loss. She'd kept writing her foolish letters—as delusional as Edna in her own stubborn way.

Even after discovering that she loved Judd, and wanted him, she'd continued the pretense out of blind loyalty. Judd had done the same. Except for the few times when emotion had brought them to the brink, they'd lived like brother and sister.

Then today, Quint's pack had arrived. Judd could have hidden it away and let her go on pretending. But he'd chosen to bring the pack directly to her, thrusting reality in her face.

And she'd behaved like a fool.

She remembered his tenderness, the way he'd buried

his lips against her palm, the way he'd cradled her in his arms. Words would have been out of place. But his actions had offered her a silent invitation to move on with him, to put the past behind and begin their new life together as husband and wife.

She should have recognized that invitation. She should have welcomed it. But the news about Quint had left her in shock. She had looked up into Judd's eyes and said the worst possible thing.

No wonder he'd gone cold. No wonder he'd left so abruptly. Judd was a proud man, and she'd wounded him.

What if he never gave her a second chance?

Hannah would always love Quint. But that kind of love wasn't enough. She wanted a husband to hold her in the night and be a father to their children. She wanted a lover, a companion to grow old with her and share all the joys and sorrows of life. When she imagined that life she saw only one man standing tall beside her—a tender, giving man with a scarred body and somber gray eyes.

Trembling, she rose from the chair, walked to the wastebasket and picked up the letter she'd thrown away. Her eyes blurred as she gazed down at the words Quint would never read. Blinking the tears away, she tore the paper in two, tossed the pieces into the fireplace and watched them crumble in the flames.

Judd steadied the buggy axle with his left hand and struggled to tighten a brace with his right. The job would have been easier with someone to help him. But he was in no mood for company.

As usual, he'd made a tarnal mess of things with

Hannah. When she'd melted against him, there in the study, he could almost have believed she was ready to move on. He'd even let himself hold her, the way he'd been aching to hold her for months.

He should have known better. Hannah might be his legal wife, but her heart belonged to the father of her child. Against all reason, she was still clinging to the hope that Quint would come home. Damn all females! The blasted woman would wait forever if need be. She would die of old age before she gave up.

The hammer slipped from his hand and dropped to the sawdust-covered floor. Muttering a curse, Judd strained to reach it, hooked it with his finger and maneuvered it back into his hand.

He loved his brother. He'd looked after Quint for twenty years, taught him to rope, shoot and ride, helped him with his schoolwork, pulled him out of more scrapes than he could count. When Quint had disappeared, he'd worn himself out searching. But there had to come a time of letting go. For Judd, that time had come when he'd opened Quint's pack and found the folded, unworn clothes.

But even that hadn't been enough for Hannah.

Maybe it was time to let her go, as well.

He had loved her since the early days of their marriage. Only the promise he'd made her, and his loyalty to his brother, had kept him from trying to win her for himself.

Early on, he'd questioned his own fitness as a husband. But now he was strong and healthy. The flashbacks about the war hadn't returned since the night he'd told Hannah about Daniel's death. Thanks to Hannah, he felt like a whole man again.

And he wanted his wife. He wanted her so much he could barely look at her without feeling the ache in his loins.

He wanted her in his arms, in his bed, for the rest of his life. He wanted to bury himself deep inside the wet satin core of her body and be her husband in every way. He wanted to give her more children—his children—to grow up with her daughter in a loving family.

But he couldn't force her. As long as Hannah was pining for Quint, she would never be his.

Judd hammered the brace into position, whacking it with twice the needed force. He'd tried to be patient, but one way or another, the frustration had to end.

He would give Hannah until the end of the holiday season. During that time he wouldn't make a move in her direction. Anything that happened between them would have to be her idea. If she showed no sign of wanting to be his wife he would put a merciful end to the torment.

He would ask Hannah for his freedom.

On December 16, Edna Seavers closed her eyes for the last time. Gretel found her that afternoon, lying peacefully beneath the peach satin coverlet, her bony little hands crossed as if someone had arranged them that way.

Two days later, after a brief service, she was buried next to her husband in the Dutchman's Creek Municipal Cemetery. The day was gray and frigid. Hannah stood between Gretel and Judd, shivering as the wind whipped her black woolen cloak around her body. She was grateful that Annie and her mother had offered to watch Clara at the house. It would have been foolhardy to bring a baby out in this weather.

The Seavers family plot was a large one. Tom Seavers's grave was marked by a wide marble headstone that would now be shared by his wife. The rest of the plot was empty ground. Who would fill it in years to come? Hannah wondered. Would Quint ever lie there? Would she?

The mourners at the graveside were few. Edna had become reclusive after her husband's death and had no close friends in town. The minister was there, of course, and Doctor Fitzroy, as well as the undertaker and Brandon Calhoun, the bank president. Judd stood a few inches from Hannah, his jaw set, his face unreadable. Hannah had taken his arm as they climbed down from the buggy and walked to the open grave, but he might as well have been escorting a stranger. Since their confrontation in the study, his manner toward her had been distant and formal, almost cold.

How could she undo what she'd done? She needed Judd, and she sensed that he needed her. But his pride had closed a door between them—a door she feared might never open again.

The minister had finished his words and was beginning the prayer. Hannah bowed her head. Beside her, Gretel was weeping, the tears flowing down her broad, flat cheeks. Al Macklin, who'd driven them to town in the buggy, stood a little apart, clutching his Stetson. His hands rolled and twisted the battered felt brim. As the first clods of half-frozen dirt thumped against the casket he turned away from the grave and walked toward the buggy.

The ride back to the ranch was long and silent. Judd and Al sat on the front seat of the buggy, hunched in their coats and lost in their own thoughts. Hannah sat on the more sheltered rear seat with Gretel at her side. The landscape was bare and bleak, with wind gusts blowing drifts of powdery snow across the road. The shaggy Belgians were coated with white, their whiskers feathery with their frosted breath. Hannah looked forward to the hot beef stew and fresh bread that would be waiting for them at the house. Edna's illness and death had drained them all. Maybe their lives would be easier now that she was at peace.

As they swung through the ranch gate and onto the drive, Gretel shifted in her seat and spoke. "Could I ask you for a letter of reference? It would help me to find another job."

Startled, Hannah turned toward her. "What on earth are you thinking, Gretel? You're like family to us! You have a job here for as long as you want to stay!"

A tear left a glistening trail down Gretel's cheek. "Thank you for that. But I have a married sister in Indiana. She wants me to come and be near her. She has sent me the train ticket already."

Judd twisted back to look at her. "Are you sure we can't change your mind, Gretel? We could use your help and, as Hannah says, you're like family."

Gretel blew her nose on a lace-edged handkerchief. "Family here, yes." She gestured toward her heart. "But my sister is blood family. Her husband has a brother whose wife died last spring. He wants to meet me. Who knows what will happen?" The color deepened in her ruddy face.

Judd grinned—the first time Hannah had seen him smile since his mother's death. "Well, in that case, I'll wish you well and see you off with an extra month's pay."

"My sister sent his picture. Not a handsome man, but such kind eyes. I hope he likes me."

"Any man who gets you should kiss the earth and count his blessings," Judd said. "Will you stay here through Christmas?"

"*Nein.* My wish is to have a real German Christmas with my sister. I was thinking to leave maybe day after tomorrow, if you can spare me."

Judd sighed. "It looks like we won't have much choice. Just promise you'll let me drive you to the station. And that you'll make us a batch of those dried apple tarts before you go."

"And that you'll help me write down some of your recipes," Hannah added.

She watched Judd settle back into the seat. Everything seemed to be changing. First they'd lost Quint, then Edna. Now Gretel would be leaving them.

Other things were ripe for change, as well. Her relationship with Judd had reached a crisis. There was no way for them to continue living as they had for the past six months. Either they would have to move ahead into a real marriage or the strain would force them apart.

Gretel's departure would leave them alone in the house for the first time. Hannah knew she wanted things to change. But with Judd keeping his proud, painful distance, she didn't know how to make that change happen.

Her one sexual experience with Quint had been a fumbling encounter in a cold barn, on a bed of prickly hay, with both of them fully clothed. All Hannah had felt was surprise, pain, embarrassment and a sense of shame that had lingered well beyond the burning soreness between her legs.

But there had to be more. Her dreams had told her that much.

The only thing her mother had ever told her about sex was that she would burn in hell if she let a boy touch her. Maybe that was why she burned every time she looked at Judd. Maybe that's what hell was—wanting someone who was just out of reach.

Hannah cursed her own innocence. She was already a mother. But what did she know about being a wife?

Chapter Fourteen

Two days later Judd drove Gretel to the railway station. Hannah watched from the porch as the buggy rolled down the long drive, passed under the gate and vanished around the bend. How easy it was to misjudge people, she thought. For most of her growing-up years she'd lived in terror of Gretel Schmidt. Yet, this morning, when Gretel was ready to leave, Hannah had embraced the good woman and wept with emotion.

She wouldn't have minded going into town to see Gretel off on the train. But the clouds spilling over the mountains were the sooty color and ragged texture of unwashed wool. The December air was sharp and damp in her nostrils. She couldn't risk Clara's health by taking her out in the weather. Besides, with Gretel gone, she would have a full day's work to do in the house.

She took a moment to check on the sleeping Clara, then started on the kitchen. First she cut up beef, potatoes and onions for stew and put them on the stove to simmer. Then she mixed some sourdough for biscuits and set it aside to rise. Judd planned to be in town until midafternoon. He'd be hungry when he got home.

By the time Hannah had washed the dishes, scrubbed the counters and swept the floor, Clara was awake and crying to be fed. She lifted the baby out of her cradle, changed her diaper and sank into the rocker to nurse. The morning was half-gone, and she hadn't even started on the bedrooms or mopped up the muddy footprints in the front hall.

Judd had insisted that they hire a replacement for Gretel, but Hannah had argued that she could manage the housework on her own, just as her mother had. Now she conceded that Judd was right. True, she might be able to take care of the house, the baby, the cooking and the laundry by herself. But there'd be nothing left of her at the end of the day. If she could give employment to some good woman and have more time for her child and her husband, why not do it?

Her husband. Hannah sighed as she shifted Clara to her other breast. Nothing had changed with Judd. And now that Gretel was gone, there'd be no buffer between them. It was time to end the standoff once and for all. And she knew of only one way to do that without making a spectacle of herself—tell him the truth.

But where would she find the words? How did a woman go about telling a man she wanted him in the most intimate, elemental way?

What if Judd had decided he didn't want her?

By noon the storm was howling in. The wind froze damp sheets on the clothesline and raised a skiff of ice on the watering trough. Cattle huddled with their backs to the storm, eyes closed against the stinging, flying snow.

Wrapped in a cloak, Hannah stood on the porch and gazed down the drive. The snow was so thick that she could no longer see the gate.

By now Gretel would be on the eastbound train. But Judd still had to drive back to the ranch. The storm could catch him on the road. And this storm was a nasty one, cold enough to freeze a man on his feet. She wouldn't take an easy breath until he was safely home.

Wind gusted under the eave, whipping the hem of her cloak and raising loose tendrils of hair around her chilled face. She had a bad feeling about this storm. Unless Judd had stayed in town, he would be on the road right now.

Last winter a farmer had died in a blizzard that started like this one. When the weather cleared, searchers had found him frozen to the wagon seat less than a mile from home. What if the same thing happened to Judd? Hannah shivered beneath her cloak as she imagined him struggling through the biting snow.

What if he didn't make it?

What if Judd were to die without ever knowing she loved him?

Judd stood at the window of the tiny railroad station café, sipping coffee that had already gone cold. Wind-blown snow clattered against the glass panes. The weather was getting worse, and he knew it might be wise to stay in town. But he'd left Hannah alone with the baby. If he didn't leave now, he could be stuck here for days.

Not that he had much reason to worry about her. Al

Macklin and his crew of winter hands were as close as the bunkhouse. If Hannah needed help, she had only to shout. But Judd's uneasiness went deeper than concern for her safety. For reasons he couldn't explain, this just didn't seem a good time to be away from her.

A glance at the clock told him it was getting close to noon. He could order a sandwich and more coffee, eat a leisurely lunch and hope the storm would break. If it didn't he could always take the horses to the livery stable and check into the hotel. But something was nagging at him, like an invisible splinter—something too persistent to ignore.

That morning, as he was hitching up the team, Al Macklin had approached him. Clearing his throat awkwardly, he'd told Judd that as soon as the weather broke he'd be leaving the ranch to live with his nephew in Arizona. He was getting too old, Al had said, for the hard work and the icy Colorado winters. He wanted to spend his remaining years in comfort with his blood kin nearby.

Al's excuses had made sense. But Judd knew his real reason for leaving. With Edna gone there was nothing to hold him to the ranch. How could he stay, when everything reminded him of the woman he'd loved for so many years?

What if Al had spoken up long ago, while he and Edna were younger? Maybe it would have made a difference in their lonely lives. Maybe they could have been happy together. Now it was too late.

Judd stared through the rippled glass into the gray world of flying snow. Was he capable of the same mistake? Was he about to let his own stubborn silence cost him the love of his life?

Suddenly it was as if an unseen hand was shoving him toward the door. He was setting the coffee cup on the counter, reaching for his hat and turning up the collar on his coat.

Hannah could wait, reason shrilled in his head. Well, maybe she could. But he couldn't. He was burning to be with her, to take her in his arms and say all the words he'd been holding back like sweet water behind a dam of pride. If she cut him to ribbons, so be it. At least he wouldn't live the rest of his life wondering what might have happened if he'd had the courage to offer his heart.

Snow blasted him like cold buckshot as he stepped outside and strode toward the waiting buggy.

The measured tick of the grandfather clock was the loudest sound in the house. Hannah had been hearing it all afternoon as she counted the seconds, waiting for Judd to appear. She'd lost track of how many times she'd stepped out onto the porch and peered toward the gate, straining to see through the blinding whiteness.

Now it was after four o'clock. The winter daylight was beginning to fade, and still there was no sign of him. Common sense told her he must have taken shelter in town, but her screaming instincts told her otherwise.

Only the housework had kept her from falling apart. Fueled by nervous energy, she'd gone through every room save one, sweeping and dusting, washing and scrubbing. Only Quint's room remained untouched, as Edna would have wished.

In Edna's downstairs bedroom, as well as Gretel's, she'd stripped the sheets and replaced them from the well-stocked linen closet. She'd taken Edna's personal things—the clothes and toiletries, the jewelry, the elegantly narrow shoes—and laid them in a cedar-lined chest. The wedding photograph of Tom Seavers and a radiantly beautiful Edna remained on the nightstand.

Maybe someday, when Clara was older, she would want to see and touch the things that had been her grandmother's. Hannah promised herself to tell Clara only the good about Edna Seavers—her fine manners, her generosity and her undying love for her husband. As for the rest—her pettiness, her impatience, her maddening superiority—these and other issues would be laid to rest forever.

Hannah struggled to ignore the rising tide of worry. Judd was a prudent man. He knew this country and the power of its winter storms. It made sense that he would decide to wait out the weather in town. So why was she growing more frantic by the minute?

By six o'clock it was dark outside. Hannah checked the stew, laid another log on the fire and braved the storm to hang a lantern from the hook on the porch. Then she sat down in the rocker to nurse Clara. The darkness deepened around them. Wind rattled a loose shutter on an upstairs window. Branches scraped against the side of the house. Hannah snuggled the baby close, seeking comfort from the warm bundle in her arms. Without Judd the house seemed huge and cold and empty.

When Clara was sound asleep, Hannah tucked her into her cradle. For a time she tried to read, but her mind refused to focus on the printed pages. She closed the book and replaced it on the shelf without remembering so much as its title.

If Judd wasn't coming home till morning, she'd be a fool not to get some rest. She checked the lantern one more time to make sure it had enough kerosene to burn all night. Then she went back upstairs, stripped off her clothes and put on her warm flannel nightgown. For the next hour she lay staring up into the darkness, listening to the sound of the wind. It was no use. Flinging on a robe and thrusting her feet into felt slippers, she pattered back downstairs, thrust some kindling into the stove and started a fresh pot of coffee.

Still restless, she wrapped herself in her cloak and stepped out onto the porch. Beyond the circle of lantern light, the night was pitch-black, the house an island in a world of blowing, swirling snow. She could no longer see the barn or the corral or the bunkhouse, let alone the gate.

There were men in the bunkhouse, Hannah reminded herself. They'd be playing cards and warming themselves at the potbellied stove. She could cross the yard, pound on the door and order them out to look for Judd. But if he'd stayed in town, she'd be exposing them to danger for nothing. And there was the risk that she'd lose her own way in the storm. If she didn't make it back to the house her baby would be left alone.

Gripping the porch rail, she closed her eyes and prayed harder than she'd ever prayed in her life. Dampness froze on her cheeks. Her lips formed words that blew away on the wind.

Please keep my husband safe... Keep him safe and bring him home.

The storm whirled around her where she stood in the darkness. Wind lashed at her skirts and tangled her hair. Light from the swaying lantern danced against the snow, a pitiful speck, lost in a world of flying white. How could she expect anyone to see it from a distance?

Her teeth were beginning to chatter. Shivering beneath her cloak, Hannah turned to go back inside the house. That was when her ears caught new sounds mingled with the wind—the snort of a horse, the faint jingle of harness and, barely audible through the storm, the sound of voices.

A lantern flared between the bunkhouse and the barn. The voices came stronger now, but clear enough for Hannah to make out words. Heart in her throat, she stumbled off the porch and into the storm. Now a tall figure was coming up the walk toward her, moving like a white ghost. With a cry, she sprinted toward him.

Judd was coated in snow from the crown of his hat to his boots. It didn't matter. She flung herself against him, and he staggered under the impact. The arms that caught her were encased in half-frozen sleeves. Frigid cold surrounded her as she clasped him close, kissing the frosted stubble on his face, kissing his icy lips.

From the darkness behind him came flickers of light and the sounds of men unhitching the horses. Judd had taken a dangerous chill. She needed to get him inside and get him warm.

She gripped his arm as they moved toward the house. "What happened out there? I've been worried sick!"

His lips moved with effort. His throat croaked out a single word. "Later."

The front hallway greeted them with a rush of warmth. Judd's hair was icy beneath his hat. He stripped off his gloves, but his fingers were too stiff to undo the fastenings of his coat. Hannah helped him work the toggles through the frozen leather loops. Then she stripped off the heavy coat and tossed it over the newel post.

Even the thick sheepskin hadn't been enough to protect him from the storm. His teeth were chattering. His damp shirt and woolen long johns clung to his chilled skin.

"In here!" She led him into the parlor where some hot coals remained in the fireplace. Laying on fresh kindling, she built the fire to a roaring blaze. Judd had sunk into a wing chair that was drawn up to the heat. Hannah worked off his boots and socks. Then she knelt on the rug in her nightgown and began rubbing the circulation into his fingers. The rest of his body needed warming, too. But his hands were the most critical. She massaged his fingers, squeezing them, pressing them to her face, kissing them with an urgency that became something more than practical need.

"There are faster ways to get me warm, Hannah." His voice was a growl. Reflected flames glinted in his eyes as his hands escaped hers to slide around her back. His palms were chilly through her flannel nightgown, but the sensation that tingled over the bare skin underneath was pure heat.

One hand tangled in her loose hair, tilting her head upward. Her heart slammed as he lifted her to meet his kiss. His lips were chilled velvet, warming against hers as he caressed her so slowly and sensually that she moaned out loud. The tip of his tongue traced a line along her lower lip, then teasingly withdrew, leaving her ravenous for more. She arched upward, lips parting, arms sliding around his neck.

His next kiss carried her deeper, molding her mouth to his. Her hands clutched the back of his head, fingers raking his wet hair, pulling him down to her. She wanted him—all of him, everything he could give her. Sweet heaven, she'd never imagined she could want anything— or anyone—so much.

His tongue invaded her again, skimming the roof of her mouth, gliding silkily along the inner surface of her lips. Hannah's response flickered and flamed. She met his thrust with her own, first timidly, then boldly, parrying until the breath rasped in his throat.

His hands had warmed. They fondled her through the worn flannel, tracing the curve of her back, rounding over her buttocks.

"You feel so good, Hannah," he murmured. "Lord, how I've wanted to do this, to touch you here…and here…"

His big palms cradled her unbound breasts, thumbing her nipples through the soft fabric until they swelled to aching nubs. Yearning sensations flowed downward through her body to pool in the dark, wet place between her legs. She felt a rhythmic, clenching, urgent pulse.

"We've…got to get you out of these…damp clothes," she muttered thickly. Her unsteady fingers plucked at the buttons on his shirt, fumbling in their haste.

He lifted her hands and kissed them. "I can do it faster." His hands moved down the row of buttons with practiced ease. Rising, Hannah stripped off his woolen shirt. The faded long johns underneath were barely damp but still cold. As he unbuttoned the upper part of them, she slid them off his shoulders, rubbing his chilled skin, feeling its smoothness and the solid steel of muscle underneath. Her husband had a beautiful body, like chiseled, polished oak. Even his scars were beautiful. She would never get tired of looking at him, never get tired of touching him.

Bare to the waist now, Judd pushed to his feet. His arms crushed her against his naked chest. His lips closed on hers, raw and hungry. His hands bunched the folds of her nightgown to find the skin beneath, cupping her buttocks, molding her breasts to his big, rough palms. His touch on her bare skin was like flame to tinder. She strained against him, wild with need.

"I don't want to scare you, girl, let alone hurt you," he murmured. "I'll try to take this slow and easy. But I might need your help with that. I've wanted you so damned much, for such a long time…. You almost drove me crazy. You're driving me crazy now."

"Hush." She skimmed his mouth with hers, then sprinkled a trail of kisses down his throat to his chest. His nipples were puckered from the cold. He gasped as her mouth found one, then the other, circling the aureole with her tongue, nipping and sucking until the warmth returned to his skin.

His fingers freed the stubborn trouser buttons. As the damp denim loosened and sagged, he guided her trembling hand downward. "Touch me, Hannah," he whispered. "Don't be afraid."

Hannah's fingers slid beneath the damply clinging

long johns. His flesh was cool to the touch. Her breath caught as her fingertips found his jutting shaft. His breath rasped in his throat as she stroked him, circled him, felt him swell and strain against her palm. Growing bolder, she explored the swollen head and let her hand creep downward to cup his solid weight. Heaven save her, he was as big as a stallion!

With a low sound he moved away from her, caught up the crocheted afghan and needlepoint pillows and flung them onto the rug in front of the fireplace. Easing her onto the makeshift bed, he stood over her and let his trousers and long johns drop to the floor. She lay on her back, looking up at him. Naked, he was magnificent, from his stormy eyes to his muscular shoulders, tapering hips and aroused maleness. Firelight rippled over his body as he lay down beside her and slipped her nightgown over her head. "You're so beautiful," he murmured gazing down at her. "Lie still, Hannah. Let me pleasure you."

Her heart seemed to stop as he bent to kiss her breasts. She moaned as he blazed a path of kisses down her belly to the nest of curls at the apex of her thighs. His hand parted her legs and slid between them, caressing the moist folds that nested inside like rose petals. Her wetness coated his fingers as they glided deeper, testing the opening into her body. Reflexively she tensed. "Lie still," he whispered. "I'd never hurt you, love."

Opening her legs wider he moved between them. Again, Hannah's muscles tightened apprehensively. It had hurt the first time, and now she'd just had a baby. Much as she wanted Judd, she wasn't sure how it would feel when he entered her.

What happened next surprised her. She felt his warm breath mingling with her dampness, felt the brush of his tongue on those exquisitely sensitive folds and the hard bead at their center.

"Oh!" It was a sound of wonder, not of pain. Her hips arched upward, pressing toward that miraculous source of pleasure as he kissed and suckled her. Sensations swirled through her body like exploding rainbows, in bursts of shimmering color.

His tongue slid deeper, dipping in and out of her wet opening. She breathed raggedly, drowning in need. Her hips bucked and ground against him as the ecstasy mounted, rippling through every part of her body. She shuddered again and again as the climax washed over her, tingling with the promise of more to come.

Rising onto his arms, he shifted forward and braced himself above her. Even without his speaking, Hannah knew he couldn't wait any longer. But she was ready for him now. Her hands reached up to him. Her legs opened wide. Their eyes met in love and trust. Then, in one long, smooth stroke, he glided into her wet heat.

There was no pain, only indescribable joy as he filled every inch of her. For the space of a long breath they lay still, lost in the wonder of their joining. Slowly he began to move, pushing deep, sliding back, then deeper and deeper still, igniting rivulets of flame that burned through every cell in her body. Her legs wrapped his hips as she strained against him, matching his rhythm with hers.

He was lost in her now, this man she loved to the depths of her soul. Breathing like a winded stallion, he drove into her, harder and faster. Wild little cries broke from Hannah's throat. She felt like a soaring comet, about to burst into a thousand pieces. As she quivered on the brink, he pushed deep inside her, clasping her hips to hold himself there. A shudder of release passed through his body. Hannah felt the warm spurt of his seed as she tumbled through space and lay still beneath him, exhausted and glowing.

It was only later, as they lay spooned in the warmth of Hannah's bed, that she thought to ask him why he'd arrived home so late.

Yawning, he pulled her closer. "Long story. I'd thought about staying in town when the storm hit. But something made me decide to come home to you. About halfway there, a woman waved me down on the road. She was half-frozen, not dressed for the weather at all."

"Who was she?"

"I didn't know her. But she said she lived on the old Hanson homestead west of town. She was looking for her boy—ten years old, she said. He'd run out into the storm to find his puppy and not come back. She figured he must have gotten turned around and gone the wrong way."

"Oh, no…did you find him?" Hannah kissed the hand that held her.

"Yes, but it took a lot of looking. We finally found the boy huddled with his pup under an old wagon. Much longer and he'd have frozen to death. Afterward I drove them home. By then the snow was so bad you couldn't see your hand in front of your face. It took me a long time to get back here."

Hannah snuggled closer, fitting her rump into the curve of his body. "If you hadn't happened along, they could've both died," she mused. "It's like a blessing, Judd. Like you were meant to come home to me."

There was no response.

"Judd?"

The sound of deep breathing told her he was fast asleep.

Hannah sighed and closed her eyes. She had agonized over words to tell Judd she wanted him. Surprisingly, no words had been needed.

After weeks of leaden skies and bone-biting cold, a warm Chinook wind swept into the valley, bringing a late-January thaw. Overnight the snow began to melt. Water puddled in the yard, turning the corral into a lake of mud. Chickadees and juncos foraged in the seed-laden bushes around the house. Cattle nosed the ground for fresh shoots of grass. The dog basked happily on the porch steps.

To Hannah, the sound of dripping water was like music. Winter would soon return. But that only made each springlike day more precious.

After lunch she'd moved the wooden rocker out onto the porch. From her arms, a blanket-swathed Clara took in the world with wide, dark eyes. At two months, she was already showing signs of her father's curiosity. Once she started exploring on her own, the little girl was bound to be a handful.

Hannah leaned back in the chair, savoring the sunlight on her face. The past few weeks had been the happiest of her life. Since that cold winter night, she and Judd had never looked back. Their love for each other had opened up a world of passionate giving that brought new discoveries every day.

They'd celebrated a modest Christmas together with a tiny tree and a few simple gifts. Earlier Hannah had bought presents in town for everyone in her family. On Christmas day, she and Judd had delivered them in their new sleigh, drawn by the shaggy Belgians. While Hannah spent time visiting with Annie and her mother, Judd had taken the children for a rollicking ride through the snow. They'd come back laughing, singing and pelting each other with snowballs.

Now, where the snow had melted below the porch, Edna's roses already swelled with the promise of buds. The past year had held more than its share of sorrows. They'd lost Quint. They'd lost Edna, and they'd lost Hannah's father. Gretel and Al had left, as well. But she and Judd had found each other, and now they had Clara. Every day Hannah counted her blessings. As her mother was fond of saying, the good Lord gave and took away, and He measured the balance in His own eternal time.

The dog raised its head, nose twitching as the smell of fresh beef tamales drifted from the kitchen. Rosita Sanchez was a widow in her forties, as lively as Gretel had been taciturn. Her English might be faulty, but her cooking was delectable. Judd's new foreman was already courting her.

From the direction of the barn came the sound of hammering. Some of the cowhands were taking advantage of the thaw to patch wind-loosened shingles. Others, including Judd and Ephraim, were riding fence, looking for storm damage. Everyone seemed to enjoy being out in the fresh air.

Clara had begun to fuss, and Hannah was about to

take her inside when she saw Judd ride in through the gate. He dismounted at the corral and strode toward the house, looking impossibly handsome in a leather vest and a gray woolen shirt that matched his eyes. His hair was tousled, his face tanned. Hannah's pulse quickened at the memory of last night's loving. Did any woman have the right to be so happy?

He paused at the foot of the steps, grinning up at Hannah and the baby. His boots were coated with mud.

"Don't track that muck up here, or Rosita will barbecue your hide," Hannah warned with a smile.

"Then how am I going to kiss my two best girls?" Laughing he kicked his boots against the side of the step and wiped them in a patch of shaded snow. Then he bounded onto the porch and swept Clara up in his arms. "How's my princess?" He waltzed her in a circle, swooped her high, kissed her curls and deposited her back in her mother's lap.

"Don't forget me." Hannah lifted her face. His lips touched hers in a light lingering kiss that sent sensual waves shimmering through her body. She strained upward, wanting more.

"Oh, no you don't!" He grinned down at her. "The rest will have to wait till after dark, Mrs. Seavers. While the sun's up, there's work to be done."

He descended the porch steps whistling, then paused and broke toward the barn at a trot. "Whoa! Not that way!" Hannah heard him shout at one of the workers.

Walking to the porch rail she followed him with her eyes. Her heart ached with tenderness. It wasn't easy for him, living with the losses he'd suffered. But he was healing. His loving, sometimes playful behavior toward her and Clara was an important part of that healing.

Judd had taken to fatherhood as if he'd been preparing for it all his life. If he still thought of Clara as his brother's child, he gave no sign of it. She was his little princess. In every way that mattered he was her father. Hannah could only hope that in the years ahead she could give him more children of his own.

Clara had begun to whimper again. Hannah was turning back toward the front door when a movement caught her eye. A rider had swung off the road and was loping his horse through the gate. As he came nearer, Hannah recognized one of the youths who delivered messages for the telegraph office.

Spotting Judd near the barn, he reined in his horse and pulled a yellow envelope out of his jacket. Still in the saddle, he passed the envelope into Judd's waiting hand. Judd fished in his pocket for some coins. Then the boy was off again, headed back down the muddy drive.

Judd ambled toward the corral, working his thumb under the envelope's sealed flap. Hannah felt a sudden chill, as if a cloud had drifted across the sun. The telegram could be nothing—an update on beef cattle prices or a reply to his offer on a prize Hereford bull. But her instincts told her otherwise.

Judd had been in contact with the San Francisco police regarding Quint's disappearance. Maybe they'd learned what had become of him, or even found his body. Whatever the news, if it was about Quint, it was bound to be upsetting.

She watched Judd unfold the telegram and read it,

trying to gauge his reaction. At a distance, his expression revealed nothing. Only his posture—rigid, as if he were standing before a firing squad—told Hannah that her husband was struggling for self-control.

Folding the telegram, he stuffed it into the envelope. Hannah waited as he walked back to the house and mounted the porch, paying no attention to his muddy boots.

"What is it?" She stared up at him. His face was pale, his eyes bright—too bright.

Judd eased Clara into his arms and handed Hannah the telegram. "Read it," he said. "You may want to sit down."

Fingers trembling, Hannah unfolded the yellow paper and read the short message.

San Francisco, 25 January 1900
Arriving Wednesday 4:35 by train. Will explain everything then. Enough adventure. Time to settle down. Tell my Hannah to start planning our wedding.
Quint

Chapter Fifteen

Hannah's legs wilted beneath her. The telegram dropped from her hand as she sank into the chair. "He's alive!" she murmured. "Quint's alive!"

Judd laid Clara in her lap, picked up the telegram and stared at it as if to make sure it was real. He looked utterly shaken.

"He doesn't know anything, does he?" Hannah forced her bloodless lips to form the question. "Your mother, the baby, you and me…" She shook her head, biting back tears. Quint was alive. He was coming home. It was joyful news. It was glorious news.

What in heaven's name were they going to do?

Judd checked his watch. "The telegram must have been delayed somewhere. Quint should be stepping off that train in less than an hour. I've just got time to hitch up the buggy and get to town."

"Judd—" She reached out and clasped his arm. The corded muscles felt strained, like knots too tightly pulled.

He shook his head, anticipating her question. "I'm

going alone, Hannah. It'll be easier all around if you aren't there. On the way home, I'll explain everything to him."

Everything? Hannah battled nausea. How could this be happening? She loved Quint—loved him in a way that had nothing to do with her love for Judd. But how could she expect either man to understand that?

Judd moved away from her. Then, hesitating, he turned, lifted her hand and pressed his lips into her palm. "Don't worry," he said. "We'll work things out for the best."

For the best. Right now that phrase could mean anything.

Hannah forced herself to smile, suppressing the one thought that was mirrored in Judd's eyes.

What had they done?

Judd was waiting on the platform when the eastbound train pulled into the station. He willed himself to relax as the pistons slowed, releasing a gush of steam. All the way from the ranch he'd rehearsed the words he would say to Quint. Now his mind had gone blank.

What the hell did a man do in a mess like this one?

He watched, holding his breath, as a tall figure in a woolen peacoat stepped down from the passenger car, hefted a canvas duffel from the platform and walked slowly toward him. Quint had put on muscle in the past ten months. He walked with the confident swagger of a man who could take care of himself in any situation.

A lump rose in Judd's throat. His brother was alive. At this moment, nothing else mattered.

Without a word he opened his arms. Quint walked

into them. The two brothers embraced like boxers in a clinch. "Lord, but it's good to be home," Quint said.

Judd found his voice. "You've got a hell of a lot of explaining to do. Come on, the buggy's out back."

Quint tossed his duffel into the rear seat of the buggy and climbed up to sit next to Judd. His face was wind-weathered, his jaw rough with stubble. He had the look of a man who'd learned some hard lessons.

Judd swung the buggy onto a quiet back road. Going through town would get them home in less time, but he wanted to talk to Quint before anybody else did. "I spent weeks looking for you in the Klondike," he said. "Then somebody sent us your pack from San Francisco. Since we hadn't heard from you, we didn't have much choice except to assume you were dead."

"Can't blame you for that, brother." Quint gazed across the yellowed fields. "Truth be told, I got myself shanghaied."

"You what?" Judd turned to stare at him.

"You heard me right. On the train, I got thinking that I wanted to see San Francisco before I caught the boat to Skagway. I saw it, all right. Ever hear of the Barbary Coast?"

"Who hasn't?" Judd had never seen San Francisco's notorious waterfront district, known to be crawling with gambling halls, opium dens and brothels. But he'd heard his share of stories. Wandering the streets, his naive young brother would have been fresh meat for any thugs or shysters who happened along.

"I went into a bar for a whiskey," Quint said. "By the time I finished my drink, the whole damned room was spinning. I keeled over and woke up on a tramp steamer bound for the South Pacific. It was work or get tossed to the sharks. I worked." He spread his hands to display his palms. They were cracked and leathered with calluses. "In Sydney I jumped ship, hid out for a while, then took a job on the docks. Finally crewed my way back to Frisco on a freighter."

"You could have written from Sydney. It might have saved us some grief." *More grief than you can imagine,* Judd thought.

"I did. But I'm guessing I beat the letter home. How's Mother?"

"Mother died last month. Passed away in her sleep. She never stopped believing you'd come home to her."

And that much was true, Judd told himself. Quint could hear the rest of the story later. "We buried her next to Dad," he said. "I like to think they're together somewhere."

Quint sucked in his breath. A fragile moment crawled past before he spoke. "Say it, Judd. I was a damned fool, going off like that, changing my plans without telling anybody. I deserved what I got. But Mother didn't. You didn't. And Hannah sure as hell didn't."

Judd let the words hang in silence. When his brother asked about Hannah the real shock would come. He wasn't looking forward to it.

"What about my girl?" Quint demanded. "Does she know I'm back?"

"She knows. She'll be at the house."

"And she knows what I said in the telegram? That I'm ready to get married?"

Judd's mouth had gone dry. He didn't answer.

"She still wants to marry me, doesn't she? Lord, but I missed that girl! Funny how you don't appreciate what's right under your nose until it isn't there anymore. When I see Hannah, I'm going to fall on my knees and beg her to be my wife!"

Judd cleared his throat. This couldn't wait any longer. "Time didn't stop for us while you were away, Quint. Hannah had your baby in November. You have a daughter."

There was a beat of stunned silence. Then Quint made a strangled sound. "Oh, Lord…if I'd known that…"

"Hannah wrote to you every week, pleading with you to come home and marry her. Her letters went to Skagway. I found the whole bundle of them when I went there looking for you. For all I know they're still there, waiting for you to stop by and read them."

Quint hung his head. His fingers raked his unruly curls. "Lord," he groaned. "What that poor girl must've gone through! If I'd known, I swear I would've done anything to get home and marry her. You believe me, don't you, Judd?"

Judd halted the buggy at the side of the road. "I do believe you, Quint," he said. "That's why I married Hannah in your place."

Quint reeled as if he'd been slammed with the side of an ax. It took seconds for him to find his voice. "Why you dirty, rotten—"

"Not another word!" Judd cut him off. "You'll hear me out, little brother. When I'm finished, you can call me any blamed thing you want to."

While Quint glowered in silence, Judd related the events leading up to the wedding and the terms of the agreement. After careful thought, he'd decided not to tell his brother the marriage had been consummated. That secret rightly belonged to Hannah, to guard or to share as she saw fit.

Hannah.

Even now, the thought of her was like a bleeding wound. Quint was the love of Hannah's life and the father of her child. Now that he'd come back to claim her, she would have everything she'd ever wanted. Judd knew that walking away from her would kill him. But for her sake, and the sake of his family, he would do what honor demanded.

"Your daughter is a Seavers, a legitimate member of our family," he concluded. "What I did, I did for her and for Hannah and for Mother. Maybe even for you. And don't expect an apology, little brother, because you're not getting one."

"I hate it when you call me *little brother.*" Quint settled back in the seat, still looking stunned. "You're saying that all you and Hannah have to do is sign the divorce papers, and she'll be free to marry me?"

Judd guided the team back onto the muddy road. "The papers will need to be filed with the court. But yes. I wanted to make it easy for her when the time came."

"But she's waited for me? She still wants to get married?"

Judd sighed, wishing the long ride would end. "I can't speak for Hannah," he said. "But I'll tell you one thing. After what she's been through, don't expect her to just fall into your arms. She's not the girl you left. She's a woman with a woman's feelings. And she's a lady, as well. She deserves a proper courtship and a proper proposal. I expect you to make damned sure she gets it."

Quint stared at him. Then a slow, knowing grin slid across his face. "Bloody hell, man, you're in love with her!"

Hannah stood on the porch as the buggy rolled through the gate and came up the long drive. With the sun low in the sky, the air had taken on a chill. She clutched her shawl tighter, shivering beneath the lacy wool.

In the buggy's front seat she could make out two men. Judd was driving the team. Quint sat beside him, bareheaded and clad in a dark blue coat.

How much had Judd told his brother? she wondered. If only they'd had time to talk before he left for town. At least, then, she might have known what to expect. Now all she could do was wait.

The knot in her stomach tightened as the buggy came closer. This was a happy day, she reminded herself. Quint was alive. He'd come home to his family. So why should she feel as if she were about to be sick?

Hannah had spent the past two hours fluttering around the house like a trapped bird. In her panic, she'd moved Judd's things from her bedroom to his smaller room next door. Then she'd stood there agonizing over what she'd done. Would it be so wrong to let Quint see the truth—that she and Judd were living as man and wife, and that they loved each other? Would that be any worse than lying to him?

She'd been on the verge of moving everything back when Clara had awakened, wet and hungry. By the time

Hannah had changed her, fed her and put her in her basket, time had run out.

The dog had been lazing on the steps most of the day. Now it raised its head and sniffed the air. With a joyous *woof,* it scrambled down the steps and hit the ground at a run. Rocketing down the drive, it reached the buggy and sprang onto Quint's lap. Quint laughed helplessly as the dog covered him with muddy paw prints and sloppy tongue kisses.

He was still laughing when Judd drove up to the porch and turned the buggy aside so that Quint could climb out at the foot of the steps. Hannah tried to catch Judd's eye, but he kept his gaze straight ahead, as if he were wearing invisible blinders.

Look at me, Judd, she pleaded silently. *Let me know we're all right, you and I.*

Judd turned the buggy toward the barn without so much as a glance in her direction.

Quint stood at the foot of the steps, the strap of his duffel dangling from one hand. He looked taller and stronger, less of a boy and more of a man than Hannah remembered. His hair wanted cutting and his chin wanted shaving. But he was alive. He was home. Her girlish prayers had been answered.

"Well, Hannah…" His warm brown eyes held a flicker of uncertainty. Tossing the duffel onto the porch, he strode up the steps and gathered her into his arms.

She embraced him—her childhood playmate, her partner in mischief, the sharer of her dreams and her first love.

But not her last love.

His kiss began gently. Then he pulled her closer. His lips grew more demanding. Hannah remained passive in his arms. She couldn't help wondering if Judd was watching them.

"Let me look at you!" He thrust her away, holding her at arm's length. "My word, but you've grown up, little Hannah Gustavson. You're a beautiful woman!"

Hannah willed her legs to stop trembling. "You're as charming as ever, Quint. But I'm not Hannah Gustavson anymore. Didn't Judd tell you?"

"He told me." Quint released her. "He also told me about the divorce papers. I'll be glad when that business is taken care of. Judd made me promise I'd court you before I proposed. I plan to do that. But not for long. I want my ring on your finger. And I want to be a father to our little girl."

Hannah stared down at the muddy porch, where the dog had settled at Quint's feet. Since Judd hadn't told her anything, she could only guess where matters stood. Judd had turned her over to his brother, laid down a few rules and was preparing to step out of the picture. Quint knew about the marriage and the baby. But he didn't appear to know that she and Judd had shared a bed. Clearly, Judd believed that was best forgotten.

Why hadn't either of them thought to ask *her* what she wanted? Did they think they could trade her back and forth like a prize heifer? It would serve them both right if she packed up Clara and left. But this was Clara's home, Hannah reminded herself. There was no way she would let pride deprive her child of the right to grow up here.

Resolving to be civil, she raised her eyes to meet Quint's. "I wrote to you every week," she said.

"I know you did. And I know that when my pack arrived you thought I must be dead. I could tell you what happened, but it's a long story. I'll save it for suppertime. Right now I want to meet our daughter."

"Her name's Clara. She's inside, waiting for you in her basket. I…" Hannah paused, battling a rush of emotion. "I was afraid you and she would never have the chance to know one another."

"It's all right, Hannah." He laid a hand at the small of her back and guided her toward the door. "I'm here now. Everything's going to be fine."

Judd came around the barn just in time to see them enter the house. He'd had no desire to watch their reunion. Seeing them together would only tighten the knot in his gut.

So far it looked as if they were picking up where they'd left off. When the time came, Judd resolved, he would sign the divorce papers, pack his bags and leave. There was plenty of room in the big house and plenty of work to be done on the ranch. But living with Hannah and Quint would be more than he could stand.

Maybe he'd go north to Wyoming or Montana, or even to Oregon. It didn't matter as long as he could find someplace open and peaceful, with grass and cattle and mountains. Someplace a lot like this one. He might even find himself a woman and start a family. But Hannah would always be a part of him. He would never stop loving her.

For the present, he had little choice except to behave

as if everything was fine. He would wash up, go into the house and share stories over dinner. When bedtime came, he would retire to his own room and try not to imagine Hannah lying beside him, welcoming his love with her sweet body.

All too soon, that sweet body would belong to someone else.

Judd splashed his hands and face at the pump, letting the icy water tingle over his skin. Scraping the mud off his boots, he mounted the porch, opened the front door and walked into the house.

Voices and laughter were coming from the parlor. Standing in the doorway, Judd saw Quint and Hannah on the settee with Clara. Quint held the baby in his arms. He cradled her awkwardly, as if he expected her to shatter like blown glass. Seeing them together, Judd was struck by the resemblance between father and daughter—the same melting dark eyes, the same thick curls and dimpled cheeks. Quint was a handsome man. Young Clara would grow up to be a beautiful woman.

Not that he'd be around to see it happen, Judd reminded himself. He wouldn't be there to watch her grow and learn, to protect her and help her over the rough spots. That realization hurt more than he cared to admit.

"I see you've met the princess." Judd crossed the room and seated himself in the rocking chair. "What do you think of her?"

Quint shook his head. His eyes glimmered with moisture. "She's…a bloody miracle, that's what she is. Those little hands. So perfect… Lord, Judd, if I'd only known…"

"Judd delivered her," Hannah said. "It was the night my father died. We got stuck in the snow on the way home. He saved both our lives, Quint."

"Then I owe you even more, brother," Quint said. "If our next baby's a boy, we'll name him after you!"

Hannah's lips parted, then closed in a thin line. Judd sensed the strain in her as she rose from the settee. "I'll leave you two to visit while I give Rosita some last-minute help. Excuse me please." She spun away and fled into the hall. Her shoes clicked across the hardwood floor of the dining room.

Was Quint pushing things too hard, too fast? Judd wondered whether he should caution him. But at that moment Clara began to fuss. Uncertainty flashed across Quint's face. He jiggled the baby, trying to soothe her. Clara's whimpers changed to howls. Quint's panic-stricken gaze met Judd's across the room. "What do I do now?" he muttered.

"Put her up to your shoulder and pat her back. She might have a gas bubble."

The baby had gone as rigid as a poker. She screamed as Quint lifted her. Quint shot Judd a desperate look. "Help me!" he pleaded.

Judd strode across the room, took the squalling child from her father and cradled her against his shoulder. His big hand massaged her bony little back. Clara began to relax. Her cries diminished to forlorn little hiccups.

"I can't believe she did that for you!" Quint muttered. "My own kid, and she doesn't like me!"

"She's just being a baby," Judd said. "Give her some time and you'll get along fine. She's used to me, that's all."

"Used to you!" Quint's lip curled. "And who else is used to you, big brother?" He rose and stalked toward the door. "I'll be upstairs unpacking. Call me when supper's ready."

Judd stared at the empty doorway where his brother had vanished. He should have known this was going to happen. Quint was no fool. The situation was a keg of blasting powder with the fuse lit and sputtering. If it blew up, Hannah's happiness would be destroyed, and the family with it.

Judd knew of only one possible way to stamp out the fire. The sooner it was taken care of, the better it would be for all of them.

Clara was chomping on one tiny pink fist. Judd brushed a kiss on her curls and laid her gently in her basket. Then he walked across the hall to his study, found the key to the desk and unlocked the top drawer.

Like most women, Rosita had taken to Quint right away. In honor of his homecoming she'd added extra touches to the hearty supper of beef tamales, enchiladas, beans and fresh tortillas. The table was set with Edna's best china, arranged on the red linen cloth that was reserved for parties and hadn't been used in years. Candles glowed in an old candelabrum that Rosita had polished to silvery brilliance. Burgundy wine sparkled in the cut crystal goblets that Edna had brought west with her trousseau.

Hannah, Judd and Quint did their best to make it a happy occasion. They put on their company faces and confined their talk to ranch business and Quint's wild adventures on the tramp steamer. But a miasma of tension hung over the meal. Judd sat at the head of the table with Quint and Hannah facing each other on either side. Quint alternated between glaring at Judd and devouring Hannah with his eyes. Judd seemed to be ringed by an invisible wall. When he looked at Hannah it was with the eyes of a polite stranger.

That look broke Hannah's heart. It confirmed what she'd already guessed—Judd had already decided to do the honorable thing and let her go. When he discovered that she'd moved his clothes out of their room, he'd take it as a sign that she agreed. Somehow she had to get him alone. They needed to reach an understanding before it was too late.

When the meal was finished, Judd shrugged into his coat and went outside. Sometimes he made evening visits to the bunkhouse to lay out the next day's work. Most nights it didn't take long. But tonight, she sensed, he'd be looking for any excuse to stay away. If he hadn't returned by the time the house quieted down, Hannah vowed, she would take a lantern and go looking for him.

Left alone with Quint, Hannah busied herself with straightening the parlor. She was plumping Edna's needlepoint cushions when he came up behind her. His arms slid around her waist. His lips nibbled the bare curve of her neck.

"Don't we have something better to do?" he murmured, pulling her closer.

She stiffened. "Have you forgotten I'm a married woman?"

"Not for long. Judd said the divorce would be simple."

She pulled away and turned to face him. "This isn't

a good time, Quint. You're worn-out and I'm still in shock. Let's both get a good night's sleep. We can talk in the morning."

His eyes narrowed. "I won't rest until I get some answers, Hannah. Are you going to be my wife or aren't you?"

"I said this isn't a good time. We need to consider what's best for Clara, what's best for us—"

"The devil we do! Clara's my baby! We loved each other! We were promised!" He loomed above her. "Bloody hell, girl, do you think I'm blind? You're sleeping with him, aren't you?"

"Yes." Hannah was surprised at her own calmness. "Judd and I are husband and wife. In every respect."

The breath hissed out of him as if he'd been gut punched. His hands balled into fists. "I knew it! That dirty, rotten, conniving bastard! He stole everything I ever gave a damn about!"

"No!" Hannah stood her ground. "I won't have you talking about your brother like that, Quint Seavers! You ran off and left me with child. Judd took me in and gave me a home. He gave me—and Clara—the Seavers name, and with it, respectability." Hannah drew herself up, her eyes drilling into Quint's. "When we were married, he promised not to lay a hand on me. Even after we fell in love, he kept that promise. It was only after your pack arrived, and we were so sure you weren't coming back—"

"You were mine!" Quint exploded. "You've always been mine! On that hellhole of a steamer, the one thing that gave me hope was the thought that you'd be here waiting for me! Now what am I supposed to do?" With a grunt of anguish he strode out of the room and down the hall. The front door opened and slammed shut with a shattering bang.

"Quint!" She plunged after him, but just then Clara, startled by the commotion, began to cry. Hannah turned back, gathered her up and cradled her close. After a few minutes the baby settled down and began chomping on her mother's lace collar.

A glance at the clock told Hannah it was time to take her daughter upstairs, change her, feed her and put her to bed. Maybe that was just as well. Chasing after Quint would only make matters worse. He needed time alone to calm down and think things through.

It was Judd who worried her. Strong, giving Judd, who was so determined to sacrifice himself for the sake of honor. Hang honor! He was the man she loved, the man she wanted for the rest of her life. How could she make him believe that?

Hannah climbed the stairs to her bedroom, closed the door, lit the lamp and dressed Clara in clean nightclothes. Then she sank into the cushioned rocker and settled down to the sweet task of nursing her baby.

The rhythmic tug of the little mouth began to lull her. Hannah yawned. She was exhausted. Everyone was. Maybe tomorrow, after a good night's rest, they'd all see things in a better light.

Her head began to nod. Her eyelids closed, fluttered open, then closed again. Tomorrow, she thought. Everything would be better tomorrow.

It had to be.

* * *

Judd stood in the cold moonlight, gazing across the yard at the house. The parlor drapes had been closed to conserve heat, but where the folds parted he could see the glow of lamplight. He had left Hannah and Quint alone together. Were they making up for lost time? Were they in each other's arms?

His restless fingers broke off a stem of wheatgrass. Crushing it in his fist, he tossed it into the mud. Sooner or later he would have to go inside. He dreaded the thought of seeing things he didn't want to see and hearing things he didn't want to hear. He'd always thought of jealousy as a useless emotion. Now he knew it was worse than useless. It was a monster. It was eating him alive.

Turning his back on the house, Judd walked down the slope toward the barn. He loved his brother and wanted the best for him. He loved Hannah, and he loved her little girl. If Hannah and Quint could be happy together, why shouldn't that be enough for him? Why was he wrestling with these ugly, selfish feelings?

He heard the slam of the front door and the heavy tread of boots across the porch. Judd didn't need to look around to know it was Quint. He'd always had a temper.

But what had happened to make him so angry? Had Hannah told him the truth?

In the concealing shadow of the barn, Judd paused and turned. Quint had sunk onto the porch steps with his head in his hands. The dog crouched beside him, nudging his arm with its nose.

Judd waited. In the house, the downstairs lights had gone out. The lamp was on in Hannah's room, soft as moon glow through the lace curtains. He pictured her sitting in the rocker, haloed by its light as she nursed her baby.

His poor, sweet Hannah, whose only sin was loving too much. How she must be hurting.

He could feel his own emotions softening, feel the ugly edge melting away. His brother was in pain, too. Somehow he needed to make things right.

He stepped into the open where Quint could see him coming across the yard. Quint's head jerked up. Rising off the step he strode forward to meet his brother.

The two came together. Quint's face was in shadow, his expression hidden from Judd's view. Judd spoke first.

"Quint, we can't undo what's—"

"You dirty, lying bastard!" Quint swung hard. His sledgehammer fist struck the side of Judd's face. Unprepared, Judd staggered backward. His legs buckled. He sank to the muddy ground.

He was still spitting blood when Quint walked away.

Chapter Sixteen

Hannah jerked awake. Her head felt muzzy, her mouth cotton dry. Clara lay in the crook of her arm, squirming and fussing, her blankets kicked off.

What time was it? She was still in her clothes, still seated in the rocking chair. She must have fallen asleep while she was nursing. Thank goodness she hadn't dropped her baby!

Bundling up Clara, she staggered to her feet. The room was chilly. Through the lace-curtained window, the night sky was just beginning to fade. The small clock on her nightstand confirmed that it was five-fifteen in the morning.

The baby was squalling with hunger. Feeding her couldn't wait for anything else. With a sigh Hannah sank back into the rocker and found her nipple. Clara latched on like a starving kitten.

Leaning back in the chair, Hannah closed her eyes. How could she have slept so soundly? It must have been the wine they'd had for supper—she and Judd and Quint, seated at Rosita's festive table.

Her heart lurched as the memory crashed in on her. Judd's remoteness and his disappearance after the meal. Quint's angry outburst when she'd told him the truth. She hadn't meant to fall asleep. She'd meant to go to Judd and explain everything. How could she have let this happen?

She could imagine it—Judd entering the dark house, climbing the stairs, finding her door shut and his clothes in his old bedroom. The message would have been unmistakable.

She had to find him. She had to talk to him before any more damage was done.

Anxiety mounting, she shifted the baby to her other breast. Clara seemed to sense her strain. She fussed and whimpered, spitting the nipple out twice before she settled into nursing again. Hannah took a deep breath and willed herself to relax. She could only hope Judd was asleep in the next room, and that he'd listen to what she had to stay.

At last Clara was satisfied. Hannah burped her and laid her in her cradle. Then, fumbling with her buttons, she opened the door and stepped out onto the shadowed landing. No one was in sight. Quint and Judd's rooms were both closed. Breathing a silent prayer, she tiptoed to Judd's door and quietly opened it.

The room was empty.

Hannah darted inside. A quick check of the bed confirmed that the sheets were clean and undisturbed. Toiletries were missing from the washstand. Most of Judd's clothes were gone, as well. The bag he'd carried home from the service was absent from its place under the bed.

In a panic of despair, she raced downstairs. It wasn't like Judd to just disappear. Surely he would leave some kind of note, explaining where he'd gone.

The first floor of the house was silent, with just enough light for Hannah to see her way. She checked the dining room and the parlor. Nothing. Maybe Judd had left a message on the desk where he kept pens and ink and stationery.

Heart pounding, she slipped across the hall and into the study. In the scant light she could just make out the open folder that lay on the desk. Leaving it in place, she crossed the room and opened the drapes. Pale gray light flooded the room.

Slowly she walked back to the desk. She didn't need to pick up the papers to know what she was looking at.

The divorce documents lay in plain sight on the polished walnut surface. Every required blank bore yesterday's date and Judd's masterful signature. All that remained was for her to fill in her own.

"Hannah."

Quint's voice startled her. She turned to see him standing in the doorway of the study, dressed but rumpled and unshaven.

"Judd's gone." Hannah struggled to keep her voice from breaking. "He signed the papers, packed his things and left sometime before I woke up. This is all my fault."

"Your fault!" Quint raked a hand through his tangled curls. "If that's what you think, you didn't see me knock him flat in the mud. I gave him a punch that would've stunned a buffalo—could've broken his jaw for all I know. He didn't even try to stop me."

"Oh, Quint!" Hannah shook her head, heartsick for them all. "We both did this. I was going to wait up and talk to him. I fell asleep and never heard him come back to the house."

"And I made a complete ass of myself last night. How could I assume you'd still want me after what I put you through? How could I blame you for moving on? I'm so sorry, girl. Lord, but I'm sorry."

He opened his arms. Hannah walked into them and sagged against his chest. He cradled her gently, like a brother. "Judd did this for us," he said. "He thought we'd be happy together if he wasn't here to come between us. Something tells me, whatever he did, it was too late."

"I love him, Quint," Hannah whispered. "I love him so much. Judd needed to hear those words last night, and I didn't say them."

Quint cupped her face between his palms. His brown eyes brimmed with emotion. "I made the worst mistake of my life when I got on that train and left you," he said. "I'll be damned if I'm going to let my brother make the same mistake!"

"What are you saying?"

He released her. "I'm going after him. If I have to track him all the way to the bloody North Pole I'll find him and bring him back to you!"

"*We're* going after him." Hannah made the decision as she spoke. "He can't have gotten far. If he's taking the train, he could still be in town. See if the men can tell you anything. I'll get Clara ready."

He hesitated, likely thinking that she and the baby would slow him down. Hannah gave him no chance to argue. She spun into the hallway and raced upstairs.

In the bedroom, Hannah dressed her daughter and packed a small valise with spare clothes diapers and blankets. It might be easier to leave the baby with Rosita. But she and Clara had never been apart, and Hannah had no idea how long she'd be gone. She took a few seconds to splash her face and smooth her hair. There wasn't time to change her own clothes. The dress she'd slept in would have to do.

When she came downstairs, Quint was waiting by the front door. He was holding a half-crumpled piece of paper. "According to the foreman, Judd took one of the horses sometime before dawn. He left this note on the bunkhouse door."

"Let me see it!" Hannah snatched the paper out of his hand. The message was terse.

Leaving on business. Pick up horse at livery stable in town. J.S.

"He's taking the train!" she said.

Quint nodded. "We don't know which way he's going, but the next train comes through Dutchman's Creek in forty-five minutes. If Judd plans to be on board, there won't be time to take the buggy. I've got a fast horse saddled out front."

Hannah bowed to reason. "Go," she said. "Do whatever it takes to stop him."

He gave her an awkward hug. Then he was off,

springing into the saddle and thundering down the drive toward the gate. Quint was the very devil on horseback. If anybody could make it to town in time, he could.

Not that Hannah planned to be left far behind. If Quint found Judd, she wanted to be there. The words Judd needed to hear could only come from her lips.

Laying Clara in her basket, she snatched up her cloak and dashed outside to order the buggy hitched.

Judd had bought a one-way ticket to Denver. It was a practical choice. He had business and banking connections there. He could take a few days to lick his wounds, weigh his choices and make any needed financial arrangements before moving on.

It sounded so sensible. Not at all as if he'd just ripped his whole damned life apart.

His gut clenched as he stood on the platform, waiting for the seven-ten train. He couldn't look back, couldn't let himself think about what he was leaving behind. If he did, he'd never have the strength to climb the steps into the passenger car.

A subtle vibration beneath his boot soles warned him of the approaching train. An instant later he saw it through the gap in the winter trees, racing along the rails, trailing a feathery white plume behind its stack. The whistle echoed across the valley, shrill and mournful on the gray morning air.

Something in him had hoped it might be late, or that it wouldn't arrive at all. But a glance at his pocket watch confirmed that the train was on time—a few minutes early, in fact.

He waited as the engine glided up to the station house and stopped in a hissing cloud of steam. The morning was cold. Judd had been waiting for several hours, resting on a bench with his feet on his pack and his Stetson tilted over his eyes. The train wasn't due to leave for another ten minutes. But he might as well board and make himself comfortable.

Hoisting his pack, he walked toward the passenger car. His gaze traveled beyond the tracks to the distant foothills, searching for something he couldn't even name. He loved this country, from the open flatland to the high meadows and craggy peaks. When he'd returned from the army hospital, he'd believed he was home to stay. Now, less than a year later, he was leaving for good.

He would write to Hannah and Quint, of course, to let them know where he'd settled. First, however, he'd give them time and distance to work things out.

And they *would* work things out, Judd told himself. Quint's temper cooled as fast as it flared. He would understand and forgive Hannah in time. Any man would be crazy not to.

Mounting the steps, Judd entered the passenger car and found a pair of empty seats where he could spread out. He'd bought a newspaper at the station. Maybe he could find an interesting piece to read.

He settled back, opened the paper and leafed through the pages. It was no good. The image of Hannah in his bed, her hair tumbling over the pillow, her arms reaching to pull him down to her, was like a brand on his soul. The memory burned deeper—her milk-swollen breasts filling his hands, silky against his face, against his lips. The warm, salty taste of her as he kissed his way down her belly to the layers of petal softness between her legs. Her gasp of delight as his mouth captured the pearl-like nub at their center…

The newspaper crumpled in his hand as he realized he was half out of his seat and on the verge of reaching for his pack to step off the train. Judd forced himself to stop. He couldn't even think of going back to her. She and Quint deserved a chance at happiness. Clara deserved to grow up with her real father.

Swearing under his breath, he lowered himself to the seat. If he could fight temptation a little longer, until the train began to move, maybe he'd be safe.

The whistle's lonesome cry quivered along the line of railway cars. Only then did Judd realize that the train *was* moving. The station house glided slowly past the window, then the cattle pens, the loading ramps and the water tower. Judd exhaled, settled back in his seat and closed his eyes. It would be a mercy if he could sleep all the way to Denver.

Hannah had driven the buggy as fast as she dared, but she was still blocks from the station when she heard the whistle of the departing train. Frantic, she pushed along the crowded main street, dodging wagons and foot traffic. Had Quint reached the train in time, or was Judd already speeding away from her?

Clara lay bundled in her basket. As the buggy jounced over a rut, she woke up and started to cry. Glancing down to make sure her baby was all right, Hannah urged the horses on. At the end of the street she could see the back of the red brick station house and the water tower that rose beyond it. She was almost there.

She halted the buggy behind the station, snatched Clara out of her basket and raced around to the platform. Her heart plummeted. There was no sign of Judd or Quint. The only person in sight was an old man reading a newspaper on a bench.

Hannah hurried into the station house. The graying, bespectacled station agent was behind the counter. He glanced up at her approach.

"Mr. Cardston, has my husband been here?" She was breathing hard and probably looked like a madwoman.

"Judd bought a ticket for Denver and got on the train, Mrs. Seavers. It pulled out ten minutes ago. I saw him through the window. Is something wrong?"

"No, not really." Hannah clutched her baby tighter. "You haven't seen Quint, have you?"

"Not a sign of him."

Turning away to hide her tears, Hannah walked outside to the platform and gazed up and down the track. Where was Quint? How could he have failed her?

Overcome, she sank onto the bench and pressed her face against Clara's blanket. She'd been so sure that Quint would be able to stop Judd from leaving. But something had gone wrong, and now it was too late. Judd was on the train, speeding his way out of her life.

"Wake up, big brother. This is where you get off."

Judd jerked to sudden alertness. Quint was standing over him. One hand rested on the emergency cord. He must have just pulled it, because the train was slowing down.

"Are you out of your mind?" Judd stared up at his brother. "What the devil are you doing here?"

Quint grinned. "I'm getting you off this train and taking you home to your wife. Come on. Let's go."

As the train screeched to a halt, the conductor bustled down the aisle, looking annoyed. "Who pulled that cord?" he demanded.

Quint's grin widened. "I did. This fellow is wanted back in Dutchman's Creek. I have orders to take him off the train and bring him in."

The small man looked Quint up and down. Quint wasn't wearing a gun or a badge, but his six-foot height, coupled with his wild hair, scruffy beard and bloodshot eyes gave him the look of a dangerous man. The conductor had his passengers' safety to consider. He wasn't about to risk a fight.

"Take him and get off, then," he snapped. "Make it fast. We've got to get this train moving."

Muttering, Judd hefted his pack and followed his brother off the train. Whatever crazy game Quint was playing, he didn't have much choice except to go along with it.

Seconds later the train had pulled away and left them behind. They were standing in a patch of cottonwoods, a half mile from town. Quint cocked his head, studying the bruises his fist had left on the side of Judd's face. "You look like the devil," he said, grinning. "Come on, let's get back to town. You can buy me breakfast."

Judd shouldered his pack and they began to walk. "You've got some tall explaining to do," he said. "How did you get on that train anyway?"

"Rode alongside and jumped aboard like a trick rider in the Wild West Show. The horse is probably halfway home by now." Quint scuffed at a rock. "It's my turn to ask the questions. Why'd you run off like that without telling us?"

"You found the papers on the desk?"

"Hell, yes. Hannah was fit to be tied. I promised her I'd bring you back. Why'd you do it?"

"Why do you think?"

"Because you're a proud, stubborn fool—too much of a fool to know when a woman's in love with you."

"You're the father of her child."

"And you're a marble-headed jackass! I'd take Hannah off your hands in a minute. But she doesn't want me. She wants stodgy old you. Can you imagine that?"

Judd walked in silence for a dozen yards. "What about Clara?" he asked. "She's your daughter."

Quint thrust his hands into his pockets. "Clara's the most beautiful, perfect thing I ever saw. I loved her from the first second I laid eyes on her. But she deserves to be raised by a responsible father who'll take care of her, not some footloose bum who doesn't even know what he wants to be when he grows up."

Judd's breath caught. He swallowed the lump in his throat. "You're saying you'd give her up?"

"Not entirely. I'd like to know her from a distance, be her friend, send a few little gifts…if you and Hannah, as her parents, would allow that, of course."

Judd swallowed a second time. "You're leaving, then? You know you're welcome to stay."

Quint shook his head. "I appreciate that. But we both

know it wouldn't be a good idea. I'm thinking I'll give San Francisco another try. It's a right lively place. Lots of excitement and pretty women. Plenty of opportunities for a young man seeking his fortune."

"Just promise you'll come back to visit—and that you'll stay the hell out of sleazy bars."

"I hear you, brother!" Quint's laughter startled a flock of blackbirds roosting in the trees. They rose in a twittering cloud, circled once, then winged toward the station where Hannah huddled on the bench, comforting her fussy baby.

Hannah looked up as the birds swooped over the platform. Her eyes followed them as they rose again, wheeled and scattered over the fields—not unlike the scattered pieces of her life.

She would sign and file the divorce papers, giving Judd the freedom to marry again if he chose. That was the least she could do for him. But she could no longer see herself married to Quint. She loved Quint in a sisterly way. But his restless nature, coupled with her own need to put down roots, would guarantee that one of them would always be miserable.

For now, at least, she would stay on the ranch and raise her little girl alone. She could do it. She would have her own family nearby, and with the foreman helping, she could manage the ranch business fine. Quint could come and go as he pleased. His room would always be ready. As for Judd...

But she couldn't think about Judd yet—couldn't imagine him far from home with some other woman in his arms. She was too raw for that. Learning to deal with Judd without hurting would take a very long time.

Gathering Clara close, Hannah rose from the bench. It was time she drove home and got the day off to a proper start. Maybe along the way she'd discover what had become of Quint.

She'd started for the buggy when she heard familiar voices. Turning, she saw them—two tall brothers walking side by side along the tracks, laughing and talking as if nothing had happened.

Thunderstruck, she watched them come closer. As Judd caught sight of her, he tossed his heavy pack to Quint and broke into a run. Clutching the baby, Hannah rushed to meet him.

They came together at the end of the platform. Judd's strong, hungry arms pulled his wife and daughter into a protecting circle. Hannah kissed him again and again, murmuring giddy, incoherent little phrases. He'd come home to her. He loved her. Nothing else mattered.

They walked back to the buggy. Judd held Clara with one arm and circled Hannah's shoulder with the other. Quint followed them with Judd's pack. As the sun rose on a bright winter day, they started home.

Epilogue

Christmas, 1902

Three-year-old Clara tugged at the ribbon on the big gold box. Her eyes danced with excitement. "I bet this is from Uncle Quint! He sends the best presents ever!"

"He does. That's why we saved it for last." Curled on the settee next to Judd, Hannah watched her daughter open the gift. Quint tended to overindulge the little girl. But how could she blame him? Clara was an adorable child, the very image of her natural father. And Quint had yet to marry and have children of his own. He was happily working as a reporter in San Francisco, where every day brought a new adventure.

Hannah surveyed the cluttered parlor with contentment. Gifts, boxes and wrappings were scattered over the floor. A bushy green pine tree, hung with handmade ornaments, stood in one corner. Burning logs crackled in the fireplace. From the kitchen came the savory aromas of a Christmas dinner—roast goose, carrots and potatoes, fresh rolls and mince pie. Hannah's entire family would be coming later, as well as Rosita and her new husband.

Judd nuzzled Hannah's ear. One hand tightened around her shoulder. The other rested lightly on her bulging belly. "How are you holding up, love?" he asked her. "I've worried about you overdoing it."

Hannah nestled against him, feeling warm and loved and protected. "I'm fine. If I can get through the next few hours without going into labor, I'll call it a good day."

"Mama! Papa! Look!" Clara had opened Quint's gift. She held up an exquisite, imported doll in a yellow lace dress and bonnet. The eyes in the porcelain face were large and brown, the hair a mass of chestnut curls. "She's just like me!" Clara exclaimed. "I'm going to have a tea party with my other dolls so they can meet her!"

Hannah sighed. The doll did look like Clara and had probably cost Quint a small fortune. Wisdom dictated that she put it on some high shelf so it wouldn't get mussed. But no, she would let Clara play with it and enjoy it. That's what Quint would want.

There was a light rap on the front door. Annie stepped inside without waiting for an answer. She was wearing the elegant dark green cape she'd made herself. Her cheeks were pink from walking over the fields in the cold.

"I told Mama I'd come early to help with dinner." She

glanced around the room. "Someone told me Quint might be here."

"Quint couldn't make it," Judd said. "Something about an important story he had to cover. He said maybe next year."

"Oh." With a little sigh, Annie shed her cape and sank onto a chair by the fire. At nineteen, Hannah's sister had grown to be a beauty. Plenty of men pursued her, but her romantic young heart belonged to just one—and Quint scarcely seemed to know she existed.

"Look, Aunt Annie!" Clara held up the doll. "Uncle Quint sent her to me. Isn't she beautiful?"

Annie knelt beside her niece. "Oh, my! She's lovely! She looks just like you!"

Clara seized Annie's hand. "Will you come with me to put her in my dollhouse?"

"Certainly!" Annie allowed herself to be led away, leaving Judd and Hannah alone in the parlor with the warm fire and the Christmas tree.

"At last!" Hannah turned toward her husband and kissed him lingeringly on the mouth. His hand slid around to massage her back, something she loved.

"Happy?" he asked her?

"Mmm, hmm." She traced a finger along his cheek.

"Did you get everything you wanted for Christmas?"

She shot him a wink. "There is one thing…but it'll likely have to wait until after this little mischief arrives."

His hand brushed her swollen breast. "I suppose it will. But then we can make up for lost time."

Hannah snuggled against him. Life was filled with hardship and uncertainty. No one could know what the future held. But today they had each other. They had this cozy room, this perfect day to hold forever. Wasn't that the real meaning of happiness?

* * * * *

Here is a sneak preview of
A STONE CREEK CHRISTMAS,
the latest in Linda Lael Miller's acclaimed
McKETTRICK *series.*

A lonely horse brought vet Olivia O'Ballivan to
Tanner Quinn's farm, but it's the rancher's love
that might cause her to stay.

A STONE CREEK CHRISTMAS
Available December 2008
from Silhouette Special Edition

"She's still very upset," Olivia told him, without turning to look at him or slowing down with the brush.

Shiloh, always an easy horse to get along with, stood contentedly in his own stall, munching away on the feed Tanner had given him earlier. Butterpie, he noted, hadn't touched her supper as far as he could tell.

"Do you know anything at all about horses, Mr. Quinn?" Olivia asked.

He leaned against the stall door, the way he had the day before, and grinned. He'd practically been raised on horseback; he and Tessa had grown up on their grandmother's farm in the Texas hill country, after their folks divorced and went their separate ways, both of them too busy to bother with a couple of kids. "A few things," he said. "And I mean to call you Olivia, so you might as well return the favor and address me by my first name."

He watched as she took that in, dealt with it, decided on an approach. He'd have to wait and see what that turned out to be, but he didn't mind. It was a pleasure just watching Olivia O'Ballivan grooming a horse.

"All right, *Tanner,*" she said. "This barn is a disgrace. When are you going to have the roof fixed? If it snows again, the hay will get wet and probably mold…"

He chuckled, shifted a little. He'd have a crew out there the following Monday morning to replace the roof and shore up the walls—he'd made the arrangements over a week before—but he felt no particular compunction to explain that. He was enjoying her ire too much; it made her color rise and her hair fly when she turned her head, and the faster breathing made her perfect breasts go up and down in an enticing rhythm. "What makes you so sure I'm a greenhorn?" he asked mildly, still leaning on the gate.

At last she looked straight at him, but she didn't move from Butterpie's side. "Your hat, your boots—that fancy red truck you drive. I'll bet it's customized."

Tanner grinned. Adjusted his hat. "Are you telling me real cowboys don't drive red trucks?"

"There are lots of trucks around here," she said. "Some of them are red, and some of them are new. And *all* of them are splattered with mud or manure or both."

"Maybe I ought to put in a car wash, then," he teased. "Sounds like there's a market for one. Might be a good investment."

She softened, though not significantly, and spared him a cautious half smile, full of questions she probably wouldn't ask. "There's a good car wash in Indian Rock," she informed him. "People go there. It's only forty miles."

"Oh," he said with just a hint of mockery. "*Only* forty miles. Well, then. Guess I'd better dirty up my truck if I want to be taken seriously in these here parts. Scuff up my boots a bit, too, and maybe stomp on my hat a couple of times."

Her cheeks went a fetching shade of pink. "You are twisting what I said," she told him, brushing Butterpie again, her touch gentle but sure. "I meant…"

Tanner envied that little horse. Wished he had a furry hide, so he'd need brushing, too.

"You *meant* that I'm not a real cowboy," he said. "And you could be right. I've spent a lot of time on construction sites over the last few years, or in meetings where a hat and boots wouldn't be appropriate. Instead of digging out my old gear, once I decided to take this job, I just bought new."

"I bet you don't even *have* any old gear," she challenged, but she was smiling, albeit cautiously, as though she might withdraw into a disapproving frown at any second.

He took off his hat, extended it to her. "Here," he teased. "Rub that around in the muck until it suits you."

She laughed, and the sound—well, it caused a powerful and wholly unexpected shift inside him. Scared the hell out of him and, paradoxically, made him yearn to hear it again.

* * * * *

*Discover how this rugged rancher's wanderlust is
tamed in time for a merry Christmas, in
A STONE CREEK CHRISTMAS.
In stores December 2008.*

Silhouette

SPECIAL EDITION™

FROM *NEW YORK TIMES* BESTSELLING AUTHOR

LINDA LAEL MILLER

A STONE CREEK CHRISTMAS

Veterinarian Olivia O'Ballivan finds the animals in Stone Creek playing Cupid between her and Tanner Quinn. Even Tanner's daughter, Sophie, is eager to play matchmaker. With everyone conspiring against them and the holiday season fast approaching, Tanner and Olivia may just get everything they want for Christmas after all!

Available December 2008
wherever books are sold.

Silhouette®
SPECIAL EDITION™

Kate's Boys

MISTLETOE AND MIRACLES

by *USA TODAY* bestselling author
MARIE FERRARELLA

Child psychologist Trent Marlowe couldn't
believe his eyes when Laurel Greer, the
woman he'd loved and lost, came to him for
help. Now a widow, with a troubled boy who
wouldn't speak, Laurel needed a miracle from
Trent...and a brief detour under the mistletoe
wouldn't hurt, either.

Available in December wherever books are sold.

REQUEST YOUR FREE BOOKS!

Harlequin® Historical
Historical Romantic Adventure!

2 FREE NOVELS PLUS 2 FREE GIFTS!

YES! Please send me 2 FREE Harlequin® Historical novels and my 2 FREE gifts (gifts are worth about $10). After receiving them, if I don't wish to receive any more books, I can return the shipping statement marked "cancel". If I don't cancel, I will receive 6 brand-new novels every month and be billed just $4.94 per book in the U.S. or $5.49 per book in Canada, plus 25¢ shipping and handling per book and applicable taxes, if any*. That's a savings of 20% off the cover price! I understand that accepting the 2 free books and gifts places me under no obligation to buy anything. I can always return a shipment and cancel at any time. Even if I never buy another book, the two free books and gifts are mine to keep forever.

246 HDN ERUM 349 HDN ERUA

Name	(PLEASE PRINT)

Address	Apt. #

City	State/Prov.	Zip/Postal Code

Signature (if under 18, a parent or guardian must sign)

Mail to the **Harlequin Reader Service:**
IN U.S.A.: P.O. Box 1867, Buffalo, NY 14240-1867
IN CANADA: P.O. Box 609, Fort Erie, Ontario L2A 5X3

Not valid to current subscribers of Harlequin Historical books.

Want to try two free books from another line?
Call 1-800-873-8635 or visit www.morefreebooks.com.

* Terms and prices subject to change without notice. N.Y. residents add applicable sales tax. Canadian residents will be charged applicable provincial taxes and GST. Offer not valid in Quebec. This offer is limited to one order per household. All orders subject to approval. Credit or debit balances in a customer's account(s) may be offset by any other outstanding balance owed by or to the customer. Please allow 4 to 6 weeks for delivery. Offer available while quantities last.

Your Privacy: Harlequin Books is committed to protecting your privacy. Our Privacy Policy is available online at www.eHarlequin.com or upon request from the Reader Service. From time to time we make our lists of customers available to reputable third parties who may have a product or service of interest to you. If you would prefer we not share your name and address, please check here. ☐

HH08R

THE MISTLETOE WAGER

Christine Merrill

Harry Pennyngton, Earl of Anneslea,
is surprised when his estranged wife,
Helena, arrives home for Christmas.
Especially when she's intent on
divorce! A festive house party
is in full swing when the guests
are snowed in, and Harry and
Helena find they are together
under the mistletoe....

*Available December 2008
wherever books are sold.*